UNEARTHED

UNEARTHED

Steve Hodgkinson

ORB
PUBLISHING LTD

Cover design:
Megan Jefferies, The Butchery

Book design and production:
DIYPublishing.co.nz

© Orb Publishing Ltd 2014

ISBN 978-0-473-29045-0

DEDICATION

*To all those who persevered in convincing me that fiction is a
worthwhile thing to do…*

ACKNOWLEDGMENTS

To Jenny Argante for her enthusiasm and expertise in editing this work

To Megan Jefferies for her amazing cover design

To DIY Publishing for publishing services

To Lighthouse for publicity services

To Eva Chan for proofreading

And to Ali for putting up with me… Really… Thanks so much.

PROLOGUE

At a glance it made no sense at all. Here in the middle of nowhere, a dapper gentleman in an immaculate pinstripe suit helped a younger chap in a lab coat up a stiff slope towards shelter. Blood and grime splattered the white coat. Shock was engrained on both faces.

In spite of everything it never occurred to them as they crested the river terrace before a crumbling bach that their killers would be waiting expectantly inside.

As they reached the crib a lone security guard swept past, but they didn't delay. The climb had been steep and the sun bright so they followed him straight in looking for somewhere, anywhere, to take a load off. Inside, the musty atmosphere spoke of a place long shut up. Squinting forward all they could make out was the burly profile of their minder silhouetted against shafts of light through cobwebbed kitchen windows.

And then all hell broke loose.

The pair were jolted back to reality by the unmistakable crack of a pistol, loud in the confines of the bungalow though muffled. The guard crumpled heavily to the ground, a tell-tale trickle of blood running out from between his eyes.

The pair froze. Shocked by the overwhelming realisation that they had stuffed up. For one moment they had let down their guard and could now be looking death in the eye.

After what seemed an age alone with their darkest thoughts someone broke the silence.

"Welcome, gentlemen. Pleased to catch up at last.

They spun as one to find the source of the greeting. They knew full well who it would be, but not how she could possibly have caught up with them here.

CHAPTER 1

WHEN SAM Miro arrived at the Institute that morning research technician Shelley Lai was already waiting.

"Have you seen it?" she said, eagerly flapping the newspaper before her. "Have you seen the report on the awards last night? They wrote such a great piece about you."

"You're joking," Sam said, feigning modesty. "I can't believe they even covered it."

"Well, they did. There's even a photo of you beaming out from behind your bow tie."

He turned to unlock his office, noting with satisfaction that a new name plate had appeared on his door overnight. Same office, different title.

'Dr Sam Miro, Postdoctoral Research Fellow.'

Pointing to it he remarked, "Now how can that be a coincidence, Shelley?" And then after a moment's reflection, "What is it about a job title anyway?"

He parked his motorcycle helmet on a filing cabinet and raked some order into his sun-bleached hair.

"Being a doctor has its merits, but what do you make of that 'Research Fellow' thing?"

"So yesterday, that's for sure," Shelley agreed, "and certainly not you!"

Sam smiled at the flattery.

"Hope not! You see, I don't think the term gives any sense of what a career in research is really about. No wonder science has such an image problem. Where's the sizzle in a name like that?"

"Ah, come on, Sam, it's not that bad really."

"I know, I know!" He sat down at his desk gesturing for Shelley to sit, too. "But it does need to sharpen up some, doesn't it? We have to get the message across that research is the future. That there's some amazing work going on in the country's research institutes. That's the story we have to tell."

"Totally agree. So is that what you said in your acceptance speech at the Young Biotech Award dinner last night?"

Shelley swept aside the organised chaos of periodicals and photocopied research papers on his desk to spread out the newspaper.

"Of course." Sam resigned himself to the loss of a week's hard thinking. "I emphasised the positive like a champion. But it was an establishment affair, if you know what I mean. You have to play the game, so I bit my tongue on the image problem."

She tapped the newspaper and began to read aloud.

"When you talk to young researcher of the year — Sam Miro — it soon becomes clear that this is no ordinary young man. For what he has is passion. An infectious enthusiasm for his research and what it can achieve that is almost addictive…"

Shelley broke off. "When I read that I hardly recognised you."

She swept her long dark hair back over her shoulder releasing a waft of jasmine in Sam's direction.

"Who is *that* guy?" she joshed. "He's the one for me."

"Yeah, right! They were banging on a bit, weren't they? But, Shelley," Sam winked, "you know what they say — believe none of what you hear and only half of what you read."

"OK, but if it's only half-right, then that's more than enough for me!"

Sam leaned back in his chair taking all of her in. The tumble of dark hair, the trimly fitted skirt and a body that seemingly danced inside her blouse. He straightened up, crossing his legs awkwardly. A flush of colour rose from his collar.

"So how about a celebratory coffee?"

"Sure." She was smiling more now. "Why not?"

CHAPTER 2

EARLY SUNDAY evening in a penthouse apartment on Wellington's waterfront. With spectacular views of high-rises set against an emerald harbour and backdrop of balding hills, the vista had an almost Mediterranean air in the setting sun. From behind the glass the radiance gave the feel of a sultry summer's day on the Riviera but the bright colours belied the reality that this was Wellington and there was a screaming southerly outside.

Bella Simcox absently surveyed the scene; watching the wind pluck plumes off distant white caps. Her mind was busy pondering her political ambitions. For too long now she'd been a coalition partner bandstanding on the green vote. But being Green Future (Kakariki a Mua) party leader wasn't doing it for Simcox any more.

Her constituency was changing and so, too, were her political aspirations. The backblocks might be where her roots were but she was so over the alternative lifestylers with their dreads and tie-dyed cardies now. They were holding her back.

Face it, girl, all you need them for is their votes. So better keep them sweet.

These days her real constituents were different, a new breed of greenie: the anti-science brigade. Middle-aged, middle-class, part-educated and anti-establishment, with beliefs fuelled by a deep distrust of government and the corporates. Conspiracy theorists to the last, they tended to be anti-GE, anti-immunisation and anti-supermarkets. Anti-everything actually, except organics, without ever really knowing why. Such were the times.

A little knowledge is a dangerous thing, reflected Simcox.

Choosing to opt out is a luxury only possible in developed countries like New Zealand. And with global warming looming her followers might not have the luxury of choice in the future.

The current rash of epidemics was also symptomatic, a consequence of the general erosion of population health measures, environmental degradation and unsafe food production practices so prevalent these days. The epidemics might make it to New Zealand and how would the alternatives cope then?

Recently Bella had noticed the media calling them super-bugs and pandemics. Scary stuff: SARS, bird flu, swine flu, CJD and *E coli*. Every day there were new developments in Asia and Eastern Europe. Sooner or later the outbreaks would spread to here. Public concern was mounting and she figured she could trade on this anxiety.

In spite of, or perhaps because of all this, her public loved her. True, the flashy image and conspicuous consumption didn't sit well with their green values, but she was such an effective champion of their cause. And she never missed a chance to poke a stick at the establishment.

She was a mistress of the politician's art of grabbing media attention — the three-second sound bite of bulleted statements. And in the current climate of doubt and insecurity, beating up on the opposition and on industry only increased her popularity.

Bella drew a long breath as she took a last look at the nation's capital. She could feel the buzz. Her polls were telling her she wasn't far off gaining the numbers. Maybe she could use the current global uncertainty to further destabilise the government and push them over the edge. That would put an early election on the cards, which could well be her big chance. The only thing needed to topple the government was a gentle nudge. And who was she to deny them that?

CHAPTER 3

MIDWAY THROUGH a three-year postdoctoral research fellowship on microbial eco-genomics, Sam Miro was going for it. In his view the planet was a mess, and New Zealand no exception.

The country's clean, green image belied its recent history of resource extraction and exploitation and of fossil fuel consumption. And the environment was suffering. He considered many of New Zealand's current practices to be unsustainable; there was a 'she'll be right' attitude that couldn't continue.

All this left Sam firmly of the view that his research would make the critical difference.

In a recent lecture he'd made plain what he believed.

"We can't go on beating up on the environment the way we are now. Take a moment and imagine New Zealand as a desert. That's how it's going to be if we go on colliding with nature as we are now."

Shock tactics for sure, but for Sam finding sustainable solutions to New Zealand's environmental problems was his *raison d'être*.

Saving the country was what he was dreaming about as he strapped his board to the roof of the trusty Kingswood after a morning surfing at Manu Bay. New Zealand is so worth the effort, he told himself looking up admiringly to Mount Karioi while flicking back matted hair and blinking sand from gritty eyes.

The view is still great even though the bush is mostly gone. And Manu Bay itself, framing the emerald waters of Raglan harbour and the break and bar beyond.

Quiet today but so often wild, the bane of unsuspecting boaties.

Yes. New Zealand is still so worth preserving.

What does sustainability really mean to New Zealanders anyway? Sam pondered as he towelled down, shimmying expertly out of his boardies into a pair of faded jeans. Does it mean scrapping the trusty Kingswood because it's thirsty for a new fuel-efficient hybrid made today from even more scarce resources? Doubt it. And where do things like my motorbike fit in? Face it, it's a shocker for sure; but hey! Nobody's perfect.

The major problem isn't fossil fuels anyway. The real issue facing New Zealand is sustainable land use as a result of current farming practices. Especially the continued degradation of our groundwater. That's the area of research to be in. That's where the serious runs will be scored on the environmental front.

And I want to be in there punting.

Sam's daydream was interrupted by his mate Wiremu Walker, who'd been surfing, too.

"You know what, Sam?" he began, laying his board out to dry. "You're not a bad surfer for a basement boffin. I don't get it though. Don't understand what it is about research that does it for you. Why not chuck it in for a quiet life here at the beach?"

Sam smiled as he rose to the challenge.

"Because a guy's got to have a proper life, bro. For me surfing's just a distraction. Catching waves is great on a day like today but it's not the main event, if you know what I mean. After all, you're a journalist. Who're you to talk? I don't see you chucking in the day job!"

"Ah, but at least I can work from home. That's a good start. What's more," continued Wiremu, "home is Raglan, which can't be bad. Photojournalism is a means to an end for me. But why science, Sam? That's what I want to know."

"Here's the thing. Because science can make the difference — pure and simple. Science will ensure a better future for us all. Isn't that enough? Also," Sam continued almost as an afterthought, "I enjoy doing what I do. That should be reason enough."

"Mmmm. I'm not convinced on a day like today. But hey! I'm too hungry to think about it. Let's head back into town for something to eat."

CHAPTER 4

GREEN FUTURE party leader Bella Simcox was still dreaming of her splendid future when the doorbell rang. The man she'd been waiting for had finally shown up. Forty-something and carrying the unmistakable signs of too many working lunches, Simcox powered purposefully to the front door to admit her visitor.

You could tell immediately Andrej Caradijc wasn't a Kiwi. The tucked-in T-shirt and drill shorts gathered by a white bowstring at the waist were a dead giveaway. The sandshoes, too — so sixties.

Bella gave him a disparaging once-over. Surely he hasn't been sitting in Courtenay Place dressed like that. As indeed he had not. Caradijc had spent the last six hours motoring down from the Waikato at her behest to discuss her project. He had no choice in the matter.

"You're late."

She spoke dismissively as she got an unpleasant whiff of the twenty or so cigarettes he'd smoked on the way. Caradijc looked away, tolerant but unaccepting of her comment. Momentarily the view from her apartment took his mind to happier times and places far away.

"It's a long way to come at your whim." He spoke with a heavy East European accent. "I hope you're going to tell me now what it is you really want."

"To be absolutely clear what I want is a PR coup," she retorted. "I need a demonstration that the government is incompetent on biosecurity matters... A storm to show the government has botched biosecurity. That's what you're about. That's why I brought you to New Zealand. Achieve this for me and I'll make sure you get residency for your family."

Caradijc looked at her in amazement. His Cold War background in the USSR meant he'd seen it all before, but even so, this was a big step for New Zealand and Bella Simcox was, after all, leader of the Green Future Party.

Caradijc didn't know exactly how to respond. Eventually he said, "You have something specific in mind?"

"Of course! But I don't want to know the details of how you plan to go about it. Is that understood?"

She took a moment to collect her thoughts, gesturing for Caradijc to take a seat.

"This is what I've organised," she continued. "I've got people in the Department of Research, Science and Technology (DRST) and they've approved a sentinel research programme to monitor a sample of Waikato farms for changes in the range of bugs found in their runoff. Here's the list of farms. You'll see the first few are doing chicken, pork and dairy. They should be your initial targets."

Caradijc reached automatically for the papers, still somewhat bemused.

"The programme is being run by a young scientist — his name is Miro — in the Institute of Land, Atmosphere and Water Research (ILAWR). Here's the list of what he's monitoring, including some of the more dangerous bugs, antibiotics, GE and the like. His milestone report tells me the programme is on track and he now has all the right analytical systems working. We also have people close to him. What I want you to do is make sure he gets some positive results in his tests. Sufficient for me to make a song and dance about. Got that?

Caradijc nodded emphatically. This woman was clearly used to getting what she wanted.

"You don't mess around, do you?" He was almost admiring. "You must be aware there are risks?"

"Then manage them!" snapped Simcox. "You're the

goddam expert. We're committed to this course of action; that's the only reason you're here."

He decided to let the matter go.

"To make sure you go undetected, I suggest you present as an ILAWR researcher yourself. We've got the gear ready for you. The cash you requested is now in your account." She fixed him with a threatening stare. "And, Caradijc, you must never come here again. If you've got any questions and to keep me updated use only my private email. Oh, and one last thing. This has to be perceived by the authorities as a major biosecurity breach. I want them convinced of a major threat by autumn and on the run. That's your task. That's how your success will be measured."

And with that she showed him the door.

What a cow! And a hypocrite to boot, Caradijc reflected as he slipped out into the twilight stowing Simcox's list of targets safely in an inner pocket as he went. How could a greenie countenance such a thing? But who was he to judge? We all do what we do for our own reasons. Like a chance to get his family back together again.

Caradijc had always known it wouldn't be easy obtaining visas for them; not in the current climate and not with his background. Simcox was still his best bet. He was desperate to be reunited. The longer they were apart the more he missed Olga and the boys.

CHAPTER 5

THE ROUTINE on Monday is always the same at ILAWR, the Crown Research company based at the Ruakura campus in Hamilton. The day begins with a science meeting at nine, and Sam was running late after the sun and action of the day before. He arrived at the seminar room at the same time as the Director and a visitor. Embarrassed, he tried to lose himself in the middle of the third row, where he was surrounded by the centre's other scientists, technicians and students.

When the Director ambled to the front, murmured tales of the weekend respectfully tapered off. Ken Judge was a wily old character, well-respected by his colleagues. Slightly stooped and arthritic from his rugby days, he showed the effects of recent inactivity mainly around his middle.

Sam was impressed by Judge, who had a rare knack for getting the best from his scientists.

"It's like herding seagulls," he would say, with a wry smile.

Though Judge clearly relished the job, his time was nearly up. The jungle drums were beating and rumour had it that Judge was to be eased into retirement. No one knew why but, ILAWR being a government organisation and given his clout, word must have come from the top.

It was evident this was not to be your average Monday get-together. The Director rarely attended operational meetings.

Judge began to speak.

"Good morning, colleagues. I took the opportunity to gatecrash this morning to introduce you to someone important. As some of you know I'll be stepping down shortly and I'm now in a position to announce my successor — Dr Iris Dent."

The room was silent. Judge was well-liked and all present knew he'd done an exemplary job in what were difficult times for science. There was an air of quiet apprehension. What would ILAWR be like under a new watch?

The Director-designate stepped forward for her say. She began with an apology.

"I understand you normally use this slot for other things and my visit was not scheduled. So I want to start by thanking you for allowing me this time."

Sam gave Dent his full attention. Judge was a class act. This new Director would have to be something special to stack up beside him.

"I'm here for an hour and I think it would be helpful if we could get to know each other. I'd also like to give you some idea of what I've got in mind for ILAWR."

Eyebrows were raised at that. The Institute had a proud tradition of environmental research and as far as most in the room were concerned it was in great shape. A strategy to meet the challenges of climate change and environmental sustainability had been developed by Judge with the input of staff, and if it was going to succeed it would have to continue full steam ahead. If anything, it needed more funding and resources given the pressing nature of the environmental situation. So what could Dent possibly mean?

Dent approached the lectern, an imposing figure pushing fifty, with something of the dominant air of an ageing netball coach about her.

"I'm guessing you're wondering where I come from," she began. "The first point is I'm an accountant focused on organisational efficiency. Not a scientist, but I still had to study for ten years without salary or any clear idea of where my career might take me. And I know I share that with you. I studied political science in the UK and did a PhD in financial control. I have worked in a variety of governmental organisations here and overseas, most recently with the National Food Safety Authority."

Huh! No science at all? Sam shifted restlessly in his seat. She'll be a fish out of water here. What relevance has that background got for ILAWR? She comes across as a career public servant.

"It's key that we're aligned in our thinking," Dent continued, "so I'd like to get a handle on what makes you tick, too."

Dent had their absolute attention but no response from her somewhat apprehensive audience. She pointed randomly to the third row.

"You. Could you briefly introduce yourself and your area of research?"

Shit! Sam squirmed as he realised he was in the spotlight. That's what you get for being late!

"Er..."

She signalled for him to rise.

"...My name's Sam Miro and I'm a postdoctoral research scientist here at ILAWR. I did a primary degree in biological sciences at Otago and a PhD in environmental microbiology at UC Davis in the US. Since returning to New Zealand I've been establishing a microbial eco-genomics group and developing a research programme funded by DRST — the Department of Research, Science and Technology."

On familiar ground, he began to relax.

"What I'm doing is investigating the microbiological ecology of leachates from Waikato farm land. Land use and water quality are real issues for a sustainable New Zealand and overall I think ILAWR is doing great work in this area. I enjoy my research as I believe it can make a real difference. The main focus is currently on profiling runoff from a cross-section of Waikato farms, but we're also researching approaches to remediation with a view to improving water quality. We already have some promising leads."

Sam finished to nods of approval from his colleagues, who waited expectantly for an enthusiastic response from Dent.

"Mmm. Interesting. To me this programme typifies where ILAWR is at and what might need to change." She cleared her throat. "Yes, indeed. When we recently reviewed the balance of activities in ILAWR we found that too many resources were being put into curiosity-driven remedial and mitigation research activities, and not enough into the key function of environmental monitoring."

Sam drew a deep breath, somewhat taken aback. He couldn't let that go. Dent could have been generalising, but he was the exemplar. He was proud of what he was doing and could be a compelling debater. He stood up again.

"Dr Dent. Please allow me to make a comment. Firstly, the programme was only funded by DRST last year and they saw real merit in the remedial as well as the monitoring aspects. Secondly, as an organisation, we don't see the point of monitoring if we don't have the means to intervene and correct the environmental challenge. Hence the research into treatments. For example, we have some encouraging data on the use of beneficial bugs to neutralise toxic bacteria in groundwater."

Dent stood there, arms crossed, coolly contemplating Miro. She said not a word.

Sam continued.

"Thirdly, review. To my knowledge when research is reviewed it is done so transparently against clear terms of reference, includes submissions from researchers and involves experts qualified to comment on the quality of science. How is it then we had no idea our research was being scrutinised?"

Dent's body language did little to disguise a mounting frustration. Judge began to think he should intervene. He was about to speak up when she beat him to it.

"Management absolutely reserves the right to review all the company's activities."

A strong statement uttered somewhat defensively.

"Accepted." Sam was on the front foot now. "So perhaps you could tell us what the terms of reference were and who was on the panel."

His workmates' furtive glances bored into him. Shut up, their eyes signalled; this isn't career-enhancing. But that was Sam when his science was under attack.

Dent shuffled papers briskly on the lectern, cheeks reddening. This was supposed to be her day and she hadn't anticipated being challenged by an upstart scientist.

"The review was internal, Dr Miro, internal! In case you don't know it, that's what management does. It manages."

Sam had got the message; she thought him well out of order. He'd better backtrack a little.

"Ms Dent. Please understand this is a science forum. We're used to robust debate here."

"And you, Dr Miro. Please understand ILAWR is under new management and things will be different from now on. For example, organisational decisions will be made by those competent to do so."

Ouch! Sam had been put firmly in his place.

With the score about equal, Dent and Judge attempted to return the meeting to normality with a few platitudes, but the damage was done. There could be no positive outcome. Dent began to toy pointedly with her mobile. Judge made a few conciliatory remarks and the meeting was over.

Listening to the outgoing Director's wrap-up, Dent reflected on what had just occurred. Hers had not been a stellar performance. Sub-par, in fact. In a lonely instant of self-reflection her track record flashed before her. Once a top student, her lack of tolerance had often derailed her progress. It was a recurring theme.

She wasn't big on people or being questioned. Dent had a supporter, though. Bella Simcox — Associate Minister of Research, Science and Technology and Green Future party leader — had wangled another chance for her at ILAWR. Stuff up this time, though, and it would be her last. She owed it to Bella to make a go of it.

She waved her cellphone airily at Judge.

"Oh, dear! Something's come up and I must fly. Let's follow up soon."

With that she swept past the remaining audience into her waiting rental and was gone.

"Ah! That went well," Judge offered, with a wry smile. He winked and added, "Not."

You could tell the ILAWR personnel were in shock. Here and there was a twitter of embarrassed laughter, but mostly there were unmistakable rumblings of discontent. Though it started quietly enough, it quickly built to a crescendo as others added their views. One thing was certain: ILAWR had changed with Dent's arrival, possibly forever.

Sam set himself apart from it all, thinking hard. There was no sign of his usual sparkle. He was struggling to deal with the ignominy of a public mauling at the hands of the new Director. He wasn't used to being the scapegoat.

At twenty-seven he had ably demonstrated the skills that marked him out as a future leader of science. Yet Sam would be the first to admit he still had plenty to learn about workplace politics. Today had been a steep learning curve. Colleagues passed by, with encouraging pats on the shoulder. There were questions and answers.

"What was all that about?"

"And what did you make of her?"

Sam put a brave face on it.

"Seems prone to theatrics, that's for sure."

"You were well and truly done over, mate."

It was said sympathetically.

"Sure was," Sam agreed.

The conversations went on over lunch and with new mana Sam was at the centre of it. Standing up for ILAWR was cool in most people's eyes. But he was preoccupied, and he soon drifted back to his desk pondering a question. What was it with Iris Dent, really?

After a while he realised speculation was futile so he opened his Outlook. No solace there; just the usual forty-something emails for a Monday — fewer than ten of any value.

He tried to settle into reading a paper but couldn't concentrate.

Soon a workmate wandered by.

"We're off to the club for a cold one. Want to come?"

"That sounds like a reasonable idea... Tell you what, I'll follow you down," he said, without looking up from his screen. "I've just received an email from Dent herself."

'I just wanted to say I appreciate that organisations like ILAWR need a diversity of views. Freethinking is to be encouraged. I have had good reports of you and your programme, Sam. You obviously have strong ideas. Your research is important to me and I look forward to working with you. Let's start over. Iris Dent.'

Hmm. An olive branch. Sam stared at the screen, signalling again to his colleagues he would follow.

His thoughts drifted back to an earlier time and place. How would his parents have rated this morning's performance? Odds on, not that highly. They'd probably have been horrified. No one saw the Director's tirade coming, but perhaps he could have done better.

Sam's mother and father wanted only the best for him. He'd had a top upbringing, no doubt about that, growing up in leafy, middle-class Auckland. His mother, Jane, was a cardiologist at Greenlane. His father, Pita, was a practising engineer; a Ngati Whatua success story. When Sam came along though, Pita had willingly thrown in the day job to homeschool the boy. Pita wouldn't have had it any other way and nor would Sam, for they were best friends.

It was harder with Jane, though; there was always a distance between them. Sometimes he had yearned for a kiss or cuddle from his mother and tried so hard to please her. Yet it seemed that whenever he needed her most she was heading in another direction. Deep down there had to be a reason for her remoteness, but until recently he could only guess at what that might have been.

It turned out Sam had been adopted. Pita and Jane had tried so hard for a baby of their own, but could never manage it. Blocked tubes or something. The pressure was destroying them so the opportunity for adoption was a timely relief. And the infant Sam was a treasure. Bright as a button, he was everything they could have hoped for. Pita said he was like new glue in the relationship; a joyous little chap with a shock of blond hair and bright, distinctive eyes.

Sam became the focus of their hopes for the future. Yet the sense of failure and the long wait must have been hard, particularly hard for Jane.

Sam knew he could not have asked for more. Who was he to complain? He should be grateful for the opportunities his upbringing had brought him. And he was. But deep down he knew it came with a certain weight of responsibility. Expectations were high and there was a need to succeed; no pressure, really. And so it was that on days like today his background weighed on him some. This was his cross to bear.

Sam shut down his PC and retired to the pub. The lads were more usually there after work, not mid-afternoon on a Monday. Today was different though because ILAWR had changed.

The first drink didn't touch the sides. The second and third were slower and the conversation grew livelier. And by dusk the assembled gaggle of researchers had solved all the big questions of life, the universe and everything.

At least, to their own satisfaction.

CHAPTER 6

So BEAUTIFUL, the Waikato on a misty spring morning in late September — almost surreal, Sam reflected, as he drove an ILAWR ute out towards one of his monitor farms. Still chilly; the low sun played off sparkling pasture and pearl-drop spiders' webs hanging from distant fence lines while the last waifs of mist danced ethereally above.

Successive farms were dotted with dairy cows or spring lambs fattening for distant Christmas markets. You couldn't get much more organic than this. Sam mused as he drove along. Sheep and cows are powered by pasture and pasture alone.

On a morning like this you could be forgiven for believing in a clean and green New Zealand. Organic almost by definition.

He was heading out from Ruakura on SH1A nor'west through Gordonton towards the Waikato River. Within twenty minutes he had reached Taupiri, dominated by the sacred burial mountain of the Tainui, and turned hard right for Orini.

Here the road wound alongside the Mangawara Stream, by this point sluggish and earthy, meandering through a wetland swamp dotted with cabbage trees and flax. The occasional pair of pukeko went busily about their chores.

Zephyrs of steam could be seen rising from the river in the morning chill highlighted by the low sun peeking through from behind. To Maori this is a mystical place; the home of a taniwha, the spirit of the river.

As he drove Sam was pondering on what an absolute privilege it was to be here on a morning like this and doing something he loved. But his thoughts were also grounded in reality, for in the end he was a scientist. The wetlands must be warm at the moment, he thought, noting the rising steam. A natural fermenter if ever there was one, heated by the rotting vegetation and peat layers below. And that's underselling it, too. More like a fusion of the physical, chemical and biological environments, he reflected. Totally amazing.

The sun was rising higher as he turned into the Mangawara Valley, a remote and fertile stretch of land with an especially temperate microclimate. Ideal for farming, with the hills of sandy loam protecting it from the prevailing coastal breeze and creating a natural suntrap for higher than average temperatures and rainfall.

Flush with new money from the Treaty settlement, a Maori iwi had bought out the local farmers in the mid-nineties and established a trust farm in the valley. At 870 hectares it had scale to enable diversification and protection against unpredictable commodity prices. It was also well-capitalised and well-run, owned by a people who were farming for the future benefit of their children. The Trust Board was also interested in the environment, recognising the major issues facing farming, and amenable to change.

For all these reasons, it had become something of a model farm in the area. The Board had jumped at the opportunity to become part of Sam's research programme — one of twenty such units dotted around the Waikato. The farm always seemed so remote when he was visiting, yet it was less than 10 km from the Waikato River, only 40 km from Hamilton and not even 100 km from the metropolis of over a million in population that is Auckland.

Sam slowed as his ute drew near to the ochre picket fence where a carved arch stretched across the entrance, proudly displaying the name Mangawara Trust Farm.

As he drove in, he saw the propeller-based spray units drenching organic kiwifruit and satsuma trees with a distinctive turquoise-coloured copper spray. Continuing on to the left, he passed the intensive chicken and pig rearing facilities run to high standards using state of the art practices. Selective breeding and improvements in management practices meant the extensive use of antibiotics so prevalent in the seventies and eighties had been all but eliminated here.

The animals were still housed indoors, but not in sow crates, and the indoor housing was for both animal welfare and environmental reasons. Recently the Trust had been pioneering a new system of cropping on the puggy lowlands unsuitable for dairying. The crops, including corn, were used as chicken and pig feed. Self-sufficiency in this cut-and-carry approach would decrease reliance on the corporate feed distributors. They weren't there yet, though, and still used fair amounts of seed and feed formulations from other suppliers.

Further on Sam reached the modern eighty-bail carousel milking shed built recently with money from the extra payout of the dairying boom. The shed was at the very foot of the valley with paths heading out laterally behind to grazing lots on the gentler slopes beyond. Directly behind the shed were the yards for sorting and washing the cows prior to milking. The yards used high pressure hoses and thousands of litres of water for sluicing out the copious quantities of cow muck that accumulated with every milking.

Sloppy, and with the heavy smell of organic waste, the green tide was hosed down into an adjacent holding pond that periodically overflowed into an open drain leading down past the chicken and pig pens and across the front paddock to spill eventually into the trickle that was to become the Mangawara Stream. There are close to a million cows in the Waikato. No wonder nitrogenous groundwater contamination was such a concern.

The foetid course of the drain was deceptively appealing in the early morning sun, glowing with iridescent hues from the interaction of light with the microbial community in the surface biofilm.

Recognising it as an unhealthy site, the drain was avoided by most. Only Sam, with his perennial fascination for bugs, ventured near. He smiled. The punters don't know what they're missing! On that thought he pulled up beside the shed right on time for the last of the morning hose-down.

He donned his branded white ILAWR overalls and gumboots and headed round the pond and down the kilometre-long path beside the drain towards the stream. Working systematically he collected samples of the discharge into disposable lab pots, carefully labelling each before placing them in an ice-filled chilly bin and returning them to the ute.

He had to keep moving but while he was packing up Sam spied the farm manager's daughter Georgina disappearing into the smoko room in the management block behind. Plans are a fine thing, but made to be changed. Georgie must be home from uni, he thought. It'd be rude not to pop up for a cuppa.

Trying not to look too keen Sam stepped out of his boots and slid across the lino entrance into the smoko room, scanning the room for the object of his desire as he went. The scene was less than social. A dozen or so farm hands sat in silence, absorbed by the challenge of their euchre hands. Mugs of tea steamed beside them. Sam felt positively over-dressed in his ILAWR cover-alls given the eclectic mix of farmyard fashion before him. Georgie sat cross-legged on a couch in the corner. Seemingly unimpressed by her surroundings she was lost in her smartphone, texting persons unknown in far-off places. He paused for a moment to take her in. She was a gem all right, with that dark hair, bronze complexion and unusually fine features.

"Hi," he said, stepping up to the couch. "On a break from uni?"

"Yeah. Good to have some time out, but not that much excitement here for a girl…"

Sam was about to reply when up stepped Georgie's father — Phil Towhai — protective as ever. Towhai was an imposing character used to getting his way.

"I've been meaning to ask you, Sam; what's with the other chap from ILAWR? Is he part of your programme?"

"Which chap?"

Phil ignored him, and continued.

"When we agreed to be involved in your programme we settled for one visit a week from ILAWR. These days it's him twice and you once. It's not on, you know. The farm isn't a bloody laboratory; the visits are disruptive."

"I have no idea what he's up to," Sam confessed. "When I asked for help with the sample collection I was told there was no one. As far as I know I'm the only visitor. Let me look into it, Phil."

"Yeah, you do that," Georgie chirped in. He appeared to have caught her interest now. "I noticed him last time I was home, so he's been coming for at least a semester. Give me your mobile number and I'll let you know when he next turns up."

Perfect! Sam smiled as he slipped a business card onto the table in front of her. Mission accomplished. That's exactly what I want; a reason to connect.

No sooner was Sam climbing back into the ute than his cellphone warbled.

"Georgie here. Take a look behind you. This shouldn't be happening, but your research mate has just arrived."

Sam craned his head out the window just in time to see another vehicle with the distinctive markings of ILAWR disappear behind the distant piggery.

"Thanks. I'll get back to you."

"You do that!"

She was definitely showing signs of interest.

Sam drove cautiously down to the piggery and parked around the corner from the mystery visitor. He sneaked a quick look. The vehicle, twenty metres or so away, definitely appeared to be ILAWR. The driver leaned on the front guard, lighting a cigarette.

Confident he could find out what he wanted to know, Sam approached the man from behind. The rear of the ute was stacked with feed bags and a sizable translucent polyprop tank nestled behind the cab. Backlit by the morning sun, the murky shadow of the liquid could be seen slopping within.

Closer now, Sam offered a greeting.

The man turned sharply, obviously startled.

"Oh, hi yourself."

"Sam Miro."

Sam held out his hand. He was now fully in view of the stranger, who seemed hesitant.

"I'm from ILAWR at Ruakura," Sam continued. "Don't think we've met. I didn't know there was anyone else from the Institute working out this way. Which programme are you with?"

The stranger was regarding him in a somewhat hostile manner now. Formidably tall, short-haired and straight-backed, he had something of the air of a military man to him.

"Here's the thing..." He started with a heavy East European accent. "...you can't expect to know what everyone is up to. I'm not based at Ruakura. I'm out of Wellington."

And with that he slopped the residue of his coffee at Sam's feet, climbed into his cab and did a wild U-turn before speeding off, peppering Sam with dust and pebbles as he went. Sam noted the registration number for later checking.

He texted Georgina.

'Need to follow up. Will keep you posted. Can u let me know when he's next out this way? Want to check what he's up 2. Thanks for the tip-off. S'

The rest of the day was wasted. Sam's mind wasn't on work at all. He visited three more farms and went through the motions of sample collection, but all he could think of was the stranger at the Mangawara Trust Farm.

Another confrontation. What was it with him at the moment? First Dent and now the aggressive ILAWR employee.

That reminded him. He pulled out his cellphone and dialled Ruakura.

"Hi, Bev," he said to the receptionist. "Could you put me through to the fleet manager, please?"

"He's in Wellington at Corp, but I can transfer you directly."

The phone clicked, rang and was immediately picked up.

"Trevor Marsh here."

"Hello. My name's Sam Miro. I don't think we've met, but I work for ILAWR at Ruakura."

"Hi, Sam. What can I do for you?"

"I have the number of an ILAWR vehicle from up here that I'm trying to trace. Can you help?"

"Sure. Someone hooning again?"

"Nothing so grand."

"What's the number? I'll see what I can do."

"BFK 657."

"Hold on."

Sam heard faint tapping of fingers on a keyboard and the metallic scrape of a filing cabinet opened and shut. Shortly afterwards Marsh returned.

"Are you sure of that number?"

"Fairly. Why?"

"We have nothing even close to it," said the fleet manager.

"What kind of vehicle is it?"

"A Hilux ute like mine," said Sam.

"Then you must be out by a mile. We don't so much as have a Hilux with a rego starting with B."

"Bugger. I must be losing it. Thanks anyway, Trevor."

And Sam hung up without further explanation.

He'd done enough for one day. Sam finished sub-aliquoting his samples, labelling them carefully and storing them in a –20°C freezer for later analysis.

"I'm out of here!"

Carefully he locked the door behind him and headed home.

CHAPTER 7

WHEN HE was doing his OE Sam didn't go to Europe and get trashed, like most young Kiwis. Instead he took a more adventurous tack touring on motorcycles in Asia, Africa and South America.

These days he lived in a fifties-style brick bungalow in Hamilton East, the walls displaying souvenirs from those formative days.

An astute stranger wouldn't be surprised to learn Sam had a thing for traditional cultures — indeed, for the sustainability of civilisations. He wanted to understand how and why they had waxed and waned; what could be learned from this.

Travel had also helped him develop essential life skills: an understanding of situations and how to handle himself in the real world.

Tonight he walked in through his kitchen, audibly sighing as he went. He slumped onto the couch and flicked on the TV to catch the last of the news and current affairs. Ads on One (as always) so he jumped to TV3 just in time to find Green Future party leader Bella Simcox expounding at her party conference.

Speaking to the converted, she was riding her familiar hobbyhorse — the dire risk to the well-being of the nation posed by the poor state of the environment, lax biosecurity and our food safety regulations. The picture she painted was sobering. An urgent need to repeal current regulations and put in place enforceable laws before it was too late. The question is not *if* there will be a major health or environmental crisis in New Zealand, she prophesied; the question is *when*.

Simcox cut a striking figure; no doubting her appeal to a growing group in society. She had presence and energy and environmental and food safety messages that Sam related to. Nor was she afraid to say what she thought; to stay on message and to take every opportunity to pillory the establishment.

With so many New Zealanders embracing the green philosophy, her willingness to stand up and be counted had greatly increased her popularity. Yet although he was empathetic with the Green cause, Sam personally found the woman overbearing and patronising. There was something about her that made him uneasy.

In closing the item the TV presenter played a clip of Simcox's election as Green Future party leader some twelve months earlier, summarising her rapid rise to prominence. Slightly younger and trimmer, perhaps not quite as flamboyant; her message was unchanged.

A final shot caught Simcox acknowledging the boisterous applause of her supporters as she left the conference hall. As she ducked into the back seat of her car, the camera panned briefly over the assembled throng of devotees.

It took a moment for Sam to register what he'd seen. Was that the stranger from Mangawara clapping and smiling in the clip? Surely not. What would he be doing at a Green Future Party conference?

Though naturally curious, he hesitated — but only for a moment. Then he went into his office and flicked on his computer, entering the search terms: TV/On Demand/Current Affairs/Green Future Party/Simcox until he found the news broadcast he'd just been watching.

He played it through, pausing again as the camera panned the crowd. Finally he was certain. That was him all right — the unidentified visitor to the Mangawara farm.

Sam sat staring at the monitor in the fading light; whether for ten minutes or an hour he couldn't be sure.

Eventually he was brought back to reality by the ringing of his phone.

"Mark here." His mate from down the road. "We're off to the Thai. Are you interested?"

"Fine," said Sam. "I'll see you there."

Thai food wasn't his favourite, but at the moment some company was exactly what he needed.

CHAPTER 8

BY THE time Sam arrived Mark and friends were well into their second Stellas; the conversation more animated by the minute. Exactly what he needed to take his mind off things.

Sam drew out a chair and settled into the frosted green bottle waiting for him.

"Hey, dude. Congrats on the award the other night." Mark slapped him on the back. "Didn't know you had it in you!"

"Me neither, but thanks anyway."

Another friend from outside work picked up on the conversation.

"Yeah, I read the citation though I have to say it was gobbledygook to me. Help me out here — just what is 'microbial eco-genomics' anyway? Can you explain — for your average office worker?"

"That's science for you," chimed another. "A touch wordy."

"Sure could connect better with your average bloke on the street," confirmed Mark.

"No argument there," said Sam. "We need to get a lot better at communicating what we're doing and why science matters. That's my number one challenge."

"Go on, give it a go then; we're listening."

Sam beckoned for another beer. "OK." He began tentatively. "Microbial eco-genomics is about how bacterial families exist together... Here's the thing; bacteria form complex communities, just like humans. They're socially interactive and fill complementary roles. For example, there are the builders, the energy companies, rubbish disposal, etc. The good guys and the bad. It's all there in what they do. And figuring out who does what and how they do it is precisely what I do."

He paused to drain the bottle.

"The study of how different bugs relate to each is the 'eco' bit. The other part is the 'genomics'; that's all about identifying genes to tell which bug is which and what they do."

"But what's the point?"

"Good question," continued Sam. "For me it's about understanding the effects of agriculture on microbial communities in our groundwater and how to use bugs to clean up after the farmers. Environmental issues are a major and I really believe this research can make the difference…"

"Yep, I get it. Some of the fishing streams around here are rubbish these days and it's all down to the increase in dairying."

"Well, maybe…"

Sam could sense he was making the connection.

"And, Sam, you'll know. We were talking about the overseas health scares when you came in. They're calling them pandemics on the telly now. Sounds serious. The Government's set up emergency planning. It can't be that bad, surely? What are the chances of an outbreak overseas affecting us here in New Zealand?"

"Another good question. Being in Godzone didn't protect us from the 1918 flu epidemic," Sam pointed out. "And these days with so much international travel we can't assume that being geographically isolated will be of much help. So I do think it's a bit of a worry, though not to the point of developing a fortress mentality."

"But they're talking about these new superbugs and diseases. What are they again, Sam, and what do they do?"

"CJD, SARS, H5N1 and *E coli* 0157."

"Yeah, that's them."

"Of all these, *E coli* should be the least sinister. It's not contagious in the real sense anyway — you catch it from contaminated food and water. It's widespread in the environment, including on our farms, but given our food standards and practices it shouldn't be a worry. Let the standards slip though and it could easily be another story. Some strains are really bad news, like the 0157:H7 variety. But we've never had an issue in New Zealand."

He realised he had their full attention and went on.

"The other bugs are more serious. They're called xenobiotics because they involve infectious agents crossing the species barrier and sometimes mutating as they go. Nasty stuff. SARS and H5N1 — bird flu — in particular might be sleeping killers."

"So what should we be doing about them?"

"In the event there was a real outbreak there wouldn't be much we could do," cautioned Sam, "except by limiting contact with other people, that is. So go bush! Big pharma is working on vaccines, but they could be years away and cost a fortune."

"No point staying away from the birds then?"

"Not much chance of that with your track record," joshed Sam.

A guy across the table leaned forward. He'd obviously been thinking hard.

"Seems to me it's all about animals. Could it be that the rise of these diseases is down to the intensification of agriculture and man's interference with nature?"

"Woo, that's deep! Yes, we do need to understand the impact of farming on the environment and too many current practices, especially overseas, are not well-informed."

"So pandemics are another result of science and technology going bad?" Mark's friend expounded. "Back to nature is what I say. I'm going to vote Green."

"Huh. Not sure I agree, but I know a lot of people that would."

Sam had come across this kind of reaction before. He leaned forward to make his point.

"The problem is that we can't turn back the clock on earlier progress, and I take the opposite view — that science and technology is the key to improving health and prosperity and the state of the planet. There isn't one challenge we face today that doesn't have science as the basis of its solution. What is true is that progress creates complexity and that many of today's intractable problems result from the more dubious consequences of earlier technological advances. That's the legacy we have to live with. And the challenge."

"I'm not convinced."

"OK. Take the car as an example." Sam was well into his stride now. "Yes, the human factor means there are accidents and they do pollute, but I don't think anyone would dispute the enormous benefit that has resulted from them as a form of transport. What we need to do is find solutions to the problems they've created and make them better. For example, through green energy."

"I can't see you selling your Holden anytime soon," said Mark. "You can't be a greenie and run a car like that, Sam. Yet somehow I suspect it'll be a while before we see you in a hybrid!"

"Hey, nobody's perfect. Anyway, enough... How about some food."

Sam was keen to end the debate.

"I reckon the safest option tonight might be to go vegetarian."

"Chemical cuisine for me, please. Nothing biological…!"

And with that the science lecture was abandoned for a serious study of the menu.

CHAPTER 9

DRIVING THE three kilometres to Ruakura the following morning Sam anticipated a productive day in the lab to focus his mind. He'd been taking things too seriously of late. Getting back to basics would help.

The day before he'd had a call from Max Logan, his PhD student, who had some data he wanted Sam to take a look at. Max had been with Sam for about a year, and Sam knew he had chosen well. Not only was Max smart; he was also resourceful and reliable. In science, such qualities were essential for success.

He had picked a good 'un, Sam reflected. Max was not a straight A student, but he did have real-world skills. Spent a year doing VSA in Kenya, builds his own computers and is into extreme sports: evidencing a degree of knowhow and independence essential for a doctorate.

A month ago Max had passed his twelve-month academic review with flying colours and was starting to get results. His project was in the area of Sam's real interest. The sentinel farm monitoring work he was funded to do through DRST was essential to develop a comprehensive picture of changes in the microbiological ecology of New Zealand farms, but to Sam it was like stamp collecting.

Despite what Dent might think, the real progress would be made by developing biological control technologies. For example, introducing beneficial bacteria to the environment to intervene and mitigate the effects of current agricultural practices, such as nitrogen runoff. Biological remediation was Sam's main interest and that's where he wanted Max to work.

Sam picked up a coffee and made a beeline for the PhD office where Max was settling in behind the computer.

"Hi, Max. How's it going?

"Hi. All good." Max ducked his head and pointed at the screen. "The data's building up."

"Great. And we're well overdue for a session, so why don't you put what you want to tell me on a memory stick and bring it round to my office? It will be more private there."

"Neat! I'll be round in five."

When he arrived, Sam took a few seconds to put Max at ease. If the guy had a fault, it was worrying too much.

"I expect you're glad the review is over, Max. You did well, so no worries, eh? Now's the time for you to get your head down and make some real progress. What've you got for me today?"

Max pulled the file up on Sam's computer.

"I'm getting some interesting results in the latest round of the growth inhibition studies."

"Go on."

"Remember you had me using the *E coli*/bifidobacteria inhibition model? I've been passaging the bifido prep and I think I've found a variant that is highly inhibitory to *E coli*. In fact, I could say toxic, especially to the more dangerous H7 variety."

He pointed to the on-screen photographs of culture dishes.

"How did you do that, Max?"

"I co-plated 0157 and the test bug and monitored growth of the *E coli* over time. Can you see it? This is a growth of 0157 in the absence of test bugs and here again with it." Max brimmed with excitement. "Major, major differences, don't you agree?"

"Absolutely. Several log orders for sure. The interaction is certainly not stimulatory or benign, so you're right. It appears to be antagonistic."

Sam straightened and signalled a little caution.

"It's definitely a good start. How many strains of bifidobacteria are you working with?"

"About twenty." Max had a glint in his eye. "I sub-cultured them from your stool sample. Remember?"

"Ah, I had a gut instinct about that. Altogether a better class of waste, but you had better try some more." Sam winked. "Now show me the range of effects you're getting with the bifido strains."

"Take this, for example; it's completely wiped out the growth. But the others have no effect."

"My God." Sam was taken aback by the clarity of the results. "What's your hypothesis, Max? How do you think it's working?"

"I've been thinking about that. Is the effect purely competitive or more than that? I'm wondering whether the variant could be toxic or predatory to 0157."

The words were tumbling out of him now.

"I tried to get hold of you to discuss it and I could see you were busy, so I did another series of experiments. Sam, I don't think it's competitive inhibition as neither space nor nutrients should be limiting in the early growth phase on agar plates."

He paused. Sam was listening intently.

"What I did next was grow out 0157 to the plateau phase where 0157 levels are stable and then add the test bugs. And do you know what I found?"

"Shock me," said Sam. "Good experiment, by the way."

"Thanks." Max was eager to continue. "At the very least there is some interference, but overall the effects are so marked that this particular strain of bifidobacteria is much more likely to be toxic."

He beckoned Sam closer to the screen.

"Look, it wipes out the 0157. You can tell immediately the *E coli* cultures have been destroyed!"

"Far out!" Sam was genuinely impressed. "Have you found anything else?"

"The effect also seems to be 0157 specific. And I'd go even further — it is demonstrating preferential effects against the enterotoxigenic H7 variety. That makes it all the more interesting. I've tested it against a raft of other *E coli* variants and other bugs and it seems benign against those. Graded effects against the other *E coli*s, but nothing like the effects on 0157."

"Fantastic." Sam was genuinely thrilled. "You might be on to something here, Max."

The two scientists settled back in their chairs and began to discuss what next: dose response curves, mechanism of action studies and genomics. Perhaps some media transfer experiments to determine whether it was the bug itself that was so toxic or something it was secreting. Either way, they agreed, this discovery had real potential for practical applications.

"Oh, one final thing," Sam told his student. "You'd better pick up an invention disclosure form. There could be a patent in this for us."

"And you know you asked me to check the effect of copper on *E coli* growth curves? Don't know where you got that idea from, but guess what? That's producing interesting results, too. At low and intermediate concentrations copper actually seems to increase bug growth. How about that?"

"Really? Thanks for that, Max. You've making good progress here."

Sam tried to remember why he'd asked for the copper work to be done in the first place.

"Oh, yes. Organic sprays. They could be a compounding factor in these environmental studies, especially on organic farms. That's worth a paper on its own. Keep up the good work, Max. You are well on track for an excellent thesis here!"

CHAPTER 10

IF THE plan was to keep a low profile in the rural heartland Andrej Caradijc could not have chosen better. At first glance the farm was totally unremarkable, though a bit of deferred maintenance and a load of top dressing wouldn't have gone amiss.

The rusting old tractor, sagging fences and pockets of gorse spoke of a place that had seen better times. The ramshackle collection of farm buildings were true to form as well: utilitarian and functional and in need of a lick of paint.

Not that the neighbouring farms were much better.

On closer inspection things didn't quite stack up. The 4WD Hilux, resplendent under a corporate paint job. The galvanised iron barn with boarded-up windows, locked sliding doors and surveillance camera. Not exactly the Waikato.

And, finally, the dogs. Definitely not your average working animals, but Rottweilers. Sturdy and well-muscled, with a suspicious and menacing air; itching to have a go.

Behind the barn was the home paddock, bordered by bush running down from the hills behind and out to the road. A few random sheep and heifers grazed lazily within. On the surface, there was not much farming going on here.

When Caradijc stepped out of the house, the dogs jumped up and whimpered expectantly. On realising he was not there for them, the whimpers changed to whining and then rose to a cacophony of howls and barks as they strained at their leashes. He ignored them and strode on purposefully towards the barn.

He, too, was in farmyard mode, to be taken at first glance as any other cocky in khaki shorts and gummies, black woollen singlet and dusty denim cap. With a wary glance around, he slid the heavy door open a metre or so, stepped inside and closed it behind.

When he turned on the lights it was patently obvious he was no ordinary farmer and this was no ordinary barn. It could have been mistaken for a modest brewery or dairy factory with stainless tanks set against white walls and a solid cement floor.

To the left was a conical spray dryer, crafted from everyday items by someone who knew what he was doing, and something resembling a giant cake blender modified from a concrete mixer.

To the right was a row of pallets neatly stacked with sacks or feed bags. The equipment and pallets suggested a working production line.

Caradijc headed for his office to turn on the computer, pausing only briefly to climb into overalls. He sat down at the keyboard and spent some minutes analysing process control data. Then he began to go about the serious business.

Taking samples from the fermentation vats he carefully measured temperature, acidity and absorbance. He could almost have been mistaken for a vintner, but the fluid was not the tell-tale red of a full-bodied Merlot, but more of a cloudy Sauvignon Blanc.

Once the measurements were systematically recorded and interpreted, Caradijc took the samples into the adjacent lab. On a long bench were a microscope, Bunsen burner and rows of neatly stacked culture plates. Caradijc donned latex gloves and a mask, lit the burner and sterilised his plate-scraper before dipping it into the culture samples and expertly spotting them on to new plates.

Working quickly he returned the lids to the plates and took them over to the incubator, removing others that had been plated earlier. Moving along he prepared dilutions of scrapings from yesterday's plates, mixed them deftly with a coloured dye and spotted them out onto microscope slides. Then he turned to the microscope, closely studying the slides and recording cell concentrations and physical characteristics.

Satisfied that fermentation was complete, he returned to the carport and drove the Hilux up to the barn. He attached a hose from the fermenter to the tank sitting behind the cab. Turning a handle on the side of the barn he watched intently as the tank filled with culture fluid from the fermenter.

Back inside he settled to the next task of the day. Still wearing the mask, he connected a hose from the fermenter via a pump to the top of the dryer and turned it on. The machine whirred into life and after a brief delay the sprayer kicked in at the top of the machine. A beige powder trickled reluctantly from the base into a waiting bucket, the process continuing for what seemed an age.

He was finished at last with the remainder of the fermenter's contents successfully dried. He carried the bucket of powder over to the mixer for the next stage of the process.

Carefully Caradijc opened sacks of chicken and pig feed from the pallets, tipping the contents one at a time into the mixer before adding a scoop of the mystery powder, a kilo of additional corn from a second distinctively labelled sack and a scoop of yellow powder from a second sack labelled ampicillin and tetracycline.

He switched on the mixer and watched intently as the contents slowly rotated. Once assured of a proper blend he transferred the contents back to the original sacks, which he expertly resealed. He repeated this operation again and again until he had dealt with every bag of animal feed on the pallet.

Then he began all over again with a second pallet of corn seed, methodically repeating the mix and seal operation until he was done. To all intents and purposes the sacks were as new, completely untouched.

By the time Caradijc was finished the sun was sinking,

but still he was not done. Sweating heavily now he lifted up the contents of the two pallets — sacks of 20 kilos each — and stacked them carefully on the back of the ute for delivery the next day.

Then he rewarded himself with a shot of vodka from the bottle in the fridge. This was not the high-tech operation of his past in the USSR. The dark days of industrial-scale preparation of biological agents for the Soviet military were long gone and it was unlikely now that a war would ever be conducted as envisaged by his masters during the darkest days of the Cold War. And thank goodness for that.

Caradijc knew the risks involved; had experienced the tragic loss of many friends and colleagues due to 'accidents'.

Yet he carried within him the learning from his early days in Kazakhstan. Essentially, the purpose behind the science remained, and in a funny way Caradijc was proud of his improvised lab in the backblocks of New Zealand.

Two shots of vodka later and the pain of his lonely existence eased.

CHAPTER 11

On a chilly spring morning with the city pocketed in fog Sam drove from Hamilton East to Ruakura for a day in the lab, his mind on the accumulation of samples collected over the last few months from the twenty Waikato monitor farms.

The samples had been safely stored in a freezer and analysis was now due to begin. Testing was threefold: chemical, for estimation of the basic minerals in effluent streams including nitrogen, phosphorus, copper, etc.; bio-actives for measurement of herbicides, fungicides and antibiotics; and microbiological analysis to profile the range of bacterial life forms present in the samples.

Additionally, Sam would test for evidence of GMO contamination of feed or produce that could also evidence issues of biosecurity. He wasn't sure why they wanted this, but the GMO screening was a request in the feedback to his grant proposal. DRST was insistent and Sam had not argued. His philosophy was to take the money and run.

Chemical analysis for the major minerals was routine these days with samples analysed in semi-automated fashion. High through-put auto analyser instruments were now commonplace in most labs. Conversely, the bio-actives were determined by more advanced LCMS technology. Whereas the auto analyser could be run by a technician with relatively little training, LCMS required skilled technicians who knew what they were about.

Sam had learned who the effective operators were in the lab and was relieved when his friend Shelley Lai was shoulder-tapped by management to work on his project.

The micro was Sam's specialty. Following his days in a

state of the art lab at Davis he was considered a leader in the techniques of molecular microbiology.

The Californians had brought new and more discriminating approaches to micro based on genome sequencing. Gone were the days of protracted cell culture methods to identify bacterial species by class, family and species. These days bugs were identified using species-specific DNA probes by high-tech PCR and micro-array approaches. What the new techniques had done was take all the art out of modern microbiology, making it faster and more specific. In turn this markedly increased the amount of information that could be generated.

Sam had extended off the learning at Davis to build a sophisticated technology platform for the measurement of community DNA. This approach allowed for the simultaneous measurement of DNA from all species in the microbiological community of a sample at once, rather than painstakingly separating and culturing each species first.

This was a brilliant conceptual leap with the potential to result in a paradigm shift in molecular microbiology. For the first time it allowed for convenient profiling of the entire range of bacteria in samples.

Sam's contribution was to make no assumptions about what species were present or to undertake any preliminary culture work, but to measure all bacteria simultaneously using a family of molecular probes. Then he could use sophisticated bioinformatic computing techniques to unravel the wealth of information obtained.

Such an approach was audacious and typical of how technology had impacted on biology by integrating chemistry, hardware and software to enable 'in silico' measurements at such high through-put and with so much power of discrimination as to blow the minds of microbiologists of the past generation.

Key to the new developments had been the linked

sciences of genomics and bioinformatics and the enormous power of mainstream computing.

Sam's analytical system had already put him at the forefront of ecological molecular microbiology globally and garnered a range of patents. He was invited to speak at major conferences and present papers in prestigious journals.

To date the technology for measuring community DNA was Sam's major claim to scientific fame and something of which he was justifiably proud. His work had gained him the recognition and respect of his peers.

This was the technology he was recruited to bring to ILAWR and which underpinned the successful award of the DRST grant that provided the funding for his current research.

Since arriving at the Institute Sam had established and carefully validated his analytical methods and this research programme was to be its first full application in New Zealand. Many eyes were on him and he was understandably protective of his work. Like most research scientists, he had his supporters and his knockers. Science is as competitive as any other field, and a repatriating Kiwi with a high profile was regarded as something of a tall poppy.

This had its upside, too, and Sam enjoyed the attention. He was a popular role model for younger scientists and technicians; an example of the new breed of scientists keen to develop a better future. But he had to be on his toes.

CHAPTER 12

He was early for his scheduled meeting with Shelley Lai, the technician assigned to help him run his sample analysis programme. Sam was hopeful of a good relationship between them. By all accounts, Shelley was great in the lab and, as he was fast finding out, fun to be around too.

To describe Shelley as a stunner was something of an understatement. Full of Eastern promise, she had the sought-after pale skin, pursed lips and sculpted nose of an exotic beauty; all set off by a statuesque body and unusual dark wavy hair. Her perfume today was a seductive blend of green tea and spice and her figure was set off to perfection by a fitted print dress.

As she entered, his jaw dropped.

"Oh, my God! Has anyone told you how amazing you look in that?"

He blurted out the words before he had time to think, then he realised he was being indiscreet.

"Oh, sorry, sorry. I didn't mean that… Didn't mean to say that, that is... But you do look great."

"Oh, Sam, don't you worry," she replied, smooth as you like on realising he was tying himself in knots. "That's absolutely fine. I'm flattered."

"It's just I'm so over the denims and micro fleece that most of the techos are wearing."

"Me, too."

She took a seat opposite.

"Sam, I'm so glad you spoke up for the Institute at the meeting the other day."

"Seriously? Thanks. I could have done better. Dent caught me off guard."

"Yes, I could tell. But you stood your ground for what you believe in — your science and the Institute. I'm excited to be working with you on this project, Sam. I'll learn so much."

He couldn't help but be touched by Shelley's disarming flattery.

"I've heard you're pretty good at what you do, too. Perhaps we can learn from each other."

"Sure." She leaned forward and patted his hand. "So let's talk about your research programme and what you need by way of sample analysis."

"Oh, that..." He snapped back from a momentary daydream. "I'd nearly forgotten."

He pulled up the Excel spreadsheet with full details.

"Let's talk to this, Shelley."

She leaned forward attentively as Sam began to take her through the programme; getting her head around the design, timelines and expected outcomes. And what he expected of her.

She made him feel like he was the only person in her world. Shelley was totally absorbed and interactive, listening intently and asking insightful questions. This was one smart woman; he was lucky to have her on board.

When he had finished she began to add some thoughts of her own. He was expecting to work through the samples from start to finish. She proposed instead a survey-style analytical programme intended to save time and enable them to focus on samples of interest.

As he listened he was impressed and his confidence grew. She knew what she was doing; best to let her do it her way.

Slowly it dawned on him that there was more going on here than a technical discussion, however interesting. The signs were all there: body language, eye contact and chemistry. He didn't want the meeting to end. After all the aggro of the last few days this felt good; it felt right.

And then his mobile rang...

"Hello. Sam here."

"Hi, doc. It's Georgie from Mangawara."

"Who? Oh, Georgie, hi. Sorry, sorry, I do remember. A bit distracted is all."

"Guess what, Sam? Our mystery man is back. Do you want to check him out?"

"Of course. I'm at Ruakura. I can be there in an hour. Can you keep him busy until I arrive? Oh, and Georgie — do you have a motorcycle helmet?"

"Sure."

"Good. I'll see you soon."

Sam turned to Shelley. "Sorry. I've got to go. Something's come up."

"Oh, that's too bad. I was enjoying this."

She sounded genuinely regretful.

"I'll press on with the samples, Sam. You have to focus on the micro, so why don't I make a start with the chemistry and bio-actives as we discussed?"

"Sounds great," said Sam. "And, Shelley. Let's catch up for that coffee and check progress in a day or so."

"Sounds good to me, but I've got a better idea. Why not come around to dinner sometime soon. There's someone I'd like you to meet."

"Oh my. What a nice idea. I'll look forward to that."

And with keys jingling and a spring in his step, Sam was on his way.

CHAPTER 13

THOUGH SAM had relished the interaction with Shelley he couldn't wait to get home. He was in the Kingswood and out the East Street gate as fast as the ageing sedan would take him, a faint haze of blue trailing behind. He needed to understand what the stranger in the ILAWR ute was all about.

Within minutes he was dropping his laptop bag on the study couch. Heading for the bedroom, he changed into denims and jacket and made for the garage that housed his newest treasure.

The motorcycle was Italian by design, gleaming and resplendent in black and orange. He'd had few chances to ride her recently and this excuse was better than most.

Swinging himself into the seat he turned the key and hit the starter button. The V-twin engine barked into life and he settled back, pulling on helmet and gloves before easing the bike out onto the road.

He gave it time to warm up as he headed out onto Gordonton Road, on the alert because this area had its hazards. The side road for Orini was quieter, tight at first then opening out into a series of wide sweeping bends arcing into fast straights through undulating country. He was swept along, reminded again of how perfect Waikato roads are for a sport bike like this.

Finally he was alone and able to give the bike its head. There was nothing to match the feeling of the wind pushing into his helmet as his speed increased. Up through the gears into top; wide open for a few seconds and then feathering the brakes to scrub off speed for the next bend.

Such power and grace.

Lay it into the turn. Suspension soaking up the bumps; bike tracking smoothly to the apex of the curve; leaning to the limits of adhesion. And then pick it up again and ease on the power, the back tyre clawing for traction and the front reaching for the sky as bike and rider are catapulted to the next turn.

Sam was going for it now but still riding well within himself. This was one of the few ways he knew to truly relax, the most fun to be had with your clothes on. So good, in fact, that for a moment he almost forgot why he was going to Mangawara.

That is, until he arrived.

CHAPTER 14

QUESTION TIME in Parliament and not the first occasion Prime Minister Jeremy Grafton had come under siege. Along with the usual bravado and banter from all parties there was no doubt the constant badgering by the Opposition was taking its toll.

Two years ago the Grafton government was on a roll with a clear mandate under MMP and driving through its reform agenda on a number of fronts. With progress came the inevitable infighting in caucus, followed by resignations, defections and scandals. Now their majority had been whittled down to one, forcing the Government into dependency on its uneasy alliances with the coalition partners.

Especially the Green Future Party.

Dark days, and Grafton's government was clinging to power by its fingernails.

Today the tension in the Chamber was palpable.

Through two hours of questioning the PM and his supporters stood staunch and steadfast on issues of education and health, inflation and immigration, food safety and the environment. No one had anything new to say, but still you could tell Grafton was at his wits' end, sweaty-browed and sneaking glances at his watch, willing the session to end.

Throughout it all an impassive Bella Simcox remained seated on the coalition benches. She had been given the Associate Minister of Research, Science and Technology role by Grafton and was also spokesperson on the environment and immigration. Frankly, a sop. A lame attempt to placate her in the Grafton government. Simcox saw the appointment as useful, but only as a temporary fix.

She was deliberating on how to play this, reviewing her meeting with Caradijc; of the effort she had gone to not only in setting him up but in leveraging her network to infiltrate ILAWR and get Miro's research programme funded by DRST. Her rationale was clear.

Simcox intended this Government to fall by engineering a demonstration of their incompetence. She was certain she would succeed. Soon she would get what she was owed.

For Bella Simcox it had been a long and winding road to the top. If she'd been even a touch more reflective she might have wondered why she was still dissatisfied with what she had achieved. Especially given her track record and success. For, after all, she was now a Minister of the Crown.

Why was this not enough?

The easy answer could be that Simcox was consumed by naked ambition; that she had an unbridled lust for power that wouldn't be sated until she rose to the very highest levels in politics. Until she held the reins of power. And that she was a woman capable of doing anything to get there.

But the question of why she was so driven ran deep indeed. There were signs in how she went about things. The uncompromising focus on control, on self-promotion and success broadly hinted at a woman who believed she still had plenty to prove.

Born to hippy parents in the back of a two-tone Kombi van, protesting was in Simcox's blood. Her early memories were of denim, paisley and love beads; of the Queen Street anti-war protests, trips on an anti-nuclear protest yacht, and camping at Bastion Point.

She was bright enough, though, and by the time of the Springbok Tour in '81 she was already beginning to question her parents. What was it with them? Why did they need to be recidivist protesters? And why live in that ghastly Coromandel commune? Even if it did work for them it was certainly no place for a self-respecting teenage girl.

So by the age of fifteen she had begun her own protest; rejecting her parents' values, their way of life and, finally, school, too.

For a time she was a wild child, dropping out to live rough in South Auckland and doing whatever it took to get by. Finally, caught in the crossfire of a gang war over a useless patch of urban desert, Bella found herself pregnant with nowhere to go but home.

What followed was a watershed moment for the younger Simcox; a sharp lesson in human nature. She soon learned that the endless summer of love that was her parents' bohemian lifestyle wasn't so free and easy after all.

Despite their rhetoric about social justice their expectations for their daughter were very different. What they wanted for her was so much more. Achievement and success, peer recognition — everything they seemingly had been unable to achieve for themselves.

Instead of being welcomed back as the prodigal daughter, the young Bella was castigated and demeaned. Her parents left her in no doubt that she had let them down and would come to nothing. The final humiliation was being packed off alone to the country for the baby's birth, all sense of self-worth now gone.

By now Bella felt gutted; desperate to get the birth over; to get rid of the child and then to prove to her parents how wrong they had been. A bitter young woman, she wanted nothing more than to succeed big time; if only to rub their noses in it.

And now here she was, sitting in the Chamber as a Minister of the Crown, holding the trump card. Bella Simcox was close to the top, but not there yet. When it happened, it would be a resounding demonstration of her ability and success. She would show them.

Then, and only then, she would have proven her parents wrong.

And got the monkey off her back, once and for all.

Forewarned is forearmed, Simcox reflected; quietly taking in the proceedings of the Chamber. When Miro's data starts to flow I will expose the government's incompetence on biosecurity. The fallout will topple them like a house of cards and trigger a general election, which I will win because I will have the numbers and because I am the undisputed mouthpiece on environmental and food safety matters in New Zealand.

A complex and risky plot; audacious enough to take out the Government in one fell swoop — and that had its attractions. It would give Simcox control and freedom to pursue her own agenda for a change, besides creating roles aplenty for her inner circle to keep them sweet.

A plan so clever that it deserved to succeed.

Simcox came out of her reverie and allowed herself to relish the caning Grafton and his colleagues were taking at the hands of the Opposition. Her silence only added to the sense of drama in the house. For now she was content to let it run — to set the scene.

Finally, in the closing moments of the session, she rose to a heavy air of expectation.

"Madam Speaker," she said, "can the Prime Minister assure the house that there have been no new breaches of this country's biosecurity that are likely to call into question the government's handling of food safety and environmental matter?"

After a long pause, Grafton responded.

"I am not aware of anything and I can give the Honourable Member that assurance!"

A perfect answer. Satisfied, Simcox sat back down.

And with that the session was over.

CHAPTER 15

THE BIKE was too distinctive and would attract unwanted attention. As Sam pulled through the gates of Mangawara Farm he hit the kill switch and coasted in behind the kiwifruit canopy, parking well out of sight. He left helmet and jacket behind and took the path towards the assembled farm buildings.

Passing the pig shed he saw the ILAWR vehicle parked alongside the storage area. Interestingly it was up on a jack with the mystery man intent on changing a wheel. Without hesitating Sam continued towards the smoko room where he expected to find Georgina.

He passed the chicken barn.

"Psst! Sam, over here!"

Georgina was crouched behind a pile of old drums at the end of the shed. He moved towards her, carefully watching to make sure the stranger had taken no notice.

"Hey, doc." Georgie kept her voice low, but was obviously excited. "It didn't take you long to get here. Did you fly?" She leaned closer. "Aren't you proud of me? I thought I'd be proactive and slow him down some."

She gestured towards the Hilux.

"Good work." Sam settled in beside her. "What's he been up to?"

"Just a bit of tyre kicking."

"I want to find out what he's doing here and then follow him. You up for that?"

"Sure am! We could use some excitement around here."

While speaking, Georgie eyed Sam up covertly. Not bad. Not bad at all for a nerdy scientist.

"Great." Sam smiled his approval. "That's cool."

With the wheel change complete the Hilux was soon back on all four tyres and Sam and Georgie started to focus on what was going on. They watched as he lugged two heavy bags into the storage room of the piggery and returned empty handed.

"What are they?" asked Sam.

"Feed bags, I think."

"Why would our friend be delivering feed?"

"Perhaps he's a philanthropist."

They fell silent as the interloper got back into the Hilux and drove over to the chicken barn, pulling up not thirty metres distant from them at the entrance to the storage shed. He repeated his routine. A sweep-around glance to ensure no one was watching and then he carried another two bags into the barn. Off again to the seed barn where he deposited yet two more.

Finally he drove round to the milking shed, where he pulled up close to the settling pond. Here he varied the process. Sam and Georgie looked on in awe as he tugged a heavy hose out from the tank on the ute to the pond. He turned a handle on the nozzle and the tank's contents began to flow into the pond.

"For fuck's sake!" It was all too much for Sam. "What the hell is he doing?"

"You tell me! You're the scientist."

The pumping continued while their quarry lit a fag and puffed on it as the contents of the tank continued to drain into the pond. When the cigarette was finished, so was the job. He wound up the hose, climbed into the cab and headed out towards the gate.

"Quick!" Sam nudged Georgie. "Let's see where he's going."

Off they dashed, emerging by the motorcycle as he pulled out onto the road.

"Your bike, Sam? Far out!"

He patted the Aprilia affectionately.

"Yep. We should manage to keep up with him on this."

By the time they were kitted up and away Caradijc was already some distance down the road. Not that Sam was worried; there was only one route for the ute to follow until it hit Orini Road and it didn't take long to locate the mystery vehicle again. When they did they stayed well back so as not to alarm the occupant.

Georgie held Sam tight; she moved well on the bike, following him seamlessly from side to side. Clearly she knew what she was up to. But then, they were only dawdling.

The ute turned for Orini and the wide open spaces of Tahuna before dodging onto the side road that ran alongside the stream at Hoe-o-Tainui. Sam noted the progression and that the route was familiar to him. When the Hilux reached its destination he immediately recognised it as another of the sentinel farms in his research programme. Hardly a coincidence. His disquiet increased as he pulled into a roadside picnic area a few hundred metres past the farm entrance.

"We won't be able to see him from here."

Georgie's voice was muffled behind her visor.

"No, but it will be hard to get into a position where we can. What we can do is check if he's shed a few more bags when he swings back. That would be revealing enough for a start."

Georgie raised her eyebrow. "How do you know he will pass this way again, Einstein?"

"Call me a dreamer, but I'm beginning to see a pattern here. This is another of my monitor farms. A coincidence? We'll know for sure if he goes to any more of my farms and they're mainly in this district."

"You're joking."

When he shook his head she was inclined to believe him.

Sam was pale and preoccupied as he tried to figure out where and why.

"So is he or isn't he something to do with your programme, Sam?"

"Not that I'm aware of. Unless it's someone checking up on me. And that doesn't explain the bags and discharge."

He half-groaned. "It gets weirder by the minute."

Georgie was frowning as she tried to puzzle it out. Sam was lost in his thoughts, and she squatted patiently beside him, before getting up to work off her frustration by kicking an old Coke can around the car park. She soon came running back.

"Quick, Sam!" she gasped. "He's coming."

They hurried out closer to the road hiding behind a stand of pines. As the truck passed by a quick glance confirmed their suspicions. The load had been lightened by a few more bags and the tank level reduced.

"Another thing, Georgie," said Sam. "The other day I got his number, but the fleet manager convinced me I had got it wrong because it wasn't on his list of company vehicles. I've just checked again and I was right — BFK 657. So how do you explain that, Miss Smartypants?"

"Duh! That it's not a company vehicle at all."

"Correct! Despite the markings."

Back on the bike they resumed discreet pursuit of the Hilux. Sitting well behind they followed as it headed out through Tahuna and across the flats towards Morrinsville. Finally, on the edge of Scotsman's Valley, it pulled into a third farm.

By the time Sam had pulled off the road into a secluded area guarded by toetoe he had partly got his head around things. Besides being his monitor farms they all shared common demographics — the relatively unusual combination of dairy, poultry and pork production, and each had a stream nearby for that matter. There was only one more farm like that in the cohort of twenty Sam was monitoring.

But one question led to another and Sam's desperation to find out what was really going on continued to mount. He turned to Georgie, his hand resting momentarily on her thigh.

"Don't bother getting off. I'm willing to bet where he's heading next."

And with that they took off helter-skelter along a myriad of sculpted Waikato roads to a picturesque farm nestled beside the Waihou spring creek off the side road to Putaruru.

Conveniently the next farm on the stranger's itinerary offered more cover. They parked under the main road bridge and worked their way upstream below the lip of a flood plain cut by the Waihou Stream.

After a kilometre or so Sam clambered up the bank to confirm their location. As he had predicted, the cluster of farm buildings belonged to the fourth in his series of monitor farms.

Watching him climb, Georgie couldn't help noticing that Sam had a great body to go with that mind of his. She smiled as she watched him. While she waited for his return she sank into the grass beside the track, taking in the crystal waters of the creek below, the clear blue sky and a line of gums on the ridge swaying gently in the breeze.

He returned shortly.

"What a jewel of a spot this is."

"I reckon." Sam settled in comfortably beside her. "I'm guessing the stranger'll be here in about an hour."

"And how do you propose we spend the time till then?" Her tone was light and teasing. "It's amazing here. It makes me feel so very..."

Giggling, she walked her fingers playfully up his arm.

"Perhaps you planned to bring me here all along."

She had Sam's attention now. He had almost forgotten who he was with; his mind too busy playing out scenarios around the mysterious behaviour of the stranger. But Georgie was a woman who couldn't help but make her presence felt.

He rolled onto his stomach and studied her carefully. She was a looker all right; earthy and tanned, with the kind of body a guy could make his life's work. Her hair had resisted all efforts of the motorbike helmet to muss it up. Her low-waisted jeans profiled classic legs and a disarming butt. And her T-shirt had risen high enough to offer a glimpse of tummy and a navel ring flashing erotically in the golden light.

Au naturel. He gazed into Georgie's eyes, the question he wanted to ask unspoken. How hot are you? And how weird is this, he reflected. This morning wild horses couldn't have dragged me away from Shelley. And now here I am with Georgie and wouldn't have it any other way. Yet I've more than enough on with work and the stranger. For me it seems to be feast or famine with girls. But it's been so long and I need the company bad.

Sam rolled onto his back and lay there in the grass daydreaming. Beside him Georgie arched her back, running elegant fingers through her hair, lips puckering suggestively. For a while he was entranced by her profile but drifted off in the afternoon sun, his imagination full of the fantasy before him.

He was brought back to full attention by a splash. Georgie, stripped to bra and panties, disappeared into the crystal waters. Immediately he was alert: wide-eyed and focused.

"Oh, God, that's as cold as," she sang out as she surfaced. "Come on in, why don't you?"

Sam stood up, not needing much convincing and with only a momentary twinge of self-consciousness, dropped his jeans. Wearing nothing but a smile and his Massimo boxers he launched himself into the bracing waters. Gasping, he propelled himself upwards to meet Georgie waiting for his embrace. Her breasts pressing into him took away his breath and any power to speak.

Her foot played up his thigh.

"What else can you do besides science?" She was teasing him again. "And when am I going to find out?"

He laughed and took her into his arms, but the waters of the spring creek were too chilly and they clambered back onto the grassy bank to spread out in the sun, hands clasped, laughing gleefully together.

"Ah, Georgie, you're sensational."

He had finally found his tongue.

She turned towards him, eyes wistful and far away, and raised her face. Sam held her to him and kissed her hard. She offered no resistance, pressing closer.

"Come on," she whispered. "Let's do it."

"You sure?"

She was smiling broadly.

"Absolutely."

To emphasise the point, she slid her hand slowly up between his legs.

"If you're up for it, that is."

"If!" Sam rolled over and pinned her body beneath him. He repeated incredulously. "If!"

"Wait."

Georgie pushed him gently aside to sit up and slip off her bra; her nipples dark chocolate on cinnamon breasts. She leaned back and wriggled out of her panties, casting them aside. Then she lay back and held out her arms.

"Oh, Georgie. *IF*?"

By now Sam was incapable of resistance. He touched her. She was cool from the water, but warming as his mouth roved over her breasts and down her belly. Oh God. The taste of a real woman, naked, open and willing. He slipped into her and all too soon it was over, though she was still smiling.

Waiting expectantly.

Watching him.

Still smiling.

Soon she was ready to go again and pushed him onto his back, sliding seductively on top. He stroked her gently and she began to gasp, rubbing against him, her eyes half-closed; rolling, misty and unfocused. The urgency increasing. And then they erupted again, backs arching, fingers stretching, toes curling with orgasmic pleasure until she collapsed onto him with delight. He held her against him until they found breath enough to kiss and giggle and kiss some more. Two human beings as one, sweaty and sated, wearing nothing but a smile.

"Far out, Georgie. That was well beyond the call of duty."

"Didn't hear you complaining."

"Did you think I would?"

She leaned on her elbow absorbed by his face. Playing fingers reflectively around his nose and eyes. Then she spoke.

"Where on earth did you get those eyes, Sam? One green, one brown, like the countryside. You're blessed, you know; one in a million."

"Don't know actually. Guess it's in my genes." He spared a thought for his unknown parentage.

"Yeah," she jested, "and we both know there's plenty in your jeans."

Then she climbed to her feet, the sunlight gilding her body, and tossed them towards him as if to reinforce her joke.

"Hey," she continued, "perhaps today has given new meaning to your work on cleaning up the environment."

"Don't know about that, Georgie, but I do thank you for giving me something so perfect to think about."

She spoke so softly Sam could hardly make out what she said.

"You're welcome, Sam. You're very welcome."

Suddenly remembering why they were there, Sam checked his watch, quickly dressed and clambered up the hill. A minute later he was back, smiling at Georgie.

"Your timing is perfect. Our man's just coming up the drive."

He was relieved he had correctly guessed this fourth location.

From the shelter of the bank they watched the now familiar routine begin.

"You know what?" Sam turned to Georgie. "We're not going to learn anything more here. I think we should head back. Judging by what's left on the ute this is probably his last stop. Maybe we should try tracking him back to his base."

He kissed her gently on the forehead and silently they walked back hand in hand, to the bike. By the time they were kitted up the ute was turning out onto the road away from them. They allowed him a minute or two and then pulled out behind.

The road meandered down from Putaruru before crossing the main road to Rotorua and heading on towards Tauranga Road. Finally on a remote stretch near Okoroire the ute slowed past a belt of trees running down from the hills behind and turned into a shingle driveway.

Sam pulled up by the trees and sat with Georgie watching the stranger park beneath a carport, stretch wearily, and pat a clamorous rabble of dogs before retiring inside.

They had found his base.

After a moment spent taking in the location Sam restarted

the bike and they retraced their steps to the nearby Okoroire pub, where they ordered beer and a plate of fish and chips. There didn't seem much left to talk about, so they sat quietly, comfortable and content in each other's company.

When they were done eating, Sam squeezed Georgie's hand.

"Come on, girl. It's getting cold out there and I'd better get you home."

Indeed, the sun was now setting. Sam hesitated.

"One thing though, Georgie. I'd appreciate it if you didn't discuss today with anyone till I get things straight in my head."

Thinking only of their interlude in the long grass, Georgie smiled broadly.

"Don't worry, doc. You're my best-kept secret!"

Soon they were speeding towards Mangawara, wanting to beat the dark. Georgie rode effortlessly behind him, matching his body moves and trusting his judgement. Sam could tell she truly enjoyed the thrill of speed.

When Sam pulled up at the farm gates she climbed off and stretched — a little cold and stiff from the day's exertions. She pulled his head close and kissed him round his open visor.

"Don't wait too long to call me, Sam. Do you hear?"

"I hear you."

And with that he hit the starter and was gone.

CHAPTER 16

SAM TUMBLED into bed and slept the sleep of the innocent, waking abruptly at dawn to face the reality of a big day ahead. Working on autopilot he was in the lab by 7.30am, knowing full well he needed to focus totally on the analyses. Unfortunately, his mind wasn't on it. Instead he sprawled back in his chair, feet on desk, supping coffee and endlessly replaying the events of the last few days. He needed to understand where it was all heading.

Of particular concern was the 'stranger' because of his unspecified connection to Sam's programme. He began to recap. The facts were these: firstly, the man is using an 'ILAWR' vehicle that doesn't check out. From that, Sam deduced he was not an ILAWR employee. If he worked at Ruakura, Sam might not know him, but he would at the very least know *of* him, particularly with that accent.

Though seemingly based in the Waikato, when challenged he had said specifically that he was working out of Wellington. Odd indeed for ILAWR. Secondly, he had a positive ID of the unknown man with Green Future leader Bella Simcox.

Thirdly, he claimed to be delivering various materials to the farms and yet the Mangawara Trust manager didn't know anything about him. Presumably, neither did any of the other farmers.

The deliveries were to Sam's monitor farms, and, as far as he could tell, only those farms. This made the matter personal and central to his research. He needed to know what was being delivered and why.

He got another flat white from the Institute's coffee machine and returned to his desk. He twiddled a pencil and fiddled with his iPod and pondered what to do. Ah, coffee, a great aid to clear thinking. Ex-Director Ken Judge used to say the coffee machine was possibly the best investment in networking and team building ILAWR ever made.

Aha! Ken Judge. Sam knew immediately that he was the man to talk to. First, he must ensure he had all the information needed. Unless there was something odd about the deliveries, he had nothing to blow the whistle on.

He needed to phone Georgie. Maybe she could get him some samples to test. He reached for his cellphone and pressed the recall button.

Finally she answered.

"Go away!"

Go away? Clearly Georgie was not a morning person.

"Hi, babe!" Sam hoped he could work through this momentary setback. "How are you?"

"How do you think? It's not even nine o'clock yet and I don't do morning." And then. "Oh, sorry, sorry... It's you, isn't it? You interrupted me, Sammie. I was dreaming of us. It was oh so good but then the phone went and you ruined it all." She sighed, then giggled. "Too bad. Still, there'll be another time. So, what can I do for you?"

"I'm trying to figure out what's behind those deliveries we witnessed. Can you get me some samples, Georgie? Spoon whatever's inside into plastic bags and tie them off. Oh, and stick a label on. Will you do that for me, please? And I'll come over and pick them up for testing."

"Beat you to the draw." Georgie was fully awake now and eager to tell him. "You're going to be well impressed, Sam. I thought of that already and wandered down to the shed after you dropped me off last night. Do you know, I couldn't tell which bags were his. The ones he delivered look exactly like any other. Bizarre, eh? We'd have to sample them all."

Georgie was in full swing now.

"But, Sam, I reckon he'll be back tomorrow. That's the pattern, isn't it? I'm going to watch him by hiding away in the shed. There's an unused office upstairs and he'll never know I'm there."

"Be careful, Georgie. I don't want anything to happen."

"Don't worry. I know what I'm doing."

"Well, OK. But really, be careful, please. By the way, I'm flattered you were dreaming about me."

"I'll ring you when I've got the samples."

Logging on, Sam surfed the online staff list to get a number for Judge. Sadly it was nowhere to be found. The man's entry had been deleted with indecent haste.

Sam frowned. He'd seen that number somewhere.

"Aha!"

The ex-Director's number was strategically fixed to the wall behind his computer. Sam dialled. Would Ken pick up? Finally he did.

"Hi, Ken. Another great day at the office?"

"Yeah, right." Ken's tone was sombre. "I'm packing."

"Ah, the ritual clearing of the desk." Sam paused. "Is this an awkward time? I wanted to have a coffee with you, but no worries."

"Always happy to talk, Sam. Meet you at the coffee station in five."

Vintage Judge, thought Sam. He's always made time for me, no matter what. And he certainly must have some stuff to work through right now.

Judge had been a great mentor to Sam and the other young scientists before him. Sam had been recruited by him, and he had taken particular note of his protégé's progress since his arrival. Equally, Sam had formed the habit of staying close to Ken, being grateful for his counsel as he grew into his new job.

Sam was waiting when he saw Ken ambling dejectedly along the corridor towards him. He rose to his feet, an unconscious gesture of respect, and fetched the older man his usual latte.

"We've got to do something to mark your departure," said Sam. "Is anyone on to it?"

"Don't know. Doubt it." Judge shrugged. "They want me out the door like yesterday, so no chance of that right now. My news and the staff meeting the other day have hit morale. Everyone is down in the dumps."

"Can you blame them? Ken, I for one don't intend to let your farewell go unheralded. But it might be better to let the dust settle on the changes, don't you think? You can be certain the staff are keen to celebrate your contribution."

They supped their coffees, and after a time Sam continued. "Why the rush to get you out the door anyway? That's what I don't understand."

"Me neither, not on specifics anyway. At my first meeting with Dent she left me in no doubt where she was coming from. Irreconcilable differences, she said. Within five minutes of our introduction she was telling me that my politics and leadership were wrong for the organisation and that the culture I had fostered at ILAWR was diametrically opposed to her intentions."

He stared dolefully at Sam.

"Strange really, especially given the recent *Herald* article which described my leadership as inclusive, participatory and transparent — all the buzz words I would have said."

He sighed.

"If that's so wrong ILAWR had better watch out because it's heading for a draconian future. My contract was up anyway, I was just hoping for a final two years to ease into retirement. It seems the contract was all the excuse needed; she was quick to tell me they wouldn't be renewing it."

"Scary stuff," Sam concurred. "The staff feel like the

rug's been pulled from under them. Me, too, for that matter, especially after the other day's theatrics. It's all a bit unsettling, isn't it? Still, I suppose we have a choice; some more than others. If my job doesn't work out, I can always head back overseas."

"Good for you, lad. That's the attitude. You'll have plenty of opportunities coming along. It's the suddenness of change that comes as a shock, isn't it?"

Ken drained the last of his latte.

"When you're young without too many commitments, change doesn't matter too much. As for me, I'll be able to concentrate on my golf and trout fishing. How bad can that be?"

Ken sat up straighter and focused his attention on Sam. "So, what can I do for you? You sounded worried. Is it about Dent?"

"Yes — well, maybe..."

Sam didn't know where to begin. He drew a deep breath and started over.

"Some bizarre things have been happening lately that I'm struggling to get my head around. I was hoping you could help."

"Such as?"

"Please. I have to assume this conversation is in total confidence and that you won't think I'm totally mad. In fact, we should probably go somewhere a little more private." He shepherded Judge into an adjacent meeting room. "You recall when we set up my farm visit programme we had to agree to limit our access. It was quite an issue — right?"

"Right."

"Imagine my surprise then when I banged into another ILAWR employee at one of the farms the other day."

"Shit happens." Judge replied pragmatically. "That's organisations for you. Sometimes the left hand doesn't know what the right hand is doing."

"I know, and I can cope with that. But Ken, this guy didn't want to know me. Told me to piss off in no uncertain terms. He reported to Wellington and it was none of my business. He's distinctive, too; got a heavy European accent, so not to be missed. I would've noticed him for sure if he was out of Ruakura."

"Wellington, huh?" Judge was unsure why Sam was bothering him with this stuff.

"But it didn't end there. The ILAWR vehicle he was driving doesn't check out either. It's like he's just masquerading as one of us. The other thing is, what he's up to. He's targeting my farms, and here's the thing — Ken, I don't get this at all — he's not taking anything from the farms he visits. The reverse, in fact. What he's doing is making deliveries of feed and stuff. Weird. So tell me, Ken. Why would an ILAWR employee be delivering stuff to my farms? Especially when the farmers don't know anything about it!"

"What sort of proof have you got?"

"Nothing yet. Only what I've seen!"

"Sam, I agree with you. It's all a bit odd, but you need to firm up on the facts. I believe you totally because I know you. But if you tried telling anyone else they'd think you'd lost the plot."

"So help me out here. Maybe I have. Can you think of an explanation?"

"No. That's not the point. Only you'll be pushing the brown stuff uphill trying to convince anyone else."

"I know, and I'm working on that. Bear in mind this has all been happening over the last two days."

"OK, Sam. And I agree it's strange. So let's stay in touch. Here's my private cellphone number. You'll be able to get me on that."

"Thanks so much, Ken. I feel very alone on this, and a bit out of my depth as it's political."

"What do you mean, political…?" Judge replied, pricking up his ears.

"I don't know who the stranger is, but I do know he's associated with Green Future party leader Bella Simcox!"

"You're joking! How do you know that?"

"I saw them together on TV."

"Well, now. That's more like it! Simcox has been sniffing around ILAWR for quite a while."

Ken was frowning deeply now as he thought about what Sam had just told him.

"You're right, Sam. This needs careful attention. Keep me posted. Oh, and Sam. I strongly suggest you keep this to yourself. Watch who you talk to, especially with the changes around here. I'll make some enquiries."

He got up and pitched his empty cup into the waste bin.

"Oh, and one last thing, Sam. Gather as many facts as you can. A few pics, that sort of thing. And hey, lad, be careful, won't you? Simcox can play hardball."

"I hear you. We'll talk again soon."

With that they went their separate ways.

Back in his office among a stack of cartons Ken ran over the damned redundancy thing again in his head. It was so out of order. He was going in a year or so anyway, and Wellington knew that.

So why the indecent haste?

Nothing lasts forever, he was old enough to know that. And it was his own damn fault that he was hurting now. Since his wife died, and with a grown-up family overseas, he'd made the classic mistake of becoming married to his work. It was all-consuming, occupying most of his waking hours and his emotional energy. He loved it: the science, the politics and the people.

Now he was being kicked for touch. No ILAWR. What could he possibly find to do?

CHAPTER 17

WALKING TOWARDS the chicken shed Georgie Towhai tried to recall the salient facts from the recent 'chain of evidence' module from her criminal law course and apply them to the current drama.

The interloper was going to extraordinary lengths to deliver bags of stock feed and it was unlikely he was doing it for fun. There had to be a motive. Outwardly the bags were indistinguishable from the standard chicken and pig feed. In fact, he was going out of his way to make them look normal. So the answer as to why he was delivering them had to lie in the contents.

Sam had the means to analyse them, but in order to do so Georgie had first to identify the bags he was delivering and then to sample them. Without this proof the story would always sound fanciful because, frankly, why would anyone bother to go to such trouble?

She had brought with her the digital movie camera her father had given her for Christmas. Like other seasonal gifts, Georgie had shown an initial flush of enthusiasm for the present, but for the last eight months it had stood idle on her bedside table, looking for a use. Light and agile, solid state, times ten zoom and it worked well in low light conditions. It would come into its own, perfect for the sleuthing Georgie now had in mind.

The upstairs office in the chicken feed store was perfect, too. She slipped through the door and ran up the stairs. No longer used, the office allowed her a good view of the storage area and the entrance, through an external window. Georgie prised open the dusty window and brushed away the cobwebs. She panned the camera over the entrance a few times to get her eye in and dusted off a convenient chair. Then she settled in for what could be a long wait, texting friends from uni to catch up on their holiday dramas as she waited.

A couple of hours ticked by and Georgie was bored and restless by the time a tell-tale crunch of tyres on gravel announced the arrival of a vehicle outside. She leapt to attention, ignoring the threat of a panic attack. After a few deep breaths, she sidled over to the window and peeked out.

Oh, God; it was him all right. For a moment she froze. Common sense prevailed and, determined to get Sam what he wanted, she switched on the camera, brought it up to eye level and focused the lens.

She panned across the ute catching the intruder as he hoisted a twenty-kilo sack of feed onto his shoulder and headed for the door. Keeping herself together, she stole quietly across to the head of the stairs and continued the sequence with shots of Caradijc entering the store below and lowering the feed onto a stack of identical bags.

He paused briefly to line it up before going back out to repeat the process. All caught on camera. How good was that? Spying wasn't so tricky after all.

When he returned to his vehicle Georgie pressed replay to satisfy herself she'd got it right. Flushed with a new-found confidence, she decided to explore what else she could get. As he went through the regular stages of hauling in and stacking up she discreetly tracked his every move. Move over, Peter Jackson!

When he had departed and she reviewed the recording, Georgie was impressed that by some miracle she could clearly identify the bags he'd deposited for later sampling and that she'd got a good clip of the imposter by the ute.

Back at the house she filled her pockets with supermarket

bags and borrowed a spoon, kitchen knife and Magic Marker from the kitchen. Back on mission to collect samples for Sam the man to do his thing with, she was just in time to see the stranger pulling out onto the road and away. No need to fear she'd been tumbled.

In the shed Georgie positioned the camera strategically on the stairs, lining it up on the stack of feed bags so she could film herself sampling them.

As she stabbed the knife into the first bag dust motes rose gleaming in a stray shaft of golden light peeking through a dusty window. Tearing open a flap to reveal the contents, she scooped a spoonful into a plastic bag before tying it off. She labelled the bag 'Chicken Test 1', standing where the camera could record her actions.

Conscious again of what criminal law required, she decided on a control to cover all angles. She plunged the knife into an unopened bag, securely shrink-wrapped, from a pallet off to the side. This she labelled, predictably enough, 'Chicken Control 1'.

Satisfied with her methodology, Georgie sampled her way methodically through the stores, finishing with the maize seed stock. She made a mental note to remind Sam that it was about to be sown out.

Finally, pleased with her efforts, she retreated outside to the shade of a tree and texted Sam.

'Hi. Treats aplenty at farm. Fancy a sample or 2? Tell me when u want to collect. X. G'

CHAPTER 18

SHELLEY LAI was plodding her way through the mound of samples Sam had delivered for analysis. His expectations on turnaround were ambitious; but fortunately high through-put analytical chemistry was what she did best. She figured that, going like crazy and assuming there were no problems, it would take about a week to get through the first round.

She was just pulling on her lab coat when the phone rang.

"Dent here."

As if one could mistake that nasal growl voice for anyone else.

Shelley froze. She had never met Iris Dent face to face and had no reason to expect a call from her now. To say she was surprised was an understatement.

"I need to talk to you about something."

Shelley had no time to respond before she continued.

"Ms Lai, you've been put on to the Miro project for one reason, and one reason only. To keep me personally updated on the trial results as they come in. I want you to get close to Miro and make sure you're fully informed. Use whatever means you think necessary." She paused. "We all know how charming you can be... As the data is processed get his interpretation of it and summarise the facts for me without delay. This is of the utmost importance and your top priority. Is that understood?"

Her tone was low and menacing.

"Oh, and about confidentiality. I will email you an independent address. All communication is to be through that address from now on. Is that understood?"

Shelley, stunned, found herself nodding. Dent obviously

took agreement for granted and continued with hardly a pause.

"Make sure you speak to no one about this. You hear me?"

This time Shelley managed to stutter her agreement.

"Oh, and one last thing," Dent continued. "I know your employment contract is up early next year. You do know that if you lose your job, immigration will pack you off on a slow boat back to China as quick as look at you, don't you? So if you harbour any hope of staying in New Zealand you'll want to make the most of this opportunity, won't you? I hope I make myself clear."

"Er, yes."

The meek reply was all a gobsmacked Shelley could manage. And with a click the Director was gone.

Shelley sank into a chair and attempted to steady herself. Surely Dent was not serious? Shelley hadn't even met the woman yet here she was being pressured by her. Blackmailed, in fact. That was not how it was meant to be in New Zealand.

Whatever the reason she'd been targeted Shelley felt suddenly very alone and powerless, uncertain whom she could turn to. Probably no one would believe her. For why on earth would Director Dent behave so despicably?

Shelley, head in hands, reflected on her own vulnerability. She was trying to be the best she could; to do a good job and lead a quiet life, desperate to put behind her the chaos and abuses of her past in China. So far things had been going so well. And Dent knew what she was talking about. Shelley did need the job to maintain her immigration status. Lose that and she'd certainly be off back to the old quarter of Wuhan.

Shelley sighed. There was nothing she could do. She returned to her work, determined to lose herself in the analyses. She was hoping against hope that if she put her mind to something else the nightmare would simply go away.

CHAPTER 19

SAM WAS on edge after his meeting with Judge. Deep down he had hoped his old mentor would tell him he was losing it; that he had overlooked some obvious explanation for the recent developments. But that didn't happen. In fact it was the reverse. He had managed to persuade Judge that something was indeed awry here. There was some dirty dealing going on that needed following up.

Sam knew he'd been avoiding the analytical work like the plague; not surprising, given the dramas of late. Yet it was patently clear that if any answers were to be found it would be in the samples. That made getting on with the analyses a first priority. The samples had been collected and a strategy for analysis agreed with Shelley. Now it was time to begin.

And that meant assaying Georgie's samples upfront. He picked up the phone.

"Hey, Shelley. Here's the thing. Something's come up and I want to include some additional samples."

"OK. What's the problem?"

Her tone was diffident.

"Oh, nothing really," he said, deliberately playing down the issue. "I want to cover the possibility of contamination, that's all. Think of them as positive control samples. I'm more anxious than ever to track changes so despite our discussion the other day I think it's essential to focus on samples from the following farms. Have you got a pen handy?"

"Yes."

Sam cited the codes for the four farms he had followed the stranger to, with a couple of others for comparison.

"I'd also like a selection of earlier and later samples if that's OK. What do you think?"

"To be honest, I don't get it, but whatever." Shelley was still stunned by her earlier conversation with Dent. "Especially after our meeting the other day. But it's your call, Sam. How do I really know what's going on? Tell me one thing, though. Why those farms?"

"Call it a hunch." He was deliberately vague. "Let's take a look at what we get, and I'll explain more later. The extra samples are in plastic bags in the genomics lab fridge. Let me know your overall sample selection and I'll make sure I do the same ones."

"Will do." She spoke listlessly.

"Shelley, is everything all right?"

"Sure. Never better." She tried to sound convincing. "One thing I'm looking forward to is dinner tomorrow evening. How about 7pm?"

"Sounds great."

Sam stared at the phone long after he'd hung up. He hadn't tagged Shelley Lai as being moody. Something wasn't right here. I'll have to be careful... I don't want things getting complicated with Georgie, either.

Shelley, too, was staring at the phone, fighting an almost irresistible urge to phone Sam back and tell him all. She burst into tears instead.

CHAPTER 20

By TAPPING his broad network of collaborators and accessing available microbial collections Sam had built up a prodigious library of bacterial species and strains. From these he had painstakingly cultured purified genomic DNA, using genome sequencing and bioinformatic techniques to identify species-specific segments of DNA. In turn, these were used to produce synthetic DNA probes that could be used to bind and identify individual microbial species in his samples using advanced micro-array technology.

In preparation for the series of analyses Sam had also prepared a batch of micro-array slides. With a state of the art robotic pipettor he had methodically produced hundreds of postage stamp-sized slides, with 384 spots on each, by spotting the DNA probes for individual bacterial species onto specific locations on the slides. The slides were then carefully stored for later use.

To perform micro-array analysis genomic DNA was extracted from the community of bacteria in samples, amplified, adjusted to standard concentration and then labelled with a fluorescent dye. The extracts were then applied to the micro-array slides and incubated. This enabled sample DNA to bind to complementary sequences on the slides before washing to remove any unbound DNA.

Fluorescence scanning was then used to reveal which spots had dye-bound DNA denoting the presence or absence of specific bacteria in the samples. Additionally, control samples and blank spots were used to ensure specificity of the method and sample dilutions to determine the relative amounts of each of the bacteria by comparison to standard DNA preparations of known concentration.

During the morning he prepared and labelled DNA extracts from over five hundred samples and in the afternoon Sam incubated them with the micro-array slides: one sample per slide. The next morning the hybridised slides were washed and then read using a sophisticated micro-array reader fitted with a fluorescence detector. The slides were scanned and images recorded. Fluorescent signals at individual locations revealed the presence or absence of individual species of bacteria in the samples. Sophisticated software was then used to interpret the vast amounts of data produced.

As he sat in front of his PC Sam wondered how well the analyses would go. His mind played through aspects of the methodology: specificity, accuracy, precision, controls and dilutions. Was his new neural network pattern recognition software up to identifying sample differences?

Most of all he wondered what the analysis would tell him. It was proceeding in real time and the major changes in microbial composition across samples would shortly be popping up on the screen in front of him.

The apprehension for a researcher doesn't get much better than this. This is what scientific research is all about. Getting your head around a new data set and recognising it could result in a major breakthrough. This is the researcher's version of the best fun you can have with your clothes on. A moment of excitement and anticipation.

For Sam this was the moment of truth.

And then the wait was over. The PC started up and the monitor blurred as screens of data rolled out before him. First by line, then as bar graphs and correlations, colour changes denoting differences and trends between samples. Data on this scale would take an age to interpret, but Sam could tell at a glance there was stuff of interest in the results. His eyes lit up as he started to get a sense of what he was looking at. The colour-coded signals were there.

The data was going to be hot.

Despite the interpretative software he also knew full understanding of what the data meant would take much longer.

He would need to focus on the recent samples if he was to figure out what was going on. Sitting at the keyboard he selected the results from the Mangawara farm, dialling in on the feed samples. He panned up and down looking for differences between Georgie's carefully collected samples. Overall it was unremarkable. The samples contained the expected range of bacterial species in the low levels normally found.

As Sam skipped through the screens he was almost convinced there was nothing remarkable there, until he got to screen five. And there it was, hitting him like a proverbial tsunami. The stranger's pig and chicken feed samples contained enterotoxigenic *E coli* 0157:H7 at such high levels they were off the scale. Unreal. Surely he must have made a mistake. But the controls were all there and everything checked out.

Sam sat at the computer for a long time surfing for explanations. Blaming the analysis, blaming himself, excluding other factors such as accidental contamination. Increasingly uncomfortable as the reality of what was before him burned into him. At first sceptical, he kept on checking, coming back always to one inescapable fact. Everything checked out.

Overall the results were mundane except for one thing. The mind-numbingly high levels of genomically pure *E coli* 0157 in Georgie's samples. What's more, the levels were real.

This was dangerous stuff. At these levels the *E coli* could easily contaminate produce and enter the human food chain with no difficulty at all.

Sam decided to find out what was happening to the pigs.

He panned for the results of samples collected from the drain where pig and chicken effluent entered. The alarm bells were ringing. The 0157 was there, too. Fairly harmless to chickens and pigs, who were really just vectors, 0157 could be lethal to humans.

That gave him an idea. The stranger had been visiting the farm for an estimated three months. Sam had been collecting drain samples for six. There was a power of data here. He began to pull up a set from a random sampling of the drain some five months ago.

Surveying the data from earlier samples he immediately noticed that all the usual microbial players in the animal effluent community were present in the samples, and showed graduated increases in abundance from the stream back up the drain to the effluent pond. No surprises there. They included the microbial faecal coliforms, gram positive and negative bacteritypes, archaebacteria and *E coli* to name only a few.

What was surprising centred on the *E coli*. Many of the expected variants of the family were present in more or less normal amounts. But the enterotoxigenic O family was almost absent from the early samples, as it should be, he thought; only present in the minute traces that might normally be expected in a farm setting.

Fast forward to the present and the 0157 levels increased dramatically coinciding with the period the stranger has been visiting the farm.

Another bombshell. The levels of 0157 were high throughout the length of the drain including the portion well up above the chicken and pig units on the run to the dairy effluent pond. How could that be? If the cows were contaminated, too, that would be most unusual.

Thinking hard, the awesome reality of what he could be dealing with came crashing down on him like a Raglan breaker in a westerly gale. Georgie and he had witnessed the stranger's activities, including the discharge of effluent into the pond. By far the most likely explanation for the findings was therefore that it was his discharge that caused the contamination of the drains with the highly dangerous H7 variant of *E coli*.

Ballistic. Sam fully understood the human health risks of this *E coli*. If the variant found its way into the food chain, in all likelihood fatalities would result. Yet deliberate contamination was by far the most likely explanation for the obscene levels of 0157 in the feed. It seemed that bugger could well be spiking the bags he delivered with *E coli*. But why?

Sam paced restlessly as the horrifying reality of what the data indicated struck home. Taken together the only reasonable explanation for the findings was a deliberate and co-ordinated programme of environmental contamination. Sabotage, in fact, was the only sensible conclusion.

What an absolute nightmare. He still hoped desperately to find he had made a mistake. It was all so unreal. Why would a person so obviously connected to the Greens' leader Simcox do such a thing. It doesn't make sense but the results were compelling.

Sam could only guess at the time he spent digesting the findings and weighing everything up. He was intent on playing out the reality of what he was dealing with and the questions it raised.

He was racked with self-doubt and concerned about his own reputation as a scientist. The whole thing was inexplicable. Something about his analysis must be off-key. He needed to double-check before he spoke out. He needed to be sure.

He decided to go home. But then the phone rang.

"Hey, doc, it's your Maori princess here."

"Oh, hi, Georgie."

He rubbed his eyes, and refocused from the surreal images of doom that had been rolling around in his head.

"Only I don't feel too much like a princess today. Must be something I ate. Don't think I'll be able to meet up later as we said. Sorry about that."

"You're ill, Georgie? That's no good." Their date had completely slipped his mind. "Don't worry about it, Georgie. Take care of yourself. I'll check in later to see how you are."

"I will. See you, hon."

With that she was gone.

Sam was concerned enough to make a note to phone her later. Then his mind returned to the problem of the data. He was mentally replaying what they knew of the stranger when the phone rang again.

"Shelley here."

God. Why was everyone calling him now? He desperately needed quality time to think. Sam forced himself to be polite.

"Oh hi, Shelley. How's it going?"

"That's the thing, Sam. I've got something of real interest here. I wasn't expecting much, you know, but I've ended up with a goldmine of data I need to run past you."

"That makes two of us. I've got data that is positively bizarre. Let's talk it through tonight."

"OK. I'll bring my notebook. Why don't you put anything you've got on a memory stick and we can talk to that as well. I could help you plot it or get it into PowerPoint or something, whatever's needed, so you have it in a form to present. I know you're busy, maybe that's a little extra I could do to help."

"Brilliant. By the way, don't go to any trouble for tonight, will you. It'd be nice just to sit with you over a glass of wine."

"Don't you worry, Sam."

When he rang off he was smiling broadly. She's an absolute gem, really. No wonder everyone thinks the world of her.

CHAPTER 21

IN HIS office, Ken Judge was finally getting into the packing, his mind as busy as his hands. As he worked he was mentally reviewing his conversation with Sam Miro. True, Sam tended to take things a bit seriously, but there was enough in what he had said to give Judge pause for thought. Something told Judge this was something that should be followed up on. But what to do? Especially as he was now on the outer at ILAWR.

The shocker for Judge was the possibility that Greens' leader Simcox was meddling in ILAWR business. This wouldn't be the first time as Judge had tumbled her interfering once before and her motives were less than honourable then to say the least.

Though she had appeared to back down, she had lost his trust. Even after he had discovered her previous interference she had still managed to make political capital of it and he had ended up being publicly castigated. Judge had not forgotten that. If she was up to something shady once again he needed some inside info to decide what it might be and what to do about it.

That conclusion arrived at, Judge picked up the phone. He was through immediately.

"Roger McWilliams speaking."

"Hi, Roger. Ken Judge here."

"What an unexpected pleasure," McWilliams responded. "I thought you'd been put out to graze!"

"Sort of, but there's life in me yet."

"I heard you were being replaced at ILAWR."

"Yeah, that's true. But I don't think of it as an end though. Rather a new beginning."

"Good man. So what can I do for you today?"

Judge and McWilliams went way back. In Judge's job he often needed insight into what was really happening in Wellington. The capital was a different world with a pulse and a language all its own and whenever Ken needed the lowdown he had used McWilliams.

A man who had the 'speak', McWilliams had made a career of doing lunch with the lads from the government departments. Picking up and interpreting the subtle innuendo of how things were said and what was left unspoken and what it meant to the business of government. McWilliams was so seriously good at what he did that he made a living from it and over the years Judge had done much repeat business with his man on the ground in Wellington.

"I need the good oil on Bella Simcox, Roger. I've heard a whisper she could be poking her nose into other people's business again. Specifically ILAWR. You'll remember she had a go at us once before."

"Yes, I remember. But why would you be bothering about that right now, Ken, given your change of circumstances?"

"Let's call it a hunch. No need to push it too far. If something falls into your lap, then fine. Otherwise we'll let it go. I'll send you my private email address. Make a few calls and get back to me when you can. Cheers, mate!"

"Hang on a moment, Ken. The devil's in the detail — who's going to pay?"

"Oh, that. I was hoping you'd do this one gratis," said Ken, ever the optimist. "A skip through to see if there's anything in it is all."

"OK, I'll allow you one freebie, but only one, for old time's sake. Call it a retirement present," he laughed. "It's the kids, you know, Ken. You can imagine. I've uni fees, cars and sports trips coming out my ears. Can barely keep my head above water, so I can't do too much pro bono. Anyway I'll make a few casual enquiries and we'll see where we get to. Talk to you later."

McWilliams hung up, more intrigued than he'd let on. There had to be something deep going on to occupy the ex-Director's mind at this time. He sniffed an opportunity.

CHAPTER 22

BY THE time Sam knocked on her front door Shelley was waiting, wiping kitchen hands on her apron as she let him in. The unmistakable aroma of Asian cooking washed over him as she opened the door.

"Come in, Sam, do come in."

"That smells amazing. Is the kitchen another of your talents?"

"Hardly."

He took her hand, pressing it warmly in his... An image of Georgie naked on the grass flashed through his mind so he dropped it hastily, taking in his surroundings instead. Simple but tasteful and comfortable. A few Asian prints and pen drawings hung from the walls.

For a guilty second he wondered whether she had read his mind. She was pale and seemed less than comfortable somehow.

"I bought you this." He handed over a chilled Sauvignon Blanc. She smiled briefly and turned for the fridge.

"Hey, if it's not a good time we can do another day."

"No, no. It's not you, Sam." He could tell she wasn't the best. "Not at all. I guess it's just — oh, everything else. Anyway, come; there's someone I want you to meet."

He followed her as she opened the door to a bedroom where a couple of small boys were busying themselves on the floor.

"This is Hua," she smiled, touching her son fondly on the shoulder. "And this is Hua's friend Chris. He is staying over."

"Hello, sport." He smiled, taking Hua's hand. "What are you up to?"

The lad barely lifted his eyes from his game.

"We were trying to get my model helicopter to fly but it's not right."

"Perhaps we can take a look."

"What a good idea, Sam. You do that while I finish the meal."

Sam sat down beside Hua who produced a one-twelfth scale helicopter.

"Wow! That's awesome. What's it not doing?"

"It won't fly straight."

"Must be the horizontal stabiliser. Let's have a look."

So the three of them started to delve into it, discussing the detail and fiddling with a screwdriver. Soon they had made some adjustments and tested it outside.

"It's wicked now." Hua squirmed with excitement. "It's never gone so well."

After a few minutes Shelley called them in, noting with some satisfaction that Hua and Sam were getting on.

"Dinner's ready when you are."

"Let's make another time and go fly it for real in the park," Sam suggested.

"Sure thing."

They turned to the table to be met by a mini-feast of honey soy chicken, stir fry and rice.

"Gosh, this is awesome."

"Oh thanks."

And the four of them tucked in, more at ease now in each other's company.

After a while Hua and his friend retreated to his bedroom.

"Can I trust you guys to take yourselves off to bed at nine?" Shelley called after them.

"Oh, mum."

"OK, then. Don't forget it's school tomorrow."

"Now to other business." Shelley turned back to Sam, seemingly more relaxed.

"Wine?"

"Sure. That was a great meal. And, by the way, Hua's an awesome little chap."

"Sure is. I'm proud of him. And I can see he likes you."

"Yeah, I hope so. I think we have some things in common." He paused. "Shall we have a look at some data now then?"

"Oh, that. OK, if we must."

Suddenly Shelley seemed remote again, not wanting to go to the results if she could help it. She turned to avoid his gaze.

"Well, it is the business of the moment," he ventured. And, after a pause, "Hey, I meant to say, thanks anyway, Shelley. You must have moved heaven and earth to get this done. It's serious progress."

"No problem. I know the work is topical so I gave it priority."

"Topical. What do you mean? So far, it's only important to me."

"Er, nothing." Shelley shifted nervously in her seat. "I don't know what I meant; it just slipped out."

"OK, let's relax. Cheers, by the way." He clinked her glass and took a sip of the wine. Shelley set up her notebook computer on the table and fired it up.

"I expect you've got your results in there," said Sam, "so why don't we start with you? Let's see what you've got."

He moved his chair closer to view the screen.

"OK." Shelley was brisk and business-like now. "I'll start at the top. I've reviewed the bio-actives by panel — you know, herbicide, insecticide, antibiotic, fungicide plus minerals, etc. — in the pond and up and down the overflow stream over time. Right? Additionally I have GE-tested the feed and seed samples. I concentrated on the farms you mentioned as particularly important, though I don't know why you think so."

"And what have you found?"

"The further back in time we go the more innocuous the samples. Like five to six months ago there was nothing of interest except a slight build-up of copper salts. As we come forward in time, especially over the last couple of months, the antibiotics ampicillin and tetracycline start to appear. Levels were low to begin with, but are building up. Also they are low in the milking shed sluicing pond, but spike up around the point where runoff from the pig and chicken units enter the creek."

"Interesting. Antibiotics, eh? Where could they be coming from?"

"I was curious about that, too, but I didn't have to wait too long to find out. Levels were up in the feed, too. Surely you knew something about this? As with the pond, the antibiotics were low or absent in earlier samples, but they're sky-high now, especially in those extra samples you gave me."

She waved her arms around for emphasis and widened her eyes.

"Out of this world. Unbelievable." This time she squared up to him. "But perhaps you already know this, Sam."

"No."

He spoke defensively and offered no explanation. He wanted to hold back from speculating until he had factored the new data into his thinking.

"Sam, the levels are dangerously high and we need to report them."

"Yes, I agree, but let's try to figure out what's happening first. Is that everything you have?"

"No, there's more, and I've got to tell you, Sam, I'm worried."

"I can see that."

She switched to another screen.

"I've been using the test you set up for BT-resistant GE corn and it's following the same pattern. We always got residual levels of contamination — like parts per trillion — as the test is so sensitive. That's to be expected for all sorts of reasons. But now; again levels are ballistic. Realistically when fully corrected for controls I estimate actual contamination of the chicken and pig feed with GE corn is in the order of two per cent. And — wait for this — the corn seed waiting to be sown out is of the order of ten per cent GE-contaminated."

She was frowning now.

"Sam, that's a major on its own, you have to agree."

Sam had thought himself prepared for bad news, but still the confirmation stunned him.

"My God. What to do?"

"For one thing we're under an obligation to report this to the Food Safety Authority."

"Before we do that we need to be absolutely convinced. You've got to admit it seems unlikely, Shelley. If we get this wrong, we'll blow our credibility clean out of the water."

He grabbed his wine and took a decent draft as if for emphasis. His programme was facing a disastrous meltdown if the figures computed, as he was sure they would. He was unable to speak and Shelley appeared to be similarly reticent.

Finally Sam asked her, "How do you interpret the data?"

"Assuming it is real — and I believe it is as I did the tests — then it shows all the hallmarks of accidental contamination. Serious contamination that we are duty bound to act upon."

He sighed.

"Yes, it certainly does. But as I said, we need to check thoroughly to be sure."

Neither of them relished the prospect but both knew in their hearts the results would be the same. Shelley was frowning again, worrying about what a delay in reporting might mean.

Sam was fixated on the contamination. The hell that's accidental. What Shelley's data did was independently corroborate his own. Different tests, same pattern of results. Almost certainly the contamination was deliberate.

Unusually for Sam he was indecisive, uncertain how to proceed. There were two major issues confronting him. First, the very real possibility of a major disaster through environmental contamination or a food safety failure, and secondly, the unimaginable prospect that this was not accidental but a deliberate and cynical act of vandalism.

The first point was of prime importance, yet faded almost to insignificance compared with the second as it would strike a blow right to the heart of the nation's biosecurity. The implications were undeniable, especially in political terms.

What was patently obvious was that the situation had to be handled carefully and there was nothing in the rule book to guide him. Heads would roll and Sam wasn't keen to see his among them. With Shelley's corroboration he could no longer avoid the conclusion that the contamination was both real and deliberate. A pattern of behaviour had been established, spatially and over time.

A text came in from Georgie.

'I hv hi temp. Dad taking me to A & E. C U l8r. X. G'

Sam was suddenly gutted. Was it possible she'd contracted gastro from the *E coli* in the samples she'd collected? He forced himself to stay calm and wait for a diagnosis.

He rubbed his aching forehead, deep in thought. From across the table in the kitchen of her Hillcrest home Shelley watched him intently and with concern.

"A problem, Sam?"

"Not entirely sure. A friend who's unwell."

"Oh, I am sorry."

She waited for him to say more, but he chose not to.

"So what have you got, Sam?"

"Here, load this up." He fished out the memory stick. "This will blow your mind."

CHAPTER 23

ROGER MCWILLIAMS had made a few subtle enquiries and found that Bella Simcox was attending a Gravitas Club dinner at a Wellington restaurant that evening.

Established by a clique of influential women, Gravitas was a somewhat secretive organisation dedicated to promoting women's interests. Ostensibly its main objective was to assist the appointment of Gravitas' members to senior positions in the public service. As far as McWilliams could ascertain this was achieved by leveraging a network of like-minded contacts in the backrooms and corridors of power.

For those in the know, the tentacles of Gravitas ran deep, using the process of judicious placement to advance its own political agenda. There were rumours of undue influence of course but so far no overt accusations had been laid against the club, and during the term of the present government it had enjoyed something of a halcyon period.

Under the leadership of its current Chair — Green Future party leader and Associate Minister of Research, Science and Technology Bella Simcox — its power and influence had never been greater.

McWilliams arrived at the trendy Italian restaurant to discover some twenty or so club members in a private room taking full advantage of Happy Hour. The mood was festive and the women animated. He chose a table strategically located to scope the action. Stealing glances from behind his menu McWilliams did his best to identify individual members. Despite the discreet lighting the group was strongly focused on its leader, hanging on her every word and doing their best to garner attention.

McWilliams scrutinised them carefully. He didn't recognise many and concluded they were mostly B-listers. He was just beginning to think the surveillance was a non-event when a late arrival swept past him and into the throng. It was unmistakably Iris Dent. Now there's a thing. That's bound to interest Judge...

McWilliams couldn't help but raise an eyebrow as Dent hugged Simcox for what seemed an age, staying close and whispering into her ear. If only he were near enough to hear.

Finally the Gravitas members settled themselves at a long table, with Simcox and Dent central among the cohort and the others fanning out in rank order. Wine was ordered and the entrées arrived as the talk grew faster and louder.

McWilliams considered his options. The men's room was off to the rear of the restaurant and to get to it he would have to pass the women. Sauntering discreetly by, cellphone in hand, McWilliams did his best to surreptitiously snap the occasion. He aimed as best he could, pressed the button, and continued on to the toilet. Damn. As he checked what he'd got in the cubicle he could see he'd missed by a country mile. Nothing for it but to try again. Emboldened by their disregard of any other presence, this time he stood outside the entrance to their private room pretending to text while he aimed and took three more shots.

Back at his table now he panned through the pictures. By some miracle one was spot on. One good picture was all it took. He phoned Judge.

"Hi, Roger here. Can you receive pictures on your phone?"

"I suppose so. It is 3G."

"Good. Take a look at this and then phone me back."

He fired them off and took up his fork.

He was halfway through his risotto when the phone rang.

"Hi."

"What an eye-opener. Dent and Simcox seem close."

"Yes."

"I guess their being together doesn't mean much on its own though, but it does rouse suspicions."

"Agreed."

"Who's the other woman in the frame?"

"Oh, that's Anne Tuakana, Deputy Director, Human Resources at the Department of State Services."

"You're joking."

"No, I'm not. Why?"

"I've never met her, but it's Tuakana who's handling my redundancy."

"Really… In that case, my friend, I think we have us a conspiracy!"

"Right. So, Roger, next task. What can you discover about a mysterious stranger from the Eastern bloc who's apparently working for Simcox?"

"Don't know, but I'll get on to it. Assuming you'll pick up the tab?"

"Guess I'll have to this time. Mate's rates?"

"You're killing me, but OK."

CHAPTER 24

"SORRY. **I** haven't had time to do as much as you with the data."

In her Hillcrest kitchen Shelley had set up her notebook amid the remnants of dinner. Without comment she pulled up the microbial genomic information from Sam's flashdrive.

"In short," he went on, "this is what I've got. The profiles were entirely normal across the farms up until a couple of months ago. Then, the dangerous form of *E coli* 0157 inexplicably increases on the same farms you found changes on. In the most recent samplings it has risen to extreme levels. Take Mangawara. Levels are up in the dairy sluice pond, spike up where the chicken and pig shed effluents enter the overflow creek and then, as you might expect, decrease slowly in the runoff."

Shelley was listening intently.

"And there's a second major peak in levels down by the kiwifruit orchard. I can't think why."

"Go on, Sam."

"0157 is a dangerous bug. As you know it's not that contagious in humans — transmissible, that is — but it is highly infectious. And as with your findings for the antibiotics, levels of 0157 are ballistic in the chicken and pig feed so that is almost certainly the source. The animals will be contaminated though 0157 is nothing like as toxic to chickens or pigs as it is to humans. They're just a means of transmitting the infection to humans. God, Shelley, it's scary."

"Yes. Scary is right. What's behind it, Sam? Or should I be saying who?"

Sam hesitated. A good question that he wasn't yet ready to answer. He wasn't entirely sure why, but for the moment he preferred not to tell her about the imposter in the ILAWR ute. But he had to offer something.

"Could it be they share a common feed supplier?"

"That's worth checking. But, Sam, the dairy cows are only on pasture, aren't they? They don't receive supplements or formulated feed. So why is 0157 so high in the sluice pond? And do you think there's any logic to the fact that both 0157 and antibiotic levels are up?"

God, she was smart.

"Doesn't make any sense at all, does it? I'm at a total loss there, too. About a lot of things, actually. I'm trying to figure out what else is going on. Shelley, that's why I'm cautious about reporting the data until we get to the nub of it. Right now I've got more questions than answers."

"Sam, the policy is clear though. You're obliged to report."

"I know that, but Shelley, there are too many unknowns. So it's not whether but when to report. I want to wait until we're clear on the facts."

"You sure? The evidence..."

Sam cut her off. "Yes, I'm sure."

Silence fell over them. Sam got to his feet. He'd let her mull it on for a few minutes more.

"More wine, Shelley?"

He strode to the fridge while Shelley stared at her notebook, thinking hard. The earlier Sam reported his findings, the more it would lessen the impact of what she was forced to hand over to Dent.

When he returned with their glasses, she leaned forward and spoke emphatically.

"I'm uncomfortable about holding off."

"I hear you."

"We've got a responsibility here, both legal and moral."

He agreed with her, but couldn't say so.

"Shelley, it's complicated... Premature action..." His words trailed off. Then, decisively, "For the moment, we can't show anyone. Understand?"

"You're the boss. I think you're making a big mistake, but OK. We hold off till you're ready." She took a deep breath. "So what do you want me to do?"

Her disapproval was patent and Sam was oddly discomfited. He leaned forward.

"Please understand. I'm new to this sort of thing and it's come as a bit of a shock. There's stuff going on behind the scenes that I need to figure out."

Unaccountably she blushed.

"Sam, it's OK. I just hope you're doing the right thing. Not putting anyone at risk."

"I have thought that through. The pigs and chickens are still too young for market. The only thing leaving the farm at present is milk and that's pasteurised. Oh, and the *E coli* in the runoff... But that shouldn't present any immediate problem. Shelley, I do realise we can't wait long."

He took her hand. She relaxed a little.

"You asked me what more you can do. If you could plot some of our data to make a presentation that'd be great. Do a few more samples to increase coverage of the other farms and, finally, see if you can't get some faecal samples fresh from the cows before the slops go into the pond."

She grimaced.

"Yes, I know. Awful. But you know Max, don't you? My PhD student, Max. He can help you with the sampling. If the cows are contaminated with 0157 that would add substance to the story, don't you think?"

Her hand was supple in his, probably the wine; but scrutinising her closely, he realised she was pale under her make-up, tense and anxious. Unlike he had seen her before.

"You are a gem, you know." She half-smiled. "Thanks for everything and sorry if I'm a tad OTT at present.

It's new ground for both of us and full on."

They sat quietly for a time. Closer and more comfortable now they were over the moment. He put an arm around her easing her gently towards him.

Sam was reflective. "...you know I think we have something pretty special going on here. We'll be better for these challenges, you'll see. They're helping us to connect... I mean, at a deeper level... Build trust and all that."

She squeezed his hand, reacting to his comment. Then opened her mouth as if to speak, her eyes misting. She stood instead and went to the sink. Leaning unsteadily against it. Then turned back.

"Please understand. I'm trying to do my best by everyone."

Sam was perplexed. Not getting the comment.

She reached for a tissue, sniffed, and wiped her eyes. Trying hard not to break into tears. She genuinely respected Sam and what his research was trying to achieve. The last thing she wanted was to go behind his back, but Dent had her over a barrel. Obviously the only reason she'd been put in with him was as a plant, a source of information. Dent was manipulating her; to be blunt, it was blackmail. And there was little she could do except comply.

And then her cellphone rang.

Shock. The caller was her Nemesis.

"Dent here. What have you got for me?"

Shelley stepped hurriedly into the lounge surreptitiously sliding the room divider across for a little privacy. Sam's interest was aroused.

"You're putting me in an impossible position." She spoke in hushed tones, dabbing her eyes again with the damp tissue. She added, in a spurt of anger, "I won't be intimidated, you know."

Dent laughed. Not at all a pleasant sound.

"I'm your last chance, Lai. Get this right and you'll be

sorted, with a secure place at ILAWR... Did you know there's new legislation before Parliament on immigration? Believe me, you need friends in high places. Think of it as us trying to help you. How bad can that be?"

Shelley tried to sum up her situation. She'd made some bad decisions in the past and she didn't want this to be another.

Born into a reasonably affluent family in a China in transition, Shelley grew up riding the wave of consumerism that gripped the country around the turn of the century. She was a looker; headstrong and foolhardy and was played along by an older guy whose money fuelled her growing taste for Western brands.

The relationship didn't last though, there was an unplanned pregnancy and pretty soon she was out on the street. China at this time was no place to have illegitimate children either. These were hard times and galvanised by a mother's instinct to protect her unborn child Shelley saw getting out as her best alternative. Stepping into the unknown was a major step for the young mother-to-be. But she did it anyway and never looked back.

When she arrived in New Zealand she carried little more than her baby boy and the clothes she stood up in. She settled well though and immersed herself in the possibilities a new life New Zealand presented. She wasn't afraid of hard work or commitment either and made steady progress.

Now she was older and wiser for the experience. In the intervening five years she had completed a master's degree in biotech, got good work experience and was making a go of it for herself and her little boy. The ILAWR job was important and she couldn't let it all slip away.

"I've got what you want. I'll get something to you by the weekend."

"That's better."

"But what guarantee do I have you'll keep your side of the bargain?"

"None. And by the way, I want it tomorrow."

With that Dent rang off and turned for approval to her friend and mentor Bella Simcox, who was licking the last of the tiramisu from her spoon.

"You got that?" she asked gleefully. "We should get what we need tomorrow."

Her reward came immediately when Simcox squeezed her hand under the table, her eyes promising what her lips couldn't speak.

If Shelley was stressed before the call she was gutted when she re-entered the room. Sam noticed immediately and rose to comfort her.

"What was all that about?"

(She was shaking and washed out.) "Nothing, Sam. A private matter, not for you to worry about."

"But I do, I do. I can see the effect the call had on you."

"Sam, don't worry, please." She was close to tears. "Someone has been bugging me is all. I'm sorting it."

"OK. But please understand. I can feel the hurt and want to help if I can. I'm here for you."

"That's sweet of you, Sam, but it's under control."

Sam was thoughtful for a moment and then continued.

"Shelley, I'm going to say this just once. I think you're totally amazing, but if we're to have any sort of future you're going to have to open up to me. I want to know the story of Shelley from the beginning. Is that OK?"

She turned to him with a hint of a smile on her face.

"Sure is." And then she kissed him full on the mouth.

Hugged him tight as though she never wanted to let him go.

"It might take a while though!"

CHAPTER 25

SHORTLY BEFORE 10pm Sam stepped out of the car at Waikato Hospital, pulling his jacket close as he did so against the chill of the spring evening. He climbed the stairs of the main entrance and enquired at Reception about the location of Georgina Towhai.

"Oh, yes. She's in Critical Care, Ward 3 in the Menzies Building.

That didn't sound good. As he strode down the corridor, now deeply concerned for Georgie's well-being, Sam was reminded again of how much he disliked hospitals, particularly in New Zealand. The austerely clinical design, staff aloofness, the astringent smell of antiseptic and the waiting. Oh, the waiting! All combined to depress.

At the nurse's station the Maori staffer was blunt. "Visiting hours ended at seven thirty," she said, giving him no chance to open his mouth.

"This is ICU, and the guidelines say differently." He gestured to the notice on the wall. "What room is Georgina Towhai in, please?"

"Oh so you want to see that one, do you? Room 14... She's in isolation now and not allowed visitors."

But Sam had already moved on.

Outside Room 14 Phil Towhai was sitting disconsolately with head in hands. Sam sat down beside him.

"How is she?"

"Bad." He lifted a face creased with anguish. "I can't lose her, son. She's all I've got."

"What exactly is wrong with her, Phil? A healthy young woman like that."

"She was pretty crook when we came in and she's much worse now. Internal bleeding."

Sam stood up and peered through the window into the sealed room where Georgie lay inert, tubes and monitors charting the course of her illness. He was shocked by the change. So recently a picture of health and vitality, Georgie had now regressed into something more reminiscent of a hollow-eyed, cadaverous Munch painting.

Heavily sedated and intubated, she was bleeding from nose, mouth and eyes — probably from all orifices. The nurse in attendance, fully gowned and masked, was busy wiping up the unsightly secretions.

"Oh, my God."

He sank down beside Towhai, welling up with anger and guilt. He knew immediately the most likely cause of her illness. Georgie must have become contaminated when she was collecting the samples.

He cleared his throat and turned to Georgie's dad.

"What have they said about her?"

"Not a lot." Phil's frustration showed in his face and in the hands tightly clasped before him. "Some sort of bug, that's all I know, and now there are complications. I forget what they called it — haemo something."

"Haemolysis." Haemolytic uremic syndrome was a definite threat to anyone infected with 0157:H7. "Phil, who's Georgie's doctor? Do you know?"

"She's under the care of a consultant — Ashby, I think his name is. Haven't seen him for a couple of hours though. Sam, I don't mind telling you I'm out of my mind with worry."

"How long since you've had anything to eat, Phil?"

"Not since breakfast."

"You've got to take care of yourself too. Who knows how long you'll be sitting here? Go and get something hot from the cafeteria and I'll hold the fort."

Finally persuaded of the good sense of this, Phil departed grudgingly for food and Sam immediately returned to the nurse's station.

"Excuse me. Is the doctor in charge of Georgina Towhai coming by any time soon?"

"Don't know. I think the Registrar will be calling round again."

"We need to see him urgently."

"I'd like to help." Sam wasn't entirely convinced of that. "But he does have other patients besides Miss Towhai, you know."

Patience was required.

"I understand that, but I have information the doctor needs to hear of the utmost importance. Will you do what you can to get him along to see us? Please."

The nurse gave him a long, considering look.

"Maybe."

Her reply didn't make him too confident of a good outcome here. Time to play the ace.

"I know Andy Ashby personally, and if I can't get action from you, I'll ring him myself."

He fished out his cellphone determined to do whatever was necessary to get to the attendant physician.

She thought it over. "OK," she said finally. "I'll make a call."

"Thank you."

He returned to the seat outside Georgina's room and settled down for what could be a long wait.

First he read Georgina's case notes cover to cover. Then, as time passed, he lapsed into a doze — replaying the events of the last few days and fast-forwarding to future scenarios. The endgame, whatever it might turn out to be.

So lost in his thoughts, he could have been there for an hour or a day…

Eventually a bevy of white coats advanced down the

corridor, and the Maori nurse stumbled to attention. One tall doctor, grey-haired and sturdy, remained behind. Behind him was Phil Towhai, with a coffee in his hand.

"Ashby here. Do I know you?"

"Hi." Sam extended his hand. "Sam Miro from ILAWR. We met last year at Microbiome — the international microbiology convention — at the Geneva Palexpo."

"Oh, right. You were part of the Kiwi contingent we went out to dinner with. Didn't you give a plenary?"

"I did. On the microbial ecology of New Zealand dairy farms."

"I remember. That's good work you're doing out at Ruakura, particularly on analytical systems!"

"Thank you. That's not why I'm here though." Sam got back to the business in hand. "That young woman in isolation lives on one of the farms I'm monitoring. And this is her father, Phil Towhai."

"Yes. We've met."

"Phil tells me she's in a bad way. Do you have a diagnosis?"

"Not specifically. Clearly she has a major systemic infection with haemolytic complications, but we don't know yet what's causing it. And our overworked health system will take another two days to identify the infectious agent."

"Good God, she could be in organ failure by then. I'm betting I can pin the bug down faster than that."

"You can? That could help. Our turnaround is not good enough, I know, but that's the reality of practising medicine in the Waikato."

Sam was reluctant to outline the likely cause in detail for fear of saying too much. Yet he had to do something. Could Ashby, handled properly, be led to the right conclusion?

"She's showing all the signs of being infected with a nasty gram negative organism of some sort, don't you think?"

"Yes. We've put her on high dose oral and IV antibiotics."

"That would work, if the bug is mainstream, but I strongly suspect it's not and I'll tell you why. I was reading that antibiotic treatment of dangerous enterotoxigenic organisms can actually induce haemolytic uremic syndrome. That is, the complication is secondary to the antibiotic treatment. Wouldn't that fit with the pattern of events here? Georgie comes in poorly — high temperature, dehydrated, with vomiting and diarrhoea. You do a good job of stabilising her and put her on antibiotics. Then, and only then, the haemolytic symptoms kick in. If we're not careful, she'll go into renal failure next."

Ashby was listening closely.

"I think I glanced at that paper, too. On that basis it has to be something extremely threatening like the H7 variant of 0157." He glanced at Georgie's father, who had stood up as if to demand immediate action. "Christ knows where she would've picked that up from. If confirmed it could be catastrophic from a public health perspective."

Phil was staring through the window at his daughter.

Sam was still anxious to make Ashby think the diagnosis was entirely his own.

"If that's the case wouldn't you be better to take her off the antibiotics before her organs go into shutdown? Counterintuitive as it may sound."

Ashby reached for Georgie's chart and flicked through the last report.

"Her temperature's coming down and other vital signs are stabilising. You might have a point there. Perhaps we could chance it."

"She's normally a healthy, active young woman. I think she'll be able to tough it out."

Sam coloured as Phil swung round to fix him with an enquiring gaze.

"Sounds like a plan."

Ashby stepped aside to instruct his attendant Registrar and the nurse on duty.

"Thanks. And if you get me a sample I'll see if I can't beat the path lab to a diagnosis."

"That'd be good."

Ashby remained somewhat bemused, glancing from Sam to Phil as if to make sense of what was going on here.

Sam shook his hand briskly. "Thank you for all your help."

"Yes," echoed Towhai. "Thank you, doctor. Thank you."

He resumed his stance by the window.

Twenty minutes later, sample in hand, Sam slipped away.

"I'll be in touch," he said. "Take care."

Phil waved a hand half-heartedly and remained where he was, a sentinel guarding Georgie against the most dire of outcomes. A parent willing fate to grant what he prayed for.

CHAPTER 26

Perhaps Caradijc believed the 0157:H7 posed no great threat because he had included potent antibiotics in the feed bags, expecting them to neutralise the bug. Perhaps he figured the risk would be minimal anyway because the monitored farms were remote from population centres.

Or perhaps he just didn't care.

The brief from Simcox had been clear enough. He was to engineer a food and environmental safety alert. Causing a major human health crisis might not have been on the agenda per se; yet the potential for disaster was omnipresent, given the deadly agents he was playing with. Whether the rationale was to create the perception of a disaster or to make it a reality had become neither here nor there.

For nature had her own ideas.

The complex natural ecology of any farming environment was doing what it does best, adapting to make the best use of the prevailing physical, chemical and biological conditions. A complex web of cause and effect was at work at Mangawara, manifest through changes in the selective pressures on individual microbial species, affecting in turn their ability to evolve and survive in the prevailing circumstances.

Changes in light and temperature, increased antibiotic levels and copper leaching in from the organic kiwifruit sprays impacted in their own way on the microbial community, challenging the individual species to adapt and increase their fitness to survive. Through it all some species lost the struggle whereas others flourished, including the 0157:H7, so recently introduced, which adapted and thrived to claim a dominant position in the microbial community.

Such was the biological diversity and adaptability of the Mangawara drain.

The high nitrogen and nutrient rich broth of the drain was ideally suited to this most dangerous form of *E coli*. Horizontal gene transfer from other microbial species markedly increased its resistance to the antibiotics. The copper leachate activated gene pathways bringing advantage in the low oxygen environment and protection against the oxidative stress caused by the high UV conditions.

Together the prevailing environmental conditions had conspired to create a perfect brew of conditions for the *E coli* to bloom.

And that is exactly what happened.

Unseen. Unknown. And unanticipated.

A tide of the rapidly increasing 0157 population spilled first from the drain into the creek that was to become the Mangawara Stream. Over the following days it relentlessly powered down the stream, tingeing it iridescent green and devastating the local wildlife as it went with its unprecedented toxicity. Finally attaining calamitous proportions 0157 drove inexorably through the natural fermenter that is the Mangawara wetlands and, undetected, spilled its bloom into the Waikato River at Tainui Mountain.

CHAPTER 27

IN A workplace given over to open plan offices the only way for Shelley to stay below the radar and prepare Sam's report was to work from home. She rose early with a blinding headache after a night of unrest and endless worrying about Dent.

She alone had responsibility for the welfare of her son, Hua, and it was never easy coping with a full-time job and the pressures of solo motherhood on a technician's salary. She loved her boy dearly, but sometimes she felt trapped. Like other single mums she couldn't escape the fear that this was all there was for her — that she was doomed forever to be alone and unsupported. But then there was Sam. Did they have a chance? She didn't want to mess that up either.

Today she had completed the school run early and was seated at the kitchen table in her Hillcrest unit with the weight of the world upon her. What had she done to deserve the contempt and abuse of a woman like Iris Dent? It was so unfair.

Shelley exhaled, wanting to rid herself of self-pity. She switched on her laptop, opened PowerPoint and pulled up the data. Sam had asked for a presentation, so that was what she would do. She had no idea what form Dent might prefer and, frankly, she didn't much care. One minute she was staunch and defiant and the next overwhelmed by despair at her own helpless complicity in Dent's campaign, which she knew instinctively boded no good for Sam or ILAWR.

By lunch time the bare bones of the presentation were there, only needing tidying and highlighting of the key points. Laid out in logical order its potential to alarm and threaten were clearly apparent, with upward-trending graphs plainly illustrating the recent inexplicable increases of antibiotics, pathogenic *E coli* and GE corn on Sam's monitor farms.

Her dilemma was laid out just as clearly in her own mind.

To get out of jail with Dent she had to forward the file to her, but to leak it would certainly blow all credibility and any future she might have at ILAWR and with Sam. She was caught between the proverbial rock and a hard place. The phone rang as Shelley was pouring boiling water into her cup of green tea. She jumped, splashing herself, thoughts scattered by the shrill sound.

"Dent here. Where is it?"

Shelley's stomach churned as she made her decision.

"I won't give it to you. I'd rather resign."

"Oh, really?" Dent sounded as if she relished the prospect of dealing with such defiance. "Why don't you sit down, Lai, and take a moment to think what it would be like if your son didn't come home today?"

"You leave my boy alone!"

Dent laughed. "Let's be quite clear, you stupid little whore. Some heavies are parked outside his school right now. If I say the word they'll pick him up, take him on a joyride and wring his neck. Do you hear me? Is there any part of what I'm saying you don't understand?"

The meaning behind the malevolent words burned deep into Shelley's consciousness and her blood ran cold. She began to shake and sank to her knees on the carpet. Without warning, she vomited.

Dully, she acknowledged her defeat.

"You've got until school's out to send me that data, or playtime will begin for real, if you know what I mean. And, Lai, believe me, if you could see those gorillas you would know they will have some fun with him first."

Shelley collapsed to the ground sobbing at the thought of

this new outrage, barely moving for ten minutes or more. Next, all hope now gone, she loaded her Gmail, attached the presentation and sent it off to Iris Dent without so much as another thought. Finally she crawled into the shower, standing below an ice-cold stream and sobbed uncontrollably until she had no tears left.

She dressed stoically and drove to Hua's school arriving early and still numb to the core. When she got there she paused, briefly respectful that class was not yet out. Then she thought, bugger this, the situation is way too serious to sit and wait. Instead she marched directly into class and collected Hua ahead of bell time without so much as an apology. Next she bundled him hurriedly into their car and sped off down the road before the encounter with Dent's hoods could become a reality.

CHAPTER 28

SAM HAD tried hard to sleep — God knows he needed the rest — but the demons could not be kept at bay. At one thirty in the morning he gave up, made some coffee, and took it through to the office of his Hamilton East home in turmoil.

He connected to work and to Outlook. As the inbox updated, a message arrived from Georgie, perhaps her last before she was admitted to A & E. He endured another pang of guilt as he opened it. In it, she referred briefly to an attached video clip.

Pay dirt! Georgie's film was a covert record of the ILAWR imposter's most recent visit to Mangawara Farm. She had got the ute and captured him as he systematically off-loaded animal feed bags and effluent. A burst of static, and now came a section on the exacting process Georgie had gone through to sample his deliveries, and set them against control feed bags from the separate stacks. Sam was impressed by how methodical she had been as she carefully identified contents from each feed bag before scooping a sample into a plastic bag and labelling it. She had taken care to ensure contaminated feed could be traced back to source and linked to the activities of the intruder.

Sam couldn't help but notice the close attention Georgie had paid to the sampling process. Head down, she had laboriously mixed the bags' contents to ensure a representative sample. All this without a dust mask.

Troubled, he forwarded Georgie's evidence to his own personal Hotmail account for safekeeping. Additionally he loaded the evidence on a memory stick and then decided to add all the other data, a process that took an hour and a half to complete. Naturally he included Shelley's PowerPoint presentation, which he hadn't even bothered to open. He knew full well that it contained a damning body of evidence on the environmental sabotage at Mangawara Farm.

As the computer worked so did Sam's mind. Why would Caradijc do such a thing? Sam could not believe he was acting alone.

Suppose Green Future party leader Bella Simcox was involved, or, worse, driving the whole damn thing. Highly unlikely, I know. Why would she be? Surely only a warped logic would lead a Greenie to do such a thing? He had nothing but supposition to link Simcox to the covert activity on the monitor farms. To make such an outrageous accusation without proof could only be terminal.

Watching Georgie's video convinced Sam it was time to elevate the matter. He sent email requests for a meeting to Dent, and separately to Judge.

He went back to bed around 4.30am and fell instantly into a deep dreamless slumber.

CHAPTER 29

Iris Dent checked and rechecked her private email with neurotic fervour. That Asian tart had better deliver. Yes! There it was. Eagerly she double-clicked on the attachment to open the presentation.

Dent sat before the screen and worked through the data. Within minutes she was rubbing her hands together in glee. This was so much better than Bella could have ever imagined and was certain to do the trick. She paused for a moment to savour Bella's pleasure, and immediately forwarded the email.

'Package attached. Everything you're looking for and more. Use it wisely. I.'

The next email was a request for an urgent meeting from Sam Miro. She considered her options. Miro was probably irrelevant now and ought to be neutralised. Briskly, Dent replied.

'I confirm I will be at Ruakura the day after tomorrow and can see you at 11am. There is much to discuss. I.D.'

Too late for now. Sam had long since fallen asleep.

CHAPTER 30

BELLA SIMCOX, Associate Minister of Research, Science and Technology, had timed her arrival to maximum effect, entering the Chamber when Parliamentary question time was more than half over.

Times were hard for PM Jeremy Grafton these days. With the economy in the doldrums his coalition government teetered on a knife edge. No wonder he looked dour and defensive. Long gone were the giddy days of his victory in the last election. Grafton was facing the harsh reality of steering the nation through a global downturn and credit squeeze. New Zealand wasn't doing that much worse than equivalent economies overseas, but being in charge of a faltering economy was a thankless task.

The latest quarterly figures made gloomy reading, officially confirming a recession. Export returns were down for the third month running, unemployment up, inflation rocketing and the high dollar calling into question Grafton's monetary policy.

Like a creature at bay, Grafton was enduring the ritual questioning on the state of the nation. He knew that the current situation would be seen by the Opposition as an irresistible opportunity to further slate and ridicule his Government.

Besides the economy there was the unsettling matter of biosecurity, hanging over Parliament and the country like a Grim Reaper. Many considered its potential implications for the overall health of the nation far greater than the looming global depression.

The questions were hurled at him like poisoned darts.

"Can the Right Honourable Prime Minister advise what

additional steps his administration is taking to secure the country against the new H1N1 outbreak in Indonesia?"

"What are the potential economic implications of a pandemic in New Zealand and how does the Prime Minister plan to manage the risk?"

"What is the current state of planning of our health system for a major emergency and can he convince us that we will be able to cope?"

Simcox was careful to keep her face neutral, after all she was a member of the coalition regardless of her real motives, but inwardly she gloated and revelled in Grafton's discomfort.

It had been a long journey and her final destination was drawing nearer with every accusatory salvo lobbed at Grafton. Yes, a long journey; almost, you might say, a protest march.

Half-listening, Bella Simcox drifted back into her past. The time in the country when she had been at once at her most happy and most miserable. It was hard, so hard, to be away from her parents. But they just didn't want to know about the pregnancy. Hard also to give birth — hard labour — and to have and to hold oh so briefly the perfect baby boy she would not be able to keep.

She tried hard not to bond with him for the six weeks they were together. Dutifully changing and holding and feeding him. But it was all too much. He was such a beautiful little person. Unbidden, his image flashed into her mind. The skin, so moist and milky. The perfectly rounded head, silky curls, so blond as to be almost white. The sparkling young eyes, so full of life and joy and adoration for mother.

Don't think about him, she self-castigated. You did all the crying; got all the grief out of your system long ago. She forced herself to unclench her hands and smooth the frown away. Put the pain back in the deepest recess of her mind. As best she could anyway.

Her attention returned to the drama unfolding in the House. Deliberately she read the questions, seemingly impassive as she heard Grafton's responses. Inside a kind of sick excitement started to well up. Careful. Careful. It's happening. Grafton is standing at the edge of a cliff but no one has the nerve to push him off. No one has the balls.

Typical.

As the questioning abated, Simcox finally stood.

"Mr Speaker, a few comments and, if I may, a question of my own."

She spoke at an unhurried pace, and with deliberate clarity.

"Honourable Members, it seems to me that the real issue here is that we have a Prime Minister with no vision or strategy for the nation." She paused for the sycophantic applause. "There is no evidence of depth or insight in his answers. Not a bit of sophistication. I regret to inform the House that I have no confidence in the Prime Minister's ability to steer us through these challenging times."

By now the House was listening intently to what Simcox was saying, some startled by her audacity, others exulting in it.

"He talks of biosecurity and the economy as if they are separate issues," she continued. "But I put it to you that they are intimately linked — one and the same. Consider for example a biosecurity event in New Zealand that has a major impact on food safety. This would have enormous implications not only for public health, but also for export returns from food as our biggest earner. If we are unprepared for such an eventuality, we run the very real risk of being locked out of our key markets."

Grafton sprang to his feet.

"Mr Speaker, this is nothing but malicious speculation. Posturing without a point, because there is no such risk."

Simcox half-smiled, alerting those who knew her best. She addressed the House.

"Honourable Members, I am going to take that as the PM's usual lame assurance that there is no current threat to the nation's biosecurity."

"Correct!" snapped Grafton, his frustration evident.

At that Simcox slapped the folder she was clutching theatrically down on the bench, opening it to reveal a ring-bound document.

"Then perhaps the Prime Minister would care to explain this report just received from ILAWR — a report with major implications... A report that signals that the worst case scenario we have been predicting for biosecurity has now come to pass. Honourable Members, fate has caught up with us. We said a breach was inevitable and now it appears we have one."

She lifted the folder and brandished it before them.

"Mr Speaker, this report documents extreme levels of contamination by a dangerous form of *E coli* plus listed antibiotics. As if that's not enough, there is GE corn on several of the Waikato farms. Honourable Members, dare I reiterate? This is precisely the danger of which you were forewarned. For some time we have said it is no longer a question of *if* there will be a major breach of biosecurity in New Zealand, but *when*. Mr Speaker, today the inevitable has occurred and New Zealand will be changed forever."

Simcox ignored the conflict of jeers and cheers that greeted the end of her speech. Instead she walked over to the Speaker and slapped the report down for his inspection.

Grafton, ashen-faced, could find nothing to say except, "I know nothing of this... "

He slumped down in his seat, head in hands.

Simcox had finally got what she wanted and the House

knew it. The Opposition had thrown so much at the Grafton government lately that eventually something had to stick. And this was it.

The PM was bewildered and broken and had nothing to say. Game over.

With callous finality Simcox twisted the knife.

"Has the PM nothing to say? Honourable Members, can we afford to show this man any pity? His incompetence is likely to result in the dismantling of all that is good about our country."

The Chamber exploded into riotous disarray. Simcox strutted away from the cacophony into a stampede of paparazzi who had rushed down from the gallery to jostle each other for a picture and comment.

"We entrusted the nation to him and he has failed us." She boomed, punching the air with a clenched fist of victory. "Ladies and gentlemen, it is time for a change."

With that Simcox departed, her sycophants trailing obediently behind.

CHAPTER 31

THE LAST few days had been harrowing for Phil Towhai. His daughter had contracted a disease that put her into isolation while she fought to recover. Georgie had come to within an inch of losing that battle, a hard thing for any father to endure. She had been totally drained and bore the scars of her near-death experience in the form of weeping sores and an incapacitating inertia, physical and emotional.

Her father was deeply traumatised and bewildered. What had Georgie done to deserve such a thing?

Towhai had sat in that mausoleum of a hospital for three days and nights with no proper sleep or substantial meals. He returned to the farm mid-morning of the fourth day only when reassured by her medical team that Georgie was out of danger. She would recover given time and more than a little TLC. Shattered, he was badly in need of food and rest.

Inevitably those lonely hours outside his daughter's room had given him pause for reflection. Georgie was all he had left now from a distant chapter of his life. He was not about to give her up lightly.

Phil Towhai had met Georgie's mother in his final year at high school. He was bronzed and physical, a star on the rugby team. She was a blonde goddess from Europe with style and social grace. On the surface they seemed made for each other, but the underlying differences were there from the start. Liz came from a privileged background. She was high maintenance with an inborn sense of entitlement difficult to accommodate within his whanau.

But young love follows the heart, not the head. Inseparable

at eighteen, dealing with an unplanned pregnancy at nineteen, they ignored the doubts of both families and were married before they were twenty.

In the years that followed Phil devoted himself to his bride, whom he loved so deeply that it hurt. After Georgie was born he worked hard to meet his wife's ever-increasing demands. But he was no investment banker, and with the nineties slump in farming the writing was soon on the wall.

Her utter hypocrisy had cut deepest. As far as he could tell they were happy — 'trying for another baby'. One morning Liz told Phil she would love him forever, kissed him passionately and left on a shopping expedition to Auckland. Never to return.

Soon it transpired that Liz had been dating an America's Cup yachtsman ever since Georgie's birth. Now the Auckland Regatta was over, the foreign crews were leaving, and so, too, was Liz Towhai, out of his life forever.

But for Georgie he might have ended it right there. Instead, he bottled his anger, increasingly silent and contained, and did his best to put his life back in order. Probably over-compensating, he became in the years that followed the consummate solo dad. He and Georgie shared everything and yes, he spoilt her. Georgie was the one perfect thing he had and she made him oh so happy.

Over the last few days he had been shocked into a realisation that Georgie had almost been taken from him, too. He could have lost his princess; a thought too horrible to contemplate on top of everything else.

Phil's mind was still heavy with such thoughts as he stepped in through the door of the smoko room at Mangawara. He knew the lads would be at morning tea and he was keen to find out how things had gone in his absence before he retired to bed.

"How's Georgie?"

The concern of his farm crew was obvious as they crowded around.

"She's going to make it, thank God... What I don't understand is how the fuck this happened."

The sense of frustration washed over him again. Deliberately he put it aside, asking, "And how are things here?"

"Fine, fine. We haven't missed you at all." That was Ross Connery, the lead farm hand. "The home paddocks are ready for the corn to be sown. We were going to knock that off today, but a couple of the lads called in crook."

"Did they? That's no good." Briefly Phil wondered if the men were skiving. "And what's up with Trev and Harley? They don't look too good either."

He pointed to the trainees, slouched at a corner table, facing the wall with heads on folded arms.

"Dunno. They're a bit off colour. Too much booze last night, I reckon."

The bell signalled the end of smoko. Most of the staff rose, stretched and departed, loading mugs in the dishwasher as they went. The two in the corner were slower to stir.

"They OK?"

"Don't think so, boss."

As Ross started towards the trainees, Phil noted how drained and unsteady they appeared. What had they been on — rocket fuel? In unison they stood, staggered a few steps and collapsed, clutching their bellies and writhing on the floor.

"Fuck me! What've you been up to?"

"Nothing," blurted Trev defensively. Harley was silent, eyes half-closed as if in pain.

Ross said, "Only feeding out to the chickens and pigs."

Phil kneeled and checked them over. "You'd better call an ambo, Ross. Quickly."

But as Ross turned for the phone another of the farm hands burst back through the door.

"What's happening, boss?" He jerked a thumb over his shoulder. "What the hell is happening?"

Phil and Ross gazed incredulously down the driveway as a contingent of Ministry for Primary Industries (MPI) Biosecurity staff swarmed towards them, swathed in white cover-all suits, masks and rubber gloves. In the distance armed police tied biosecurity warning tape across the driveway while a helicopter thumped ominously overhead.

"Who's in charge here?" a senior Biosecurity Officer demanded as he burst through the door.

"I am." Phil stepped forward.

"My name is Peter Smart. I am head of Hazard Containment at MPI Biosecurity. Under the Biosecurity Act (2003) and other relevant legislation I am enacting emergency measures to secure this farm. A major biosecurity threat has been detected and as a consequence I am quarantining the facility and all who work here."

His audience were shocked into silence.

"No one is to enter or leave without my express permission. Do you understand? As of now this operation has a restricted access order on it. The farm is locked down and closed to business until further notice. It is an offence under law to withhold your full co-operation. A solicitor has been contacted and will be here shortly to advise you of your rights and obligations. Do you have any questions?"

"None."

Phil was at a total loss as the nightmare continued. He sank heavily down on the nearest chair.

Smart was scanning the room.

"What's up with them?" He indicated the groaning trainees.

"You tell me!" was all Phil could offer. "We were about to call an ambulance."

CHAPTER 32

Sᴀᴍ ᴡᴀꜱ pulling into Ruakura when his phone buzzed. Three new messages — all delayed, he noted.

The first was a confirmation of his meeting with Dent.

The second was a brief and intriguing note from Ken Judge.

'Hv u checked the news. Come round asap for a heads up.'

He panned down to the third message from Shelley.

'Pls talk to me b4 Dent. Need to explain.'

What was all that about?

But the major surprise came when Sam walked into the main foyer. When he had left the previous evening it was a familiar and totally unremarkable reception area. This morning, however, it had been transformed into what looked like the nerve centre of a disaster relief operation. Wide-screen computers on trestle tables, whiteboards, frantic staff with heads together one minute then scurrying off on some urgent task the next.

As he stopped to survey this astonishing scene, the clamour of activity subsided. Momentarily he was caught in the crossfire of multiple enquiring stares before the workers returned to the task in hand. Something was up and Sam felt instantly alone. He was relieved to find Max only a few paces away.

"What's up?" he enquired.

"What!" Max stared at him in disbelief. "You haven't heard."

"No, Max. Enlighten me."

Sam had figured that he was missing something big here.

Max had just opened his mouth to reply when over the drone of busy researchers came a bellow from Iris Dent.

"Miro! My room. Now."

Sam quailed at the thought of another encounter with the new Director. But no sooner had he started reluctantly to follow her than he was intercepted by Shelley Lai.

"Sam," she stammered breathlessly. "We have to talk."

"Can't right now, Shelley. I've been summoned by the Ayatollah."

"We must! It's about her."

"OK, OK." She was clutching a tissue. Had she been crying? "Don't worry. I'll come and find you afterwards. Or you can call me."

Her gaze flicked to Dent, who was watching them both attentively. Shelley paled and darted away. Dent beckoned to Sam imperiously and went into her office. Sam was forced to set aside any concern for Shelley and hurried forward, halting again when he saw Max.

"Quick, Max!" Sam said, grabbing him by the arm. "What's with all the theatrics?"

"Man, you should know! It's your farms. They're all fucked up. We have a major biosecurity alert here."

CHAPTER 33

Ex-Director Judge was on his third espresso. He was fuming at his enforced redundancy, for no sooner had he been shown the door than there was a major biosecurity alert. His track record demonstrated that it was in situations like this that he was at his very best. Judge's decisive action had made the critical difference in several problematic situations before.

News of the alert had reached him as the briefest of brief reports from the grassroots back at the Institute. The details were sketchy, but sufficient to ring alarm bells. Young Sam Miro was apparently up to his eyeballs in the mire; Judge urgently needed his perspective. He texted Sam and got no response. When his phone rang he snatched it up eagerly.

"Hi, McWilliams here."

Not Sam's pleasant tenor, but the deeper bass of Judge's Wellington contact.

"You've heard about the goings-on in the House?" McWilliams continued with hardly a pause. "Apparently it's all happening in the Waikato!"

"Yes; still waiting to get the details though."

Judge saw no point in speculating on an alert to which he could add nothing specific.

"Ah, yes. You'll be out of the loop now. And here was I hoping you could fill me in."

"Sorry," apologised Ken. "I've been completely excluded though, frankly, there are bugger all of us left who can handle situations like this. I'm hoping it'll blow over as quickly as it blew up."

"You bet! Ken, by the way I've been digging around on that Eastern bloc associate of Simcox. You asked for the lowdown on him."

"Good man. What have you come up with?"

"I'm not exactly sure what I've got. I phoned a mate of mine who used to work for Simcox. He left a few months ago under a cloud; thoroughly disgruntled. He said you'd have to be into S and M to work for that bitch from hell."

Judge laughed.

"He told me that about eighteen months ago she helped a guy from Russia get an immigration permit. Turns out my man did some of the spade work. It was an unusual case so it stuck in his mind. He still had some of his computer files from that period and was able to track back."

"Great. What did he find?"

"The Russian is one Andrej Caradijc and he came in on a two-year visa as an environmental policy adviser to Simcox some fifteen months ago. Whatever that means. Some sort of consultant, I guess."

"This is good stuff, Roger. Where'd he come from?"

"After the break-up of the USSR he lived in Kazakhstan. Before that he worked in a city called Sverdlovsk, for what it's worth. That's all we know."

"You're joking! Sverdlovsk, you say?"

"Yes. So what?"

"I could tell you, but I'd have to kill you." On reflection Judge thought it wiser to backtrack. "Never heard of it."

"Ha ha, you had me going there."

He could always check out Sverdlovsk in Wikipedia.

"Did your contact add anything else of value?"

"Oh, not really. Nothing you don't know already I suspect."

"Go on."

"For one, he thinks she's psychotic, has Asperger's or something; a real head case. He sounds quite cut up by the experience. Can't help but reiterate what a nightmare it was to work for her. On the one hand he said she could be so charming and persuasive. When she wanted something done she could be really convincing; to hell with the consequences. He said she can make you feel like you're the only person in her world, like the sky's the limit if you play her game. Certainly she does have legions of minions bowing to her every wish and there's a real buzz around her office. So she must be doing something right. On the other hand, cross her and you soon know she's got it in for you."

"How so?"

"Well, my man is no angel, you understand, so when he was asked to leak a bit of dirt on the Opposition to the media he did so. Thought it would be a bit of fun. Next thing though he was being asked to rig a Wellington hotel room with cameras so she could get one over on a senior official from the Ministry of Research, Science and Technology who had a taste for prostitutes. Can only guess why she wanted to do that... Anyway he refused and their relationship turned sour. Before he knew it he was subject to all manner of abuse. Didn't go into the details but it appears he took as much of it on the chin as he could, but there was a scene where she really went at him. He had no alternative but to level a bullying complaint. It was managed down and soon after he left under a cloud. When you talk to him you can tell he is still carrying baggage over the affair. Poor chap."

"Huh. No surprises there from my perspective. You know she has put me through the mincer before!"

"Sure do."

"Anyway, thanks, Roger. I need to make a couple of calls now. I'll get back to you later."

"Cheers, mate."

McWilliams hung up. Ken stayed by the phone, chewing over the information. McWilliams' business was mainly innuendo and gossip but if Roger was right about Sverdlovsk, it was massive.

Where the hell was Miro? He needed to talk to him urgently!

CHAPTER 34

A WEEK is a long time in politics including office politics. Ken Judge's old office had been completely expunged of the personal touch he'd brought to it — the mementoes, certificates and photographs that had defined the man. All absent now. Stripped back to its stark grey walls, the room now had a repressive, authoritarian air.

Dent had planted herself pointedly behind the Director's desk, her sour expression clearly signalling the tone of the meeting to come. She said nothing, and after a brief pause Sam waded in.

"Dr Dent, I called this meeting because I need to brief you on matters concerning the monitor farms."

"That's rich!" she snorted. "A bit late for that, don't you think?"

"What?" Sam frowned, puzzled. "I have no idea what this is all about," referring to the alert outside. "If it's to do with 'my' farms, I have no clue what's happening, what information is out there or where any information may have come from for that matter. It's outrageous that I haven't been included if this relates to my programme."

"Where I got the information from is none of your business, Dr Miro, but thank Christ I did. Fortunately, other staff at ILAWR seem to have a stronger sense of duty than you. Let me remind you of your absolute responsibility to report evidence of biosecurity breaches without delay. My question is this: why did you not comply with this obligation?"

"Er... Dr Dent, the data may not be all that it seems, that's why. I needed time to sort things out."

"What things?"

Sam took a deep breath and spoke earnestly to her.

"If it's my farms you're talking about I have evidence of a very grave nature. It seems likely the contamination was not accidental and might have come from within ILAWR!"

Dent took a deep breath, taking her time to process Sam's comment. This couldn't be taken lightly. Quite the opposite, especially if Miro had tumbled over more than he should have. Did he say he'd got evidence? Jesus. That would be a fucking nightmare. Game over. Where is Simcox? We're in crisis mode here. Dent drummed her fingers on the desk, thinking hard.

Then she gave Sam a look of such abhorrence he almost cringed. And before his eyes ILAWR's new Director went into one of her more spectacular meltdowns.

She leapt out of her seat, storming around her desk to loom over him like some interdiction interrogator.

"You fucking little upstart. Who do you think you are? You've screwed up by not reporting the breach and now you're cooking up some fanciful notion of conspiracy to cover up. That's cheap, Miro, very cheap, and it won't wash. Not for one second. You've shirked your responsibility to report. I'm going to make sure you never work in science again. You're finished — kaput. I'm suspending you forthwith for serious misconduct pending a formal process."

Sam cowered under her withering onslaught. He opened his mouth to protest but could find no words to speak. He stared at the Director and struggled to come to terms with her actions.

Dent reached for the phone. "Get security in here immediately!"

Within minutes two Polynesian bruisers were knocking on her door.

"Escort Dr Miro off the premises. Remove his access, security passes and laptop. Make sure he has no contact with any ILAWR employee on the way out and secure the contents of his office!

"Oh, and by the way, Dr Miro," she called after him as they frogmarched him through the door. "Don't forget you're still bound by the Institutional Confidentiality Agreement!"

Next Sam was making a long walk past the assembled researchers, flanked by the blue-uniformed security guards and out into the mid-morning sun. For a moment he stood there, stunned. Fixed in the enquiring stares of his ex-colleagues, trying desperately to comprehend what had just happened. Then he turned and walked to his car.

Driving out of Ruakura not knowing whether he would ever return, he glanced into the rear view mirror.

In the distance, outside the main entrance, stood Shelley Lai, gazing forlornly after him.

CHAPTER 35

BEST MATES Pete and John had made a habit of trout fishing the twilight rise for as long as they could remember. For fishing was in their blood.

These days, they agreed, the lower Waikato was not what it used to be. Over the last few seasons, what with the increased dairy farming and nitrogen runoff, the water quality had deteriorated and trout numbers declined.

While the rainbows and brownies were still the prize, nowadays they couldn't afford to be too choosy. After all, fishing was mainly an excuse for a bit of a lash, a few laughs and a couple of beers. How bad could that be? With trout on the decline, they turned their attention to the next best thing.

The local streams were getting something of a reputation as a koi carp hotspot. The introduced goldfish, regarded as a mongrel, was known to grow to a metre or so in length and was said to be great sport when caught on a crossbow line.

What's more the decreasing water quality was having the reverse effect on carp, with numbers multiplying fast. Koi carp were officially declared a pest and fair game for fishing with no restrictions.

Pete and John reckoned they were up for this carp lark and so here they were out on the Mangawara on a sultry spring evening hoping for a bit of sport and a few laughs with their new rigs. They parked up alongside the wetlands on Orini Road in the shadow of Taupiri mountain.

"Waders, ya reckon?" Pete enquired.

"Nah! It's warm enough. Jeans 'n' runners will do."

"OK. This is going to be a hoot, I tell ya."

"Provided you can hit a fish with that thing and, mate, I doubt you could hit anything smaller than the milking shed."

"Shut the fuck up. I'm the business. Bet you can't so much as draw that thing of yours. Much less hit anything."

The banter continued as they sidled down onto the river terrace and alongside the main flow. Here they fell silent, surveying the river for signs of action. Nothing yet. The two men moved on until they came to a turn where the stream was deflected around a bank.

"Strange," said Pete. "Not so much as a dickybird."

"Nah."

They continued upstream.

"Cor," John gasped, "what's that pong? Not you, is it? Or d'you suppose something died?"

"Dunno." Pete scanned the surrounding area. "There's a couple of dead sheep over there."

"Bugger me, there's a few dead pukeko over here too. Wonder what caused it?"

"Hard to say. Probably some loony with a gun. Anyway, John, we should cross here."

Pete eased himself into the flow. The thick mud sucked at him and the water lapped around his waist.

"Phew. Not that warm yet. Mind you don't get shrinkage."

"Sweet as, mate. I'm longer on a cold day than you'll ever be."

John reached the other bank first and lit a cigarette as he watched his mate navigate the swampy reach.

"Huh, more stinky pukeko here, too," he called out. "What's causing that, do you think?"

"Dunno."

Pete cupped some water in his hands and splashed his face to cool down.

"I tell you what, this water's a funny colour today. Kind of iridescent, like petrol in a puddle."

"You're dreaming, mate. I can't see any difference. Come on, let's go fishing."

Continuing upstream, they still couldn't find any evidence of the elusive carp.

"Where the fuck did they go?" John was getting frustrated. "The last few times we've been here and didn't want the bloody things, they were all over. Now we do, they've buggered off back to Japan. That's us; without bad luck we'd have no luck at all."

"Give it a rest, mate." Pete was a perennial optimist. "They'll turn up."

Even he began to wonder after another reach with still no sign of koi carp. A smouldering silence had replaced the banter as it began to dawn on them this was not going to be their day.

"What do you reckon then? Been going over an hour now and still nothing."

John sat down, surveying the options.

"Yeah, and I feel a cold one coming on. But I say we keep moving. We've got an hour or so of daylight left. Let's give it one more reach!"

"Better be worth it or you're buying!"

They walked on in silence, preoccupied with the curious case of the absentee carp.

Before long Pete became aware of another problem. At first the discomfort was almost subliminal, no more than a tickle. Next it was a bit of an itch. A few strides further and the matter was pressing. He stopped behind a bush and scratched his buttocks; sadly, with little effect.

He continued along behind his mate, trying to be stoic in the face of the reality that this thing, whatever it was, was not going away. The itch, intensely irritating, had spread to his crotch. Pete broke off as it became intolerable, a fire in his pants that he had to put out once and for all.

He found a convenient ponga and dropped his trousers

to inspect the problem... To his horror his private parts and crotch were red and bloated and covered in throbbing welts as if someone had taken a stick to them. His old fella was more like a half-deflated party balloon than his pride and joy.

Further on John, too, had abandoned all pretence of discretion and was scratching the hell out of his nether regions staring in disbelief at the thing that used to be his penis.

"Jesus! It must be the water," he yelled, while pulling up his pants. "C'mon, we're out of here."

As he swaggered over to Pete, backside jutting out and legs apart, John could easily have been mistaken for a fifty-year-old K Road hooker on stilettos instead of the sprightly young chap he was. He was worried stiff, and when he got to his mate, he recoiled in horror. Pete's face had the lurgy too, whatever it was. He couldn't disguise his shock.

"It must have been when you rinsed your chops."

Pete's face was puffy and swollen, his eyelids closing fast.

"God, you look like you've been three rounds with the Tuaman!" But John could no longer make light of this situation. "C'mon, Pete, c'mon. We're out of here! Forget your crotch and your face. We've got to get going and tough it out!"

"We'll have to cross back over!"

"Too bad! If we want help, we're going to have to put up with whatever's in the fucking water. I don't care if it's nuclear coolant fluid!"

In the gathering gloom as they turned back towards the river the men finally stumbled on what they'd come here to find. From the bank a fallen tree extended out, partially blocking the flow. Behind it, trapped by the current, was a twenty-metre slick of flotsam and jetsam, a weird tapestry in silver and orange.

They stared and stared. The water was layered with hundreds of dead and dying carp floating belly up.

"So that's where they went," said Pete. "No wonder it stinks here. C'mon, let's go, before we end up like that."

"What in God's name could have caused that?"

"Dunno, but hope someone else does if we're going to get fixed up."

Crossing back over the river redoubled their torture, but the two men were made of stern stuff. On they struggled to the road, though by the time they neared the car they were beyond scared. Rather it was a state of inexpressible fear overlaid by the agony of their extreme reactions to something incomprehensible in the Mangawara Stream. Pete could tell John was struggling to breathe. In the grip of something that resembled an extreme attack of asthma, Pete could tell John would be hard-pressed to make it. Neither of them had much time; they had to get to A & E without delay.

"Get in, get in," he yelled, as he tugged open the driver's door. John lagged behind and he doubled back to help, half-carrying, half-dragging his mate into the back seat. He slammed the door shut and floored the Falcon and spun the wheel, laying a long smoky track of rubber as he headed back to the main road.

"For fuck's sake!" John whispered. "Watch what you're doing or we'll be done for dangerous driving."

"It's been a while since anyone's mistaken me for a boy racer."

Pete's mind was racing as he slowed the car at the SH1 intersection of Gordonton Road. The clinic is closer in Huntly, they should head for there. Once there was a gap in the traffic he shot out and gathered speed as he raced towards the Mangawara bridge in the direction of Huntly.

There was an immediate sense of relief. They were heading for the help they needed, and he could afford to take a deep breath. For a moment Pete relaxed his grip on the wheel and allowed himself to scratch his balls.

That mere instant of inattention was all it took. When he looked back to the road he realised they were going way too fast for the tight approach to the Mangawara bridge. He dabbed the brakes, slammed the Falcon down into second and threw it sideways, sliding out to meet the double yellow.

Bad idea.

Peering out through the spotty windscreen into the last of the sunset Pete recognised the double beams of a monster milk tanker bearing down on top of them. There was nothing he could do. The Iveco ploughed into the side of the Falcon and reared up over the bonnet and cab, splattering the two men inside like raspberries in a blender as it went.

Then the tandem truck careered on though the railings and into the dark waters of the Mangawara below. The stream erupted in a tower of spray as the truck and trailer split open releasing a flood of milk as it went.

A gross disruption to the serenity and yet the turmoil soon subsided. The natural flow of the Mangawara soon returned, and the milky stream continued on its journey out into the Waikato River and on towards Auckland.

"God, what a mess!"

The St John ambulance driver stood with his assistant on the bridge approach surveying the chaos below. He pointed out where the truck had completely taken out that side of the bridge.

"It's down there somewhere," he said. "Not that you'd know it right now. And the car! Totally unrecognisable. We can't so much as tell how many people were in it."

"What do you suppose caused it?"

"Oh, I dunno. A moment's inattention, I guess. What a waste."

The assistant gazed down at the waters of the Mangawara,

beaded with phosphorescence in the waxy light of the new moon, barely hinting at the deadly secret within.

"Still," he said, "it's a lovely evening to die."

"True. The water certainly looks inviting tonight."

He gestured towards the team of emergency rescue divers clambering in and out of the water as they tried desperately to get to the truck driver. Presumably he was now long dead in his submerged cab.

He turned away.

"Not such a bad job that, eh? Being a police dive squad member."

CHAPTER 36

SAM WAS only slowly coming to terms with the shock of it all. He badly needed to talk things over so he headed round to his old boss and mentor, Ken Judge. He found Ken poring over his notebook. When he saw Sam approaching, he opened the patio slider and beckoned him in.

"Where've you been?" he said urgently. "I left you a message."

"Up at work being grilled by the Ayatollah." Tersely. "Scary morning. Did you know I've been suspended?"

"No. What for?"

"For not declaring a biosecurity breach."

"Why didn't you?"

"Here's the thing, it's not what it seems."

The two men were seated opposite each other at the table. Ken still clutched his notebook in his hand. He listened intently as Sam went on.

"I know for a fact the foreign chap from ILAWR I told you about is up to his eyeballs in it. I've got evidence the tosser has been deliberately contaminating my farms. I needed breathing space for a day or two to fill in the gaps, that's all. That's why I hadn't spoken up."

"You're joking. Sam… You sure it's deliberate?"

"Absolutely. And I don't know how the data got out or what's happened since because I've been out of circulation for a couple of days. I tell you what though. Only a couple of us had all the info and it sure as hell wasn't me that spilled the beans."

"Really?" Ken sat back and thought about it. "Sam, somehow your data found its way into the hands of Simcox and she tabled it in the House yesterday. It's bigger than

Ben Hur, you know. Uproar in question time, PM acutely embarrassed and — well, the long and the short of it is that it'll probably bring down the government."

Sam struggled to grasp the implications. "You sure?"

"Absolutely. MPI Biosecurity has stepped in to quarantine the affected farms and surrounds."

"Ah! That explains why Ruakura looks like Mission Control this morning!"

Ken waved his notebook. "I've got some bits of the jigsaw puzzle too, and we need to put it all together. But first, how about a coffee to help us concentrate?"

As Ken frothed the milk, Sam turned to watch the breaking news on TV. A reporter stood under the arch proclaiming the entrance to Mangawara Farm, now festooned with distinctive yellow biosecurity alert tape.

"...all we know at this time is that following revelations in Parliament yesterday of a significant contamination event in the Waikato, Biosecurity operatives have stepped in to secure several local farms including this — the Mangawara Trust Farm — a high-profile Maori operation located in the Mangawara Valley not far from State Highway One. We are expecting a statement from MPI shortly. What we can see is that the farm has been locked down and that there are at least thirty Biosecurity staff on site including several in cover-all isolation suits. They appear to be busily sampling the site..."

"Full on, isn't it?" Ken set down two flat whites. "I can already tell they're rummaging around like bulls in a china shop. My experience tells me these events require decisive leadership. You only get a brief window to get your head round the problem and must act immediately to nip it in the bud. If you don't, it quickly balloons out of control." He sat and lifted his cup. "Breaches like this can undermine our credibility with trading partners as quick as look at you."

Sam turned these new developments over in his mind as he absent-mindedly sipped his coffee.

"Anyway," Ken continued, "let's cut back and fill in the gaps we can. How do you know the place is contaminated?"

Sam took a moment to collect his thoughts.

"We've been collecting samples from the monitor farms for six months or so, but only recently started the analyses. I've been working with Shelley Lai, our lab techo. We noticed almost immediately that the measures were unremarkable until about two months ago. More recent samples show skyrocketing levels of a dangerous form of *E coli*, high levels of antibiotics in the formulated chicken and pig chow, and GE contamination of the feed and corn stocks waiting to be sown out."

Ken whistled.

"Seems uncomplicated in a sense, though," he rallied. "An issue with the feed suppliers, perhaps?"

Sam shook his head.

"Ah! So what's the real problem, then?"

"The contamination doesn't follow any of the normal rules from a biological perspective. That's why I've been struggling with it. One example: the extreme contamination with the killer form of *E coli* in the dairy sluice pond is extremely unusual. That got me to wondering. Then I had a word with Phil Towhai who runs Mangawara."

"Not a bad bloke. A bit dour."

"Yeah — and we'll come back to him. He's been through a bit lately. It was Phil who first drew my attention to the other ILAWR visitor to the farm. Turns out his visits began about the same time the contamination levels started to rise."

"Interesting, but proof of nothing."

"Yes, a bit of a so what, except for two things. The stranger, whoever he is, didn't want to pass the time of day with me and his ILAWR vehicle didn't check out. Then I noticed from the analytical work there was a correlation between the timing of his visits and the sites of contamination."

By now Ken was leaning forward. "Go on," he urged. "Tell me more."

"You remember I said he was delivering stuff, including feed. Well, the contaminated sacks are the sacks he delivered, and only those. We have it all recorded. And so far as we can tell it's only the farms he visits that are contaminated."

"You sure?" The light was finally going on for Ken. "Fuck me!"

Sam nodded solemnly.

"Beyond a shadow of a doubt. I followed him. And we know he's tipping stuff into the sluice pond, which probably explains the extreme *E coli* levels up there. I know for a fact he visited all the farms that are now in lockdown."

The two scientists ruminated in silence over this shared information.

"You have been busy," said Ken. "What did you mean about recording the deliveries?"

"Phil Towhai's daughter Georgie did that. She videoed one of his visits and took samples from the feed bags he dropped off. Bingo! She's got it all there on camera. The levels of contamination were ballistic in the bags he delivered and only those bags."

"You're the man." Ken rose to stretch and patted Sam approvingly on the shoulder. "We'll make a real scientist out of you yet! But why didn't you spill the beans on him there and then?"

"Bear in mind we've only had the data for two days. And, Ken, it turned out to be a dangerous business sampling those feed bags. Poor Georgie collapsed soon afterwards and is in intensive care with an acute infection." He grimaced. "Her infection shows all the hallmarks of the enterotoxigenic varieties of *E coli* we found in the bags and on the farm. Ken, it was touch and go with her! She almost karked it."

Momentarily overwhelmed, he got up and paced around until he was in control again.

"Hard thing to say, but Georgie's infection is grist to the mill. We're testing samples from her now to confirm the infectious agent but ten to one it's the same as the *E coli* variety in the bags. She'll make it now, thank Christ. But it's been fucking scary all the same for me and for Phil. What this episode tells me is there's a very real risk to public health, too. And notwithstanding the buffoons out at the farm we need to consider what to do about that aspect, too."

"I can see that."

"I could show you the data and evidence of contamination; it's all there and safely stowed. But I don't think there's much to be gained, Ken, because it all checks out. The question I wanted to ask is why would anyone do such a thing?" He was fuming. "It beggars belief… And why my programme and how did the fucking info get to Wellington in the first place? Seems like I've been deliberately targeted."

"Well, now. I think I can add to this… Allow me to explain my own theory." Ken had been putting the jigsaw together. "And, Sam, it's not pretty."

Sam sat down heavily, preparing to hear something else he didn't want to.

"I'm not one for conspiracy theories, mind you, but this scam shows all the signs. Let me tell you what I've come up with after doing some background work. Your stranger's name is Andrej Caradijc and he was brought into New Zealand as an environmental consultant." Ken paused for effect. "By Simcox!"

"I knew it."

"And get this, Sam. His field of expertise is biological warfare, no less."

"You're joking, right?"

"Ever heard of a place called Sverdlovsk in the old USSR?"

"Can't recall."

"That's where our man comes from. Sverdlovsk used to be what the Russians called a 'closed city'. It's in the Ukraine about 1500 km east of Moscow and the restricted access was because Sverdlovsk was involved in top secret military research. The entire city was given over to production of biological agents for use in war — anthrax, smallpox and the like. During the Cold War it was massive, but there was a major leak there around 1980 and a shitload of people died. It was like the biological equivalent of Chernobyl, and, with the fall of the Iron Curtain, the operation was shut down. I'm guessing a score of WMD scientists became redundant!"

"Fuck!"

"Fuck indeed. Sverdlovsk is common knowledge now, but you've got to remember it was at its peak in a completely different era. I don't expect he's making biological nukes or whatever in New Zealand, but hey, he might well know how."

Ken got up and refilled his cup.

"The other thing is that Simcox and your new boss Iris Dent are in bed together. Literally, by all accounts."

"No!" Sam half-laughed. "You have been busy, Ken."

Ken tapped the side of his nose, and winked. "It's not what you know but who! And there's a third connection. Ever heard of a woman called Anne Tuakana?"

"No. No idea."

"Allow me to enlighten you. Tuakana is from State Services in Wellington. She's the one handling my redundancy from ILAWR."

"So? You've lost me there!"

"Turns out Simcox, Dent and Tuakana all belong to

a women's club called Gravitas, which is dedicated to promotion of women in the civil service. Sam, they're all in this together! And my redundancy was part of the plan to get to you."

Sam sat down abruptly, factoring in this new information. Ken was silent, allowing him to put it all together. The conclusion was inescapable. Eventually Sam said aloud what he was thinking.

"Call me an idiot, but let me tell you what I think I'm hearing. You say Simcox has been sniffing around ILAWR and we both know she's been banging on forever in Parliament about the shambolic state of our biosecurity..."

He paused. Saying it aloud only made it seem more unbelievable.

"I know, I know. Completely wacko, but, Ken, hear me out on this..."

"Don't worry," Ken encouraged. "I can see where you're going with this. Keep it coming!"

"Here's the thing! Maybe Simcox got sick of waiting for a random biosecurity event to happen that she could create a stink about in the House. She decided to cook one up instead. You see where I'm going with this? She brought in — what's his name? — Caradijc — who of all people on the planet might well have useful experience in such matters..."

Ken nodded.

"That's what it's beginning to look like to me, too. And it goes deeper, much deeper, doesn't it? She needed someone to tamper with things. And she needed someone to measure it — you. And she had to be able to extract the information from ILAWR. So what'd she do? She made sure your monitoring research proposal was approved by the research funders. Then she tapped her network in Wellington to make me redundant and installed her crony as Director instead. I bet she used Dent to shoehorn the data out of your group as results began to come in too. Once she'd got what she wanted she didn't need you any more. You were suspended to shut you up. How's that for a theory, Einstein?"

"Not only weird but almost unbelievable. Sounds more like a Le Carre novel to me than a day in the life of a scientist down under. That stuff doesn't happen here."

"I'm seriously thinking it does, and right now. That's where the facts are leading us."

"There's something else I couldn't make sense of before, that ties in now," continued Sam. "I'm an environmental microbiologist with no interest in measuring GE in seed and crops. Imagine my surprise when they said they'd fund my research proposal on condition I monitored for GE as well. I said yes; I wanted the programme to run, but I never did understand why they wanted me to do that. After all plenty of other groups monitor GE. This explains it. They wanted GE because it's high profile and with me they had a one-stop shop to get some results."

He fell silent, brooding. He was roused again to action when Ken said, briskly, "OK, then. Let's test the hypothesis. What important things don't we know?"

"A few." Sam ticked them off on his fingers. "One. Simcox and Caradijc are connected, but is he acting on her instructions? Two. Where is he getting the stuff from to spike the farms? Three. We can't be certain yet if Dent is part of this or how the info was leaked." He was struck by another thought. "And, Ken, there's the matter of how to manage the biological risk. We need to give some serious thought to cleaning up the mess. It could cause chaos. Now that the news has broken I guess Caradijc will be keeping a low profile. Oh, and I forgot to tell you I tracked him and know where his base is. Probably we need to take a closer look at that, too. We'll have to be bloody careful though."

"So we've got a bit of work to do then, lad."

"Where should we start?"

"Fill in a few more gaps and then blow the whistle. Take the file to Wellington or alert the press or something. Blow the thing wide open and round them all up. Can you email me everything you've got, Sam? I'll write up something believable. We have to do this properly. My God! The political ramifications are enormous."

"OK. Let me on your computer and I'll forward you the whole goddam file."

Sam worked steadily while Ken brewed more coffee, but soon he was sighing audibly at the keyboard.

"What's up, lad?"

"Could swear I forwarded every last file to my independent web account. Even checked it had arrived. But it ain't there now! How does that happen? Nobody else has access."

Sam pulled a memory stick from his pocket. "Good job I've got it all backed up here."

"Thank Christ for that! We're nothing without the data. Copy it over to my computer before we lose that, too, and create new email accounts for both of us."

He brought the mugs over to the table.

"We need to take things a bit further," said Sam. "What do you say to meeting here again tomorrow evening and see what we've got?"

"Good plan."

Sam took back his memory stick and stood up from the computer. Ken settled himself at the keyboard and started to read what was there.

CHAPTER 37

BOTH MEN jumped when suddenly there was a sharp rap on the patio slider.

"Who's that?" Ken stared at the intruder.

Sam went to open the door.

"Oh, it's Shelley Lai, the technician who's been working with me."

He motioned her into the room.

"Ken, this is Shelley. I completely forgot, but she wanted to see me, too. Ken she's the only other person with access to the data. How did you find us here, Shelley?"

She ignored his question. White-faced and tense.

"You promised you'd talk to me, Sam."

"You're right. Sorry. I've been as good as fired, and, in my defence, I needed some time out."

He pulled out a chair for Shelley. "Have you met Ken Judge? You've probably seen him around work."

"Hello, Dr Judge." Ever polite, she stood up and shook Ken's hand. "It's an honour to meet you, sir. "She turned to Sam to answer his question. "I followed you here. I wanted to tell you how sorry I am."

"Why? I don't understand."

"It was me that passed your data to Iris Dent."

Now Shelley had their full attention. Beneath their accusing stares she lost control, and started sobbing. Ken handed her a folded hanky and poured another cup of coffee. She sat down and cupped her hands around the mug.

"I had no choice," she whispered.

"I asked you to wait," said Sam, rankled. "All we needed was a bit more time."

Shelley struggled to keep it together. "She blackmailed me," she wailed. "She threatened me."

"Who?" said Ken.

"Dent."

Shelley was crying too hard to go on. Sam sighed and sat down beside her, placing a comforting arm on hers.

"How so, Shelley?"

"She threatened to kidnap my son if I didn't do what she said!"

Sam and Ken exchanged glances, uncertain what to believe.

She scrubbed her face with the hanky and sighed.

"I know it sounds ridiculous," she said, straightening in the chair. "But it's true. At first I couldn't believe what she was saying, and then I was so frightened I started to tape her calls. Listen to this."

Shelley reached into her handbag and pulled out her cellphone. She put it on the table and turned on the speaker to replay the conversation.

'Dent here. Where is it?'

'I won't give it to you. I'd rather resign.'

'Oh, really? Why don't you sit down, Lai, and take a moment to think what it would be like if your son didn't come home today…'

Sam listened with mounting horror as the recording played out.

"Jesus," Ken uttered, aghast at the exchange. "I knew Dent was a nasty piece of work, but I had no idea she'd stoop to this. We need to be very careful."

"Agreed."

By now Sam was forehead to forehead with Shelley, fingers gently stroking her cheek.

Eventually she spoke, relief apparent in her tone. She had so needed to share her predicament and knew instinctively both men were now on her side.

"She's certainly not big on social graces."

Sam gave her a comforting squeeze.

"You'll be all right now," he reassured. "What you've done is brilliant. You mustn't worry, Shelley. Anyone would have done the same in the circumstances. We totally understand, don't we, Ken?"

The older man nodded, still frowning as he processed what he'd just heard.

"I've had to fight to survive in the past, but that's another story," she said. "But this is different. Tell me what you think it is all about."

Sam regarded her solemnly. Things were complicated enough. She hadn't been prepared to just lie down and take it from Dent. But all the same, how much could they really afford to tell her at this point? The less people implicated the better.

"You've done well, Shelley. Very well. What you've told us changes the game but Ken and I have been playing catch-up, too. To be honest we're not yet sure what's going on ourselves. Your question is a good one but can I hold off answering until we've figured out what Dent is really up to ourselves?"

"OK… I'm persuaded, but just for the moment."

With the air cleared between them, the three sat together with a new sense of comradeship.

After a time Sam got up and said, "I think we have to do more to protect you, Shelley. Could you and Hua go and stay with friends?" What was dawning on him was that the more time he spent with Shelley, the more he cared. His affection was becoming deep, very deep and the bond between them growing.

"There is someone like an aunty to Hua across town. I could visit and talk to her."

"Why don't you do that? Ken and I need to work things through anyway, so you pop over and see her and when you're organised I'll help you move in."

"Aside from staying somewhere safe I think it's best

that you carry on at work as if nothing has happened," continued Ken. "Don't talk to anyone about this though. And you haven't seen us. Shelley, you can be our eyes and ears in ILAWR. There might be other ways to help in due course."

Shelley was listening intently.

"Why don't we talk again when you've visited your friend?" continued Sam. "Give me a call and I'll meet you at your place and help you pack up a few things."

"Thanks. That'd be great."

Shelley stood and headed for the door with evident relief, even managing to return Sam's smile. He gave her arm a reassuring squeeze. She fell into his arms for a long time, and then he showed her out.

"What a girl!" Sam turned back to Ken excitedly. "She's moved this thing forward in leaps and bounds. She's proved for sure that Dent is involved; that she's almost certainly the one who leaked the material to Simcox."

"Mmm." Ken was thoughtful. "It also proves we're up to our eyeballs in this. Sam, I've got to say I don't know what you're so pumped about. I'm feeling gutted myself. These people are dangerous."

Sam sobered some. Ken was correct as always. He sat down, sighing.

"You're right. This is way serious. And, Ken, thanks for being here for me. I don't know how I'd cope if it wasn't for you."

"Hey, don't go all soft on me, lad! Remember, I need you too. So let's call it a day and meet here tomorrow evening to see where we've got to."

CHAPTER 38

IN HER office Iris Dent contemplated the morning's events. With the Miro developments there was much to discuss. She dialled Bella Simcox's private cellphone.

"My dear! How are you?"

"On a roll. Been talking to the media all morning. Grafton is making a press statement at three tomorrow. Odds on he'll resign. Fantastic, eh?"

"That's great news, Bella. So all on track then. Listen, I rang to update you on developments here. I think we might need to cover up. This morning I met with Miro, the scientist who's running the monitoring programme. Obviously he was miffed we'd released his data."

Simcox snorted derisively. "Tough."

"Right. But, Bella, when I asked him why he hadn't informed me of a biosecurity threat in the usual manner he made an interesting comment. He said the contamination wasn't what it seemed. That it was deliberate and caused by an ILAWR employee. In other words — he's on to Caradijc."

"Shit. Sounds like this Miro has a trick or two up his sleeve and is not to be underestimated."

"He's bright enough, that's true. Bella, I suspended him to make it harder for him to talk to anyone else."

"Probably the best thing to do. Iris, now we've got what we want it might be better to shut the Caradijc operation down anyway. Call it risk management. I'll phone him. What say we meet at his farm tonight around dusk to talk to him about it? I was coming up anyway."

"Sounds good to me."

With that Dent rang off, relieved Simcox was OK with her handling of Miro.

CHAPTER 39

IN THE predawn Sam lay sleepless in his bed contemplating the prospect of being unemployed. He'd never been in that situation before; was more used to being headhunted and offered his choice of three or four opportunities. A golden boy indeed...

A prospect even more worrying niggled at the back of his mind. He buried his head in the pillow; intent on ignoring whatever it was that threatened his peace. But with the first few notes of the dawn chorus, it all came rushing back. Simcox, Dent and Caradijc — the fucking conspiracy that threatened to destroy not only his career, but a Prime Minister's rule, New Zealand's environment and also its international reputation.

He could turn and walk away... Yes, if he was another sort of person.

He had to face the facts. This wasn't just about him any more. It was about doing the right thing by everyone involved. And there was no one else. Or no greater cause. It was about saving the country.

The thought was scary, so scary that Sam gave it away and climbed out of bed. Within minutes he had showered and was flicking on breakfast TV as he walked into the kitchen.

On screen a reporter was presenting from outside Waikato Hospital. Sam stopped in his tracks to listen and watch.

"We have received unconfirmed reports of an outbreak of serious infectious illnesses clustered in the northern Waikato region. MPI has so far declined to comment on whether they are connected to the major Biosecurity operation presently under way in that area. We do know that three of the affected individuals are

from the same rural community as the quarantined farms. One is a young woman aged around twenty and the other two are local farm cadets. Additionally a team of five Police Dive Squad members were rushed to A & E late last night after attending an emergency call-out to a motor vehicle accident at Mangawara Bridge on State Highway One. It is understood there were three fatalities in the collision, which involved a milk tanker that crashed off the bridge into the Mangawara Stream near the Waikato and a private motor vehicle. Details of the divers' conditions have not been released, but we understand them to be serious. At this time we are awaiting statements from the police, hospital staff and Biosecurity officials…"

Jesus! Sam switched off, despondent. This thing could be escalating. He'd better head out and take a look. As he bolted down two slices of Vogel's and an espresso he fired off some texts.

'Ken. Did U C the news? Any connection between that cluster of sickness & quarantined farms? Will take a look. This thing could be moving to the next level. Sam'

'Hi, Georgie. U up for a visit? I'm heading your way, could drop in. Sam.'

And one last thing. Sam reached into his pocket and fished out the back-up memory stick with the key information on it. Where to hide it? He didn't want the data falling into the wrong hands. His gaze roved over the cookie jar, couch cushions and paintings on the wall. He finally decided to tape it behind the toilet bowl. He smiled. Dent and Simcox are deep enough in the shit. That's the last place they'll think to look.

That done Sam shrugged on his motorbike jacket and helmet, fired up the Aprilia and sped out through Hamilton East and onto the main road north at Cobham Drive. Approaching Taupiri, he was slowed by a tailback, and by the time he got to the Mangawara he could see why.

The bridge looked as if it had been hit by a bomb, side railing mangled and the road torn apart by the passage of the articulated milk tanker into the murky depths below.

Sam pulled over into a nearby car park and walked back for a closer look. Startled, he noticed immediately the deep green iridescent hue of the stream, the almost psychedelic glitter of the surface layers in the early morning sun.

He was snapped back from his contemplation of this troubling reality by a shout.

"Hey, you! No rubber necking. Beat it."

One of the policemen on duty was making it clear he wasn't welcome there.

Back on his bike he meandered round onto Orini Road for a further inspection of the Mangawara. Immediately he took his helmet off he was struck by the stench of decay rising from the swamp. Something was badly wrong here. Why hadn't it been reported?

Curious to understand the cause he dropped down onto the river bank, which only increased his concern. The wetlands were quieter than usual in the stultifying air, and there laid out before his eyes was a sprawl of dead animals — birds, sheep, a horse and, in the river, hundreds of dead fish.

He pulled out his cellphone.

"Hi, Shelley. Did you sleep any better last night?"

"Oh, hi, Sam! Yes, much better, thanks to you chaps. I thought the only thing for it was to curl up and die, and now I have a way forward. I'm so grateful, you know. By the way my friend is taking Hua and me in for a few days too. So it's all good. I was telling her all about you, Sam. She can't wait to meet you."

"Hey, that's nice. Thanks to you, too, for hanging in there, Shelley, you've added a lot to the case... On another matter, I'm out at Orini and I've got some real concerns about the Mangawara Stream. It looks like a goddam sewer."

He paused, thinking of what to say next.

"Could be a coincidence, but I can't help wondering if it's a result of the contamination at the farm. I think we need to take some samples and do the microbial panel of analyses on it urgently. Shelley, listen. This could be serious. The farm contamination is one thing, but my concern is that the introduced bugs have upset the local ecology and set off a toxic bloom."

"Oh, Sam, that is scary."

"Yes, it is. I can't tell yet, but if my theory is right there's no telling what might happen. Worst case, we're headed for a real disaster. Do you think you'd be able to get out here and sample the stream? Then give the samples to Max to assay. Don't tell him where they came from — just say they're an absolute priority."

"No worries. I get it. Anything else?"

"Shelley. Honey, please be very careful. It's imperative you use a full isolation suit. The last thing we need is you getting sick, too! No easy job either, so take your time and use sterile technique. It won't be easy so allow yourself plenty of time. Is that all right?"

"Sure, Sam. I'm happy to help." She added, "I'm so glad you still feel able to rely on me."

"Of course I do. Yesterday is behind us, I know we're together on this now. Let's get together soon. Call me when you've done the sampling, won't you?"

"Will do."

"Bye, Shelley — and thanks again."

Almost immediately Sam rang off, his phone vibrated to announce the arrival of a new text.

'Hi. Happy 4 U to drop in. Don't get your hopes up tho. I look and feel like road kill. X. G'

Somewhat flustered by this disturbingly close juxtaposition of one girl with the other, he texted back.

'B there in about an hour bearing gifts.'

That promise rang hollow as he realised how difficult it would be to carry anything resembling a present on the bike. No flowers, then. Instead Sam made his way to the French bakery and loaded up with croissants and *pain au chocolat*. He stowed them neatly under his jacket and set off for Mangawara.

Predictably the farm was a hive of activity overrun as it was by Biosecurity staff, police, TV crews and one or two ILAWR vehicles. Not a hope in hell of getting in there. Still, as Georgie's place was located up the hill beyond the farm boundary it would offer a reasonable view.

The rumbling of the big V-twin signalled his imminent arrival and by the time he got to the forecourt Georgie was waiting by the open front door. As he removed his helmet, Sam was struck by the contrast between this Georgie and the one he'd first got to know. The effervescent sparkle and round curves of a few days ago had been replaced by hollow eyes and sagging, anorexic angles.

He so tried not to, but his first glance must have betrayed the shock he felt at the sight of her pale face and gaunt body.

"Oh, please don't stare!" Her eyes were misty and her voice cracked as she spoke. "I wouldn't have seen you if I'd thought..."

She tapered off as the tears came. It was all too much for Sam as well — the long pent-up pain and stress, his feelings of responsibility and inadequacy, and Georgie, crying too. He stepped forward and folded her in his arms, and misted along with her.

"Ah, Georgie. I'm so sorry. You didn't deserve any of this."

How long they clung together like shipwreck survivors, he didn't know. Eventually, as the sorrow washed out, they were able to step back and be calm. Sam brushed the tears from Georgie's cheeks with his thumbs.

"How are you really, Georgie?"

"I'd like to say never better, but it wouldn't be true. This thing has really knocked me, Sam. Apart from looking and feeling like crap, I've got zero energy." She turned and led the way inside, saying over her shoulder, "Hopefully I'll come right soon."

"You will and there'll be no stopping you. You'll soon have the boys beside themselves again."

"Huh!" Georgie seated herself at the table. "Sam, you must know, you're the only one I want."

Sam was flattered, but cautious.

"Ssh, Georgie. One step at a time, huh?"

"Sure. Only there's nothing like what I've been through to make me realise what's important."

"I understand, OK, but there's a lot going on, and I have to sort this mess out first. I feel so responsible."

"Responsible for what?"

Phil Towhai had just entered and picked up the last of the conversation. And it was obvious he wasn't best-pleased to see Sam.

"Oh, hi, Phil."

Sam stood and held out his hand. Phil ignored it and went over to the sink.

He washed his hands, and dried them on the kitchen towel before turning.

"Yes… What exactly are you responsible for, Sam?" he demanded.

The last thing Sam wanted right now was confrontation.

"Georgie, I brought some goodies for morning tea. Any chance of an espresso before we chat?"

She nodded and went over to fill the jug. As she walked past her father to reach the sink, Sam noticed her brushing his arm reassuringly, doing her best to allay his anger.

Phil said nothing more but stood pointedly with his back to Sam. From the window he could survey the Mangawara Trust Farm, crawling now as it was with officials. He ignored the hiss of steam and the aroma of fresh-ground coffee percolating in the machine. Sam thought it best to say nothing and busied himself setting the pastries out on a plate.

Eventually though he had to speak.

"Fresh croissant, anyone?"

"Please!" said Georgie. "I've been hanging out for some real food."

Finally Phil turned to face them, his mood no less disagreeable. Sam knew he'd have to tread carefully.

Phil sat down, and nodded thanks to Georgie as she set plate and mug before him.

"Sam, listen. I've been fobbed off, bandied about and fucked around for three days now. If someone doesn't start explaining things to me soon I'm going to explode and, believe me, it won't be pretty! Just answer three things. What's really up with the farm, what's your role in all this and what has Georgie's illness got to do with it? How hard can that be?"

Sam could tell Phil wasn't to be meddled with. He was at his wits' end, sick with worry, mad with anger and wound up like a spring. If he didn't put Phil's mind at rest, there'd be a major eruption.

"Phil, my role, as you know, is the monitoring programme. About a week ago we started to detect some unusually high levels of dangerous bugs, GE corn and other things wrong on your farm. The levels were outside all normal guidelines and had to be reported. It went straight to the top, as you know."

"Come on, lad, that much is obvious. But how did it get contaminated? There appear to be only three farms affected, but the whole area gets its supplies from the same merchants."

Sam knew he was on dodgy ground here. He didn't want to tell Phil too much; the man could be a loose cannon. He was also aware Georgie knew far more than he wanted Phil to know at present.

"You're right. It could be that all the farms in the area are contaminated," he said. "But those three are the only ones I've been monitoring."

He reddened as Georgie fixed him with an enquiring stare. When he said nothing, she had to speak. She knew Phil needed answers.

"Come on, Sam, you have to do better than that. What about the stranger?"

"I knew it!" Phil banged his fist down on the table and leapt to his feet. "I knew something else was going on. What's this about the stranger? Spit it out, man."

Sam's brain went into overdrive, trying to recall what Georgie knew. Father and daughter waited expectantly for him to deliver.

"Phil, there is something else but we don't know for sure it's connected. Remember the other ILAWR vehicle? Georgie and I witnessed him doing some strange things, delivering feed, for example. But we're not absolutely sure yet whether it's his feed that's contaminated. I did make enquiries and he didn't check out, but I got myself into such serious bother doing it that I've been suspended and I'm now facing possible misconduct charges. So, Phil, I just don't know. Sorry."

Sam could only hope his selective use of the facts would be enough to head off confrontation. Eventually, to his relief, Phil moved on.

"Could Georgie's infection be related to the contamination?"

"Could be, but again, we won't know that for sure until her lab results come through."

"You know two of the farm hands have since been admitted to Waikato with similar symptoms."

"I heard something about that on the news, but I didn't know they came from here. What work do they do around the farm?"

"Odd jobs is all," said Phil, "they're only cadets. Things like feeding out to the chickens and pigs, hosing out the milk shed and so on."

"Yes, well, if you were to ask me I'd say they probably did catch the bug on the farm." Sam knew he was being frugal with the facts. He had to keep a lid on things. "What we don't know is whether that bug is a result of the stranger's activities."

Georgie was frowning now so he hurried on with what he had to say.

"Please understand it's difficult for me to do much to speed things up now I've been shown the door at ILAWR. I do know how you feel though, Phil, and I'll do what I can. I'm still in close with some of the lab staff. I'm also following up on the stranger and I'll keep you posted."

No response from either of them.

"Hey, isn't the best news of all that Georgie's over the bug? Isn't that amazing? She needs time to recover and plenty of TLC. But no worries, Phil. I'm absolutely convinced she'll soon be back to her spectacular best."

Phil allowed himself to relax a little.

"I'll have to limit your visits then."

Sam smiled but wisely said nothing. Phil seemed to be settling.

"Sam, I want you to keep me fully posted. Tomorrow I'm meeting the Biosecurity Manager. What do you think I should be asking him?"

"I promise I'll keep you informed, Phil. As for Biosecurity, I wouldn't be feeding them any information. So I don't think you should be discussing the stranger. Remember, you're the victim here. What I'd be doing is demanding to know what progress is being made on cleaning up your farm and when you can expect to have it back again."

Now they'd talked things through Phil returned to his office, seemingly at ease. Georgie and Sam sat down on the couch.

"Sam," she observed, after a minute. "I can tell you're not coming clean."

Sam feigned innocence as best he could.

"Why do you say that?"

"I don't think what you're saying adds up! For example, if you're so sure the stranger is at the centre of things, why don't you just report him to the police?"

Jeez! There were no flies on Georgie. Sick or not, she was one insightful young lady. Sam hesitated. How much could he afford to tell her?

After a moment, he replied.

"Georgie, you're on to it, but you'll have to trust me a bit longer. You see there's another layer of complexity in all this. Wellington is involved and it goes right to the top. I don't know who we can fully trust ourselves. I do have good help, though, in the ex-Director of ILAWR, Ken Judge, who has all the right connections, so hopefully we'll be able to piece it all together soon and blow the whistle on it."

"Sam, you'd better be careful. These people must be pretty screwed, and that means they'll stop at nothing."

"Yeah. You're right. But, please, Georgie — do I have your confidence on this?"

"Of course, provided you promise to be on your guard and keep me fully up to speed with what you're doing."

Sam squeezed her hand, gently, for even her bones felt fragile. He drew her close and cuddled her. It felt good to be shielded for a time from the grim reality of his world even if she wasn't Shelley.

CHAPTER 40

A THRONG of media with assorted equipment including TV cameras and microphones filed hurriedly into the main auditorium at the Beehive in response to the hastily called press conference. The press had been having a field day. Speculation was rife and there was a heavy air of anticipation that the government would respond to Simcox's ambush by resigning and calling a general election. Only through such drastic measures did it have any hope of regaining its mandate from the people.

The auditorium was packed to the gunwales when on the stroke of three a door adjacent to the stage opened and a stoical Jeremy Grafton entered and proceeded directly to the lectern. Richie McCarthy, Chief of Staff of the Prime Minister's Office, stepped up onto the stage to start things off.

"The Prime Minister will shortly read a prepared statement. There will be no questions at this time. A series of supporting press releases will be released at 5pm in time for the evening news. We thank you for respecting protocol. Now, Prime Minister Grafton."

"Members of the press, thank you for responding in such short order to the notice of this announcement.

"It is with great sadness and regret that I have decided to tender my resignation.

"You are all aware of the findings tabled in the House two days ago of a major biosecurity breach in the Waikato. This has occurred in spite of my very best efforts to develop a biosecurity policy to protect this nation from such threats, so ultimately I consider myself culpable for the failure.

"It would be easy to demand accountability from the

chain of command in MPI and Biosecurity itself. However, I have no direct evidence of shortcomings on their part. What is true is that they function within a legal and operational framework that my administration developed and funded. As a consequence, on reflection, it is my view that the accountability for the current crisis sits with my office and in particular with me as PM. In other words I have decided the buck stops here."

He paused briefly to allow the murmurs from the floor to die down.

"Since the announcement of the threat I have spent much time with officials getting a full briefing and understanding of the issues. My advice and judgement is that this is a matter of grave concern and of the utmost importance, with serious potential to do lasting harm to the nation both in respect of its economic and fiscal well-being and the health of its citizens. So although the real gravity of the threat has still to be resolved I consider I have no alternative but to resign and call a general election. Only this way will New Zealanders have a chance to say for themselves who they wish to lead the country out of this crisis.

"So this afternoon with a heavy heart I tendered my resignation to the Governor-General. At that time I expressed my regret about the current situation and acknowledged to His Excellency that the electorate should have the right to choose the administration it wants to take the country forward. It is for all the above reasons that I have resigned.

"Finally we discussed the window of opportunity that exists for an early election. In consideration of all relevant matters I now confirm the date of the election for Saturday November 27th. That is ten weeks from now. I will step down as PM effective immediately and the PM role will be assumed by the current Deputy — David Whangapa.

I will remain in Cabinet until the election to support David and assist with transitional arrangements. I have yet to consider whether I will stand for re-election. A decision on my political future will follow shortly.

"I would like to thank everyone who has supported me through my term. Thank you to the press as well for their objectivity in this matter."

With that PM Grafton turned and solemnly left the auditorium. He didn't look back.

Sitting in front of Parliamentary TV, Ken Judge witnessed the breaking news. Magnanimous of Grafton. He has certainly done the right thing here. By falling on his sword he has kept his integrity.

He might just get a second chance when they blew the whistle on Simcox's nasty little scam. Certainly apart from this crisis and the misfortune of having to govern through a downturn, Grafton has not done such a bad job.

He switched off the TV and texted Sam.

'In case U had had any doubt U can B certain now yr research of high impact. Did U C the news? The biosecurity fiasco has brought down the govt. PM resigned, election called for 27 Nov. C U 2nite. KJ.'

At Ruakura Iris Dent watched the telecast in the privacy of her office. Her efforts had paid off. Hopefully Bella would reward her well. She shot off a quick text.

'Well done U. Way to go.'

She got a reply after the briefest of delays.

'Yes. Our turn now. Epic media attention tho. Good time 2B out of town. C U at Caradijc @ 7pm. X.'

CHAPTER 41

Where the stand of bush marking the boundary of Caradijc's hideout ran down to meet the road, Sam killed the engine of his motorbike and coasted quietly in behind a convenient screen of toetoe. Jumping the fence he made his way cautiously up through the bush to a point some 400 metres from the road adjacent to the ramshackle collection of farm buildings.

Once there he stopped to survey the scene. The barn was the closest building, some 200 metres away across an open paddock. Beyond that, against the house, Caradijc's Hilux was parked under the carport. Bugger. He must be home.

Sam stood there considering how best to cross the paddock without drawing attention to his presence. If he crossed here, the barn would block his view from the house. On the other hand, Caradijc might already be in the barn. What to do? God, the last thing he needed was to be caught red-handed. Indecision crept in. Should he wait until dark or give it a miss completely? But the sun was sinking and would be directly behind him while he was in the open. The glare should be enough to hide him from view, he surmised.

The time was right to do it. So he did.

Nonetheless, Sam sidled up to the boundary fence with some trepidation. Snooping around other people's property wasn't your average day at the office. He placed his hands on a convenient post and stepped gingerly onto the middle strand and swung a leg over. In that most precarious of positions, straddling the barbed wire, he discovered at least one good reason for his apprehension.

The fence was electrified. He was brought back to earth by a God almighty thump between the legs and ejected unceremoniously into the paddock. He lay there writhing for a good five minutes, heart racing, before he clambered shakily back to his feet. God, that hurt. Things could be going better.

He brushed himself down and decided he couldn't stay where he was. A mad dash across the paddock brought him to the relative security of the barn wall, where he paused for a watchful moment. No sign of movement, no sound from the barn. Perhaps he could risk a peek. Sam repositioned himself where he could peer through a crack in a boarded-up window.

He could tell immediately this was not your average barn; more like some kind of do-it-yourself process lab. To his expert eye the stainless steel tanks, the dryer and mixer spoke of a microbiology fermentation plant of some scale and sophistication. Sam tried to reassure himself. It could be anything. Think the best.

As he leaned against the wall, deep breathing, he decided to check in with Judge and punched out a text.

'Out at Caradijc's. He has a custom built micro lab here all right. Back yard WMD maker? Might not make dinner. C U a.m. S'

Within a few seconds came a reply.

'Don't be a dickhead, Sam. B bloody careful. U R not James Bond. K.'

Yeah, right. Sam was getting into his work now. No one in the barn so he'd try for a closer look. He scanned the building for a side entrance, but there was none. He'd have to try for the main door, which would take him out into full view. Sam stood there for ages convincing himself there were no signs of movement from the house or surrounds, and then, suitably pumped, he went for it. Reaching the main door he quietly slid it open and gently closed it behind him. He paused briefly to check if he'd attracted any attention. There was only the distant barking of a dog so Sam turned his interest to his surroundings.

The one thing immediately evident was that Caradijc was no average punter, but a microbiology expert of some note. A skilled craftsman too, with a knack for fabricating complicated devices from everyday items. A bit rich in the circumstances to find your enemy had a No. 8 wire mentality!

The more he looked, the more he was impressed. Everything in the lab confirmed that Caradijc had specialist knowledge of large scale fermentation, and to someone with Sam's trained eye it was extraordinary. Terrifyingly so. If it wasn't for the fact that he was up to such dirty tricks, this was a man Sam could seriously relate to.

Enough. He was there for a reason and so when the wonder of it all subsided he turned back to the business of the moment. Using his mobile phone Sam took a series of photos: overview shots and close-ups of equipment and feed bags including some open bags of corn he suspected were GE. Finally he photographed the impressive process control laboratory and QA sheets containing recognisable codes for E coli 0157.

Next he located some sample pots, a mask and gloves and went about collecting samples from the equipment carefully labelling them and zipping them safely into his jacket pocket. All went well until, as he was thinking about sneaking out again, he heard the sound of cars on the drive. Sam scooted over to the window in time to spot Caradijc emerging from the house to greet the newcomers.

The true gravity of his predicament dawned on him as the assembled party turned and headed towards the barn. He was trapped. Fuck! What to do? If he left now, he'd be tumbled.

Turning, Sam made a dash for the best hiding place in the barn, over beside the fermenters. He ducked in behind two pallets of feed bags only seconds before the door opened and the group stepped purposefully in.

"Yes, you've done well." A woman's voice, vaguely

familiar. "So well in fact that it's mission accomplished. What we need now is to cover our tracks."

Sam craned his neck around the furthest pallet to catch a quick glimpse and was struck by the earth-shattering reality of what was he was looking at. The voice belonged to Green Future party leader Bella Simcox and also standing there with Caradijc was his boss, Iris Dent. Game over.

The conversation continued in the fading light.

"What do you mean by cover our tracks?" asked Caradijc.

"For a start get rid of this equipment, turn it back into a normal barn again. The last thing we want is any connection between us and your activities. Also, you need to respray the ute as a matter of priority."

Caradijc was obviously taken aback by the finality of it all.

"What about the future and our agreement?" he ventured.

Simcox laughed. "There is no future, Caradijc. Your job is done. When you've finished the clean-up you're free to leave the country. I'll make sure you're fully paid up including the bonus."

"But my family, immigration..." Caradijc spoke with an air of hollow desperation. "You promised."

"Get over it. It's not going to happen. Couldn't possibly in the current climate."

Sam could tell the tension was rising. He also knew this was a once in a lifetime opportunity to get a snap of them all together. In these surroundings a picture would be the most damning evidence of all.

Struggling in the confines of his hiding place, he pulled out his phone again, zoomed the camera at the conspirators and pressed the button.

In the next instant Sam's world changed, possibly forever. In the gathering gloom the automatic flash had turned itself on and the group was frozen in a burst of brilliant white light.

When the shock hit him what followed for Sam was the spine-numbing realisation he was done for!

Simcox and her team stared at Sam, first startled then with growing rage as it dawned on them there was an intruder. Sam took the opportunity of their momentary indecision to burst through the group and out into the yard, bolting quickly around the side of the barn and into the paddock.

"It's fucking Miro," shouted Dent, as they turned to follow.

"Get after him!" screamed Simcox at two heavyweights slouched nonchalantly against the cars. "Kill the bugger!"

If Sam had been in any doubt about a threat to his personal security it was completely dispelled by her spine-chilling command. He increased his pace and dashed across the paddock towards the fence line.

Behind him Caradijc had released the dogs and they growled and bayed as they rapidly gave chase. He could hear them closing rapidly and as he approached the fence the mongrels were snapping at his heels. He ran straight for a post and with centimetres to spare, planted both hands on top and vaulted over.

The dogs leapt up at the fence and Sam heard them shrieking with pain as 20,000 volts surged through them. He spared a quick glance back to where they howled and contorted on the grass, but he didn't delay. Instead he powered through the bush to his bike. The slap of cutty grass and the prickle of blackberry thorn meant nothing to him now. As he ran the whining of the dogs subsided to be replaced instead by the roar of powerful European cars being floored and spun around in the shingle. Above it all Dent bellowed instructions to Caradijc.

"Burn the fucking barn. Now!"

Sam wasn't waiting around for the fireworks. He pulled on his helmet, gunned the motorbike and smoked it out onto the road. Behind him two sets of headlights emerged from the driveway.

Sam accelerated hard down the straight, noting with satisfaction the cars' lights fading into the distance. Cold comfort though, for as he rounded the first bend the road tightened and he knew that his pursuers would soon be upon him. He left his braking late and dived deep into a series of slow turns, trying hard not to scuff off speed. In spite of his efforts a rapid glance behind confirmed they were closing now. It was all on.

Soon enough, Sam felt the metallic scrape of his footrest on a car door as a powerful black Mercedes tried to run him off the road. With disaster looming the road opened up again and he was able to pull clear, reaching insane speeds as he changed into top. It wouldn't be enough, though. Ahead was a stretch of shingle where he would easily fall into the grip of his pursuers.

What to do? Sam was thinking hard and as he rounded a fast left-hander it came to him. He had to pull off and head back the way he'd come. In the distance at the end of a short straight he spotted a house on top of a hill with a drive winding up between the hedgerows. Perfect. Sam switched off his lights to disguise the manoeuvre as best he could.

Once in the driveway he deftly turned and waited to see if he'd been spotted. Seconds later he could tell the skulduggery had worked. The Mercs sped by in hot pursuit without so much as a sideways glance. Sam waited a few seconds more then pulled out in the opposite direction and headed at a good clip for Hamilton East.

By the time he reached home the pounding in his chest had just about subsided. His breathing returned to normal and he was beginning to let his guard down.

Big mistake.

Sam stepped up to the patio door intending to text Ken straightaway. His wrists were grabbed and pinned from behind and, as he was bundled in through the door, his cellphone flew unceremoniously out of his hand and fell into the garden.

Sam half-turned to glimpse two massive thugs, all suits and shades, as a club-like fist crunched into his cheek. He recoiled, bending double as a baseball bat was driven deep into his guts. His eyes opened to be treated to the sight of a size 14 Doc Marten as it ploughed into his face.

He lay on the edge of consciousness, lights flashing and the room whirling around him. He could barely make out what the man was saying.

"What'll I do with him then…? You sure you want that…? It'll cost extra."

Then the obligatory slosh of cold water as his captors tried to revive him.

In the distance Sam made out the other man carrying his computer, laptop and spare drives out to the car. Meanwhile, the other heavy stood over him, goading him with the baseball bat.

"Where's the camera then, eh? Come on, you turd. You're just making it worse for yourself."

Curled up on the floor Sam tried to grasp what was being asked of him. Camera — what camera? Ah! They were after the photos. He patted his trousers and his attacker immediately bent down and rummaged through Sam's pockets, scattering sample tubes in all directions.

"Don't fuck with me, sunshine! Where is it?"

Common sense dictated to Sam he come up with something to stop the ever-imminent threat of the baseball bat. He had an idea.

"Try the table by the door; think I dropped it there as we came in."

The thug picked up a digital camera that happened to be there, waiting for repair. Satisfied, he slipped it into his pocket.

"Good. We should have a drink to celebrate."

He brought out a half bottle of single malt from Sam's cabinet.

"Open up! I want you shit-faced."

Remorselessly he forced Sam's face upwards and poured the scotch down his throat until the bottle was empty. Sam fell back, retching, whisky splashes stinging face and eyes.

"Did ya enjoy that?" Now his assailant held a bottle of gin. "Seconds, perhaps?"

That, too, was upended deep into Sam's gullet. And then he was on a helicopter rotor, the world whizzing by. Fuzzy thoughts came and went. Shelley and Georgie. The conspiracy. Ken.

Nothing made sense any more and he closed his eyes against the lights and the spinning. But that was worse.

Next he was dreaming of being half-lifted, half-dragged, his feet scraping the ground. He was inside a car and on a bridge, below him the Waikato River. A fall, the chill of water closing over him. He was gasping in a terrifying glutinous dark. So cold. So cold. A futile struggle. The bubbles rising above him and dispersing into the night.

A cold grey dawn wreathed with mist on the Waikato River path at Memorial Park, with only the occasional jogger to disturb the ducks. Only as the sky began to lighten did two runners notice something like a hastily discarded rubbish sack lying half-buried in the river mud.

"Bob. There's something not right about that."

"Why? What do you reckon it is?"

"Don't know. Think it moved." He had slowed now and stopped, staring. Next he took a hesitant few steps towards the misshapen bundle.

"Oh, God. I think it is a body."

The other runner, impelled by curiosity, joined his partner.

"What, dead?"

"Got to be, by the look of it..."

The pair jumped back nervously as a hand rose aimlessly from the sludge, barely disturbing the mist.

"Call 111, Wayne."

He did so as the crumpled, half-broken body struggled to break free of the ooze.

"They said to wait here and put him in the recovery position."

Gingerly they obeyed instructions. The lump in the mud seemed hardly human, and they stepped back hurriedly.

"What do you think? A druggie or failed suicide?"

"Don't know. Let's leave that for the paramedics to find out."

A siren wailed forlornly in the distance.

"That's them now. Go and wave them down here, Bob. This guy's going to need all the help he can get if he's to make it."

CHAPTER 42

KEN WAS on his second espresso and getting more anxious by the minute. He'd texted Sam a couple of times the previous evening with no response and still nothing this morning. He tried to connect once more, but all to no avail. If he wasn't worried before he was now. By the time he'd finished breakfast he had resolved to drive over and check on the lad.

His worst fears were confirmed as he pulled into Sam's drive. The Aprilia lay ominously on its side with helmet and gloves scattered haphazardly around. The patio door was open and the living room looked for all the world as if it had hosted a pub brawl — upended chairs, empty booze bottles and Sam's bike jacket crumpled on the floor.

Sam himself was nowhere to be found.

What on earth had happened here? Ken sat down heavily on the couch, fast-forwarding possibilities; paralysed by indecision and his growing concern for Sam Miro. He should call the police; but what if Simcox had contacts there, too? Not impossible. He didn't know what was best any more.

He'd just decided to bite the bullet and call the constabulary when he heard a cellphone ringing nearby. Ken traced the sound to the garden by the patio door. A moment later he'd recovered the cellphone and dusted it off.

"Hello!"

"Hi, Sam. Shelley."

"Shelley, it's Ken — on Sam's phone!"

"Oh! I wasn't expecting you, Dr Judge. Sorry, sorry. Is Sam there?"

"No. When did you last talk to him, Shelley?"

"He texted me last night to say he had some priority samples for analysis that I should collect. Why, where is he now?"

"That's the point. He's gone AWOL and I'm worried." As he spoke, he saw the tubes spilling from Sam's jacket. "I think your samples are here, though, so why don't you drop around to collect them?"

"Sure, why not? See you later."

"Oh, and if Sam does turn up, please get him to ring me straightaway."

Ken sat and fiddled with Sam's phone. The mystery was deepening by the minute. He thumbed through the recent call and message lists. No surprises there. Eventually he reached the camera file where he found a multitude of pictures. He began to surf through, recognising immediately what he was looking at — technical shots of a fermentation plant. Caradijc's, in all likelihood.

Ken was about to pocket the phone and head for his car when he got to a photo of people. He squinted to get a better view of the tiny screen. The realisation of what he was looking at struck him like a left hook on a cold morning. Dent and Simcox standing in front of a fermenter with a tall, straight-backed man between them. That was Caradijc, beyond a shadow of a doubt.

How on earth did Sam get a photo like that? No wonder he's in trouble. Maybe they tracked him back here and dealt to him.

Oh my God. What to do?

What to do?

CHAPTER 43

NOTHING AT first. Then random thoughts. Faces he ought to know and things he should be doing. Places, past and present.

He couldn't move. He couldn't speak. A wave of fear, ice-cold.

Nothing again.

Light, too bright for his eyes to bear so Sam closed them again and drifted off.

Figures in blue and white coming and going.

Still drifting in and out but with anxiety now about his inertia. Things pressing on his mind he couldn't form into words. He tried to get up.

Big mistake. Nothing worked.

Can't move. Can't speak.

And God it hurts.

"Hello! Hello! Can you hear me?"

Still no words, so Sam blinked twice. He wanted to speak, but he was tired and confused.

"Too soon obviously! Give him another sedative and electrolytes and we'll try to bring him back later."

"Yes, doctor."

He was waiting when next they returned.

"Ah! Can you hear me?"

Sam nodded vigorously and then wished he hadn't.

"OK. Help him sit up and get the lines out of his mouth."

"What's your name?"

Good question. He thought hard about it and muttered,

"Shaam..."

"Sam? Oh hi, Sam. Welcome back. You're lucky to be here, young man. Not many jump off that bridge and make it."

"Jump?"

"You smashed yourself up pretty good."

Sam abandoned his efforts to make sense of it all.

"...is there a phone I can use?"

"Not so fast. You need to rest up for a day or so and then we want you to see the psych team."

"To hell with that! All I need is a cup of tea and an aspirin. Oh, and a phone."

The doctor patted his shoulder knowingly.

"We'll be back later."

Sam waited until they had left the ward and then hauled himself into a sitting position. He rested and then swung his legs around to the side of the bed. That required a longer rest and, God, it hurt. Jumped off a bridge? Put through a compactor, more like.

When he stopped being dizzy, Sam checked the occupant in the next bed. The old bugger was sound asleep. Sam shuffled as best he could through his roommate's bedside table, picked up the phone he found there and dialled.

"Judge speaking."

"Hey, it's Sam."

"God, you sound rough. Where are you? I've been scared shitless."

"Me, too. I'm at the hospital. Can you come and sort them out? They think I tried to top myself."

As Ken exited the lift and walked down the corridor to the ward he had absolutely no idea what to expect. Generally speaking, Sam could take care of himself; but this attack demonstrated they were now playing in a different league. The threat made to Shelley, the assault on Sam by Dent and Simcox's hired thugs, scraped up no doubt from

Wellington's seedy underbelly, made that explicit. The lowlifes they were up against were capable of anything.

None of this speculation prepared Ken for the reality of what confronted him when he turned into Sam's room. Hit by a bus would be an understatement.

The grin Sam attempted was more of a grimace, pulling on the stitches around his mouth; and then there were the two black eyes and other scrapes and bruises.

His jaw dropped and he stood there, staring.

"Oh, get over it, Ken."

Ken took his cue from this well-rehearsed nonchalance.

"You have looked better," he said collapsing heavily into a bedside chair. "I thought those bastards had got you for good."

"Yeah, well, they had a good go, I tell you — but they won't get a chance to do that again. Talk about stereotypes. The two of them were like ponced up pro wrestlers. You know, all dark suits, wraparound shades and fake tan. Ghostbusters on steroids. I doubt Simcox found minders like that through her Wellington club."

"Scary stuff, huh?"

"Yes, but enough of that. Ken, you've got to get me out of here."

"Hold on, Sam. Let's take five and talk about this." Ken had no idea of the extent of Sam's injuries. "You take it easy and I'll check with the staff what the deal is. Why did they think you tried to kill yourself?"

"Apparently I was found in the river under the Bridge Street bridge so they assumed I'd jumped."

"So how did you get there?"

"No idea. After they beat the stuffing out of me at home they filled me full of booze and everything's a blank after that. They probably dumped me there to float away. I guess they wanted to make it look like an accident, or worse, a suicide attempt."

"Lucky escape."

"Yes. One down; only eight lives left."

Tired by all the talking, Sam fell into a sudden doze. Ken watched him as he slept. He'd always wanted a son, but it hadn't happened. His daughters were grown up, married and flown the coop — one in Australia, the other in the UK. He'd have to hope for a grandson. In the meantime, Sam Miro was a good substitute.

Ah! The lad was awake again.

"You're smiling, Sam. Who've you been dreaming about — Shelley?"

"You might think so. I couldn't possibly comment."

Sam tried hard to crack a smile; grimaced instead as he raised himself on to his elbow.

"How did you get on with the doctor?"

"He said you're dead lucky. No broken bones, some minor internal bleeding and brain swelling, a few stitches. If you take it easy you should be good to go in a couple of days. They do want you to see someone first. Like you said, they think you jumped, that you're depressed."

"The thing I'm depressed about right now is that I can't get a decent meal in here. I'm starving. Ken, you did put them right, didn't you?"

"Yes, I did manage to convince them you can pass for normal. You didn't have any ID on you, Sam, so you were a bit of a mystery man. I filled in the background and that changed things. You're free to go when you're ready. You'll have to keep your feet up for a week or so though."

Ken cleared his throat, and said, gruffly, "One thing, Sam. They wanted to know your next of kin. I didn't have a clue so I told them to put my name down. You don't mind?"

"Of course not." Sam ducked his head. "Families can be complicated, and I don't think mine would relish seeing me in this state. My parents are great in the good times, if you know what I mean; but they've never been the sort you turn to with a problem. You'll do just fine!"

Ken squeezed Sam's hand, and was relieved when the nurse came in and indicated his visit had lasted long enough. He walked away quickly as a mist of emotion descended on him. The Miro lad was beginning to matter a lot.

They kept Sam in hospital until he could prove he was fit enough to take himself off for a shower, eat semi solids and keep his pyjamas clean. Finally he was released into Ken's care and they headed home, mostly in silence. The journey wasn't that long, but tiring enough for Sam to agree to rest in bed. After a long sleep, he was primed for a recap.

"I suppose you could use an update on the drama, Ken?"

"That'd be good, though you might be surprised what I've been able to figure out myself."

"First off, I learned I'm not cut out for this. It was no fun; in fact, I was scared shitless... I did have a nose around Caradijc's place and it was everything we suspected it might be. He's got a DIY biological weapons plant there, the toerag! A regular back yard terrorist, if you ask me."

"I'll make it easy for you, Sam. I know all that and I'll tell you why. I was worried and went round to check on you. Your house was a bomb site, by the way, but I've sorted it. Your phone rang and I flicked through it and found the pictures. Simcox, Caradijc and Dent together! A masterpiece, Sam; a dead giveaway. All we need to take them down. I've downloaded the pics and put them into the report. But it's what happened next that I'm not so clear about."

"I was doing OK until the flash went off as I took that pic. They weren't over the moon at being snapped and gave chase. Set the dogs after me and tried to run me off the road. And when I got home they had their goons waiting. Did me over big time then dumped me in the river. To drown, I guess." Sam shook his head. "Still can't believe it happened."

"Like I said, you're one lucky bastard! Oh, by the way, Sam, I haven't been totally idle while you were lying in bed! I got the samples to Shelley."

"I expected nothing less."

"You up for a beer?"

Sam nodded and Ken got two out of the fridge. He ordered pizza and came back to continue the discussion.

"Seriously, though," he said, "there's nothing like adversity to focus the mind. We've been sucked into this torrent and swept along with it. How could either of us expect this kind of dirty dealing to be going on in Godzone? Unreal. Plus it's getting more sinister and murky by the minute. Neither of us asked for this kind of grief, yet here we are up to our necks in it. Let's take stock for a moment and consider what to do. When you went missing, I seriously contemplated going to the police."

"Yeah, well, we can't, can we?" Sam was indignant. "Simcox is seriously corrupt; over everything like a rash."

He pointed his bottle at Ken. "I'll tell you something else for free. I thought it'd be safe to go home after the chase, but they were waiting for me. Explain that to me. She had to get my address from somewhere PDQ. It's not listed so where? I wouldn't put it past her to have the police in her pocket, too.

"You serious?"

"I am. And I'm not dead either, so I expect they'll be back to finish the job — a scary thought, eh?"

Sam paused to accept another Steinlager from Ken, and reflect on what he was saying.

"Probably should make that the last for now."

"And another thing while we're on about her contacts and connections. Losing those files on my webmail might not have been an accident either. Yeah, maybe I did stuff up; it wouldn't be the first time. Except for one thing. I swear I saw them in my inbox after I forwarded them. I'm betting someone hacked into my account and deleted them. What that tells me is we can't be too careful, or underestimate her. One positive is they don't know you and I are working together. That's something. But it can't last long.

"Good thinking, Sam. You can't be too bad!"

"Huh! I've had worse, but not much."

"But you're right," Ken went on, "we do have to plan the next stage. And I think you need to keep a low profile for a while, Sam. You could use some time out anyway. Why don't you go home to your parents?"

"What, looking like this? I'd never hear the end of it. Good point, though. I guess I could visit my mate at the beach."

"Good idea."

"Given all of this, what do you think we should be doing with the info?" Sam continued. "Who should we be taking the evidence to?"

"I reckon the only person we can trust absolutely is Jeremy Grafton himself, given how much he's got at stake. I've met Grafton a few times; we should be able to get to him through my Wellington mate. What do you reckon?"

"Sounds good to me."

"Let's do it then!"

The phone rang.

"Hi, Ken. It's Shelley. I'm so worried. Any progress?"

"Yes, he's back. I'll put him on." Ken handed the phone to Sam. "It's Shelley."

"Oh, thank God. Sam, how're you doing?"

"Hi, Shelley. Oh my, it's great to hear you again. But believe me. I've been better. I'm sure Ken told you I was beaten up by Dent's offsiders and spent a couple of days in hospital. I'm not bad now, but you won't want to be seen in public with me for a couple of days."

"Oh, Sam. Are you sure you're OK?"

"Don't worry, Shelley. Soon will be."

"Thank the Lord we didn't lose you."

Her concern was warmly expressed, and Sam was grateful, misting even. Shelley was a sweetie, and though he knew now he wanted more with her there was still the matter of Georgie to work through.

"Sam, I've got the assay results you asked for."

"Brilliant, I'll put you on speaker so you can take us through them."

"No surprises in the most recent samples. High levels of the same enterotoxigenic *E coli* 0157:H7 strain that we've been seeing in samples from the farms. Where'd you get them from?"

"I'll explain later. Let's just say for now I think I've tracked the contamination to its source. And these are samples from there."

"Interesting! They have exactly the same genetic fingerprint as the earlier samples from the farms, so it's fairly conclusive. I hope you're able to hang a conviction on the perpetrators with this!"

"Us, too. What about the other samples from the Mangawara?"

"Again totally dominated by the contaminating strain of *E coli*, with all the other microbial bit players of the stream ecology present as well."

"So, no surprises there…"

"Sam, please wait; there's more. We know already that levels are high, but imagine my surprise when I saw that the levels increase the further away from the farm we go. They rise cataclysmically down towards the main road bridge. My take on that is the wetland conditions are good for this strain and it's proliferating as it moves downstream. I'm wondering whether we have a toxic *E coli* bloom on our hands in the wetland swamp."

"No chance you mixed up the samples or anything dumb like that? It can happen."

"Oh please, Sam. You know me better than that. Anyway Max was with me when we sampled so he can confirm!"

Sam was disturbed, to say the least, by Shelley's news.

"What's the gradient across the swamp, Shelley? How much do levels increase?"

"As you know they were high to start with — like five million of this strain of *E coli* per millilitre of water in the drain. That's how we picked this thing up in the first place. And then — wait for this, Sam! — they increase another thousand-fold over the length of the stream down to the main road bridge. So levels are approximating five billion cells per ml by the mouth."

"Jesus! That's almost fermenter levels of the bug. That's colossal! That wetland swamp must have textbook conditions for this strain to grow. Perfect storm conditions for cooking up an *E coli* bloom. Remember the main road crash? This most probably explains why the divers got so crook after they went into the river. Nobody could have contemplated this kind of outcome. Not even Simcox. But it's well out of even her hands now!"

Ken was more than a little troubled by the dialogue between Sam and Shelley.

"We all know it doesn't pay to bathe in this crap, but what if we were to drink it?"

"With this strain at such mammoth concentrations you'd be gone by lunch time, I reckon."

"How much would you have to dilute it to make it safe?"

"Massively."

"Because you might not realise this, but the intake to the Auckland water supply from the Waikato River is downstream from the mouth of the Mangawara Stream!"

All three of them fell silent as they contemplated the enormity of this revelation.

Finally Shelley spoke.

"Can you guesstimate how much the stream contents would be diluted before the intake?"

"Based on river flows I'd say only about two hundred-fold," reflected Sam. "So the bloom would still represent a threat."

"The water is fully treated before it is pumped to Auckland though."

Ken was seeking some reassurance.

"True, but it's still a worry and I'll tell you why. With bugs at these sorts of obscene levels they tend to split open when they are treated and filtered, spilling high levels of toxins into the water. So even if the water is devoid of bacteria, after treatment it could still contain poison and remain lethal."

"We must get the plant shut down. Like, yesterday!"

"I agree, but I don't think they'll be keen to do that." Shelley was clearly troubled. "I was reading that Auckland's drought is now critical after the dry winter. The West Auckland reservoirs are low and they are heavily dependent on the Waikato source!"

"This is a major," Sam said emphatically. "This thing has the potential to bring Auckland to its knees. Imagine that."

"In different circumstances there could even be some justice in that," said Ken. "What it demonstrates though is that it doesn't pay to stuff around with nature. You can never be sure what you're going to end up with."

"Ken, what'll we do?"

"Without a doubt the first step is to report it together with a compelling recommendation to get the plant shut down forthwith. We should write it up now and I think it is best that you submit it, Shelley, so that it doesn't look like we've had any input. I think it's best that you bypass ILAWR as well. Don't bother submitting it through Dent. She'll bury it. Probably best to take it directly to the guy in charge of the Biosecurity operation — what's his name again? — Oh, yes. Peter Smart. Then we'd best get on the phone to Wellington."

Sam remained thoughtful, and Shelley made no further comment.

"I'm wondering whether we can be more proactive." Sam's mind was racing. "Ken, what do you want me to do?"

"Nothing. You're off to Raglan, remember? Doctor's orders."

Shelley was listening intently as Ken continued. "Shelley is more than capable of taking care of this. And I don't intend to loll around while you're resting up in Raglan either."

CHAPTER 44

THE BEST Sam could find on the car radio as he drove out through Dinsdale towards Raglan was election build-up on the National Programme.

"Good afternoon, everyone.

"The country is increasingly moving into election mode and in breaking news we can confirm that former prime minister Jeremy Grafton will not be standing for re-election. Grafton's current second-in-command in the Social Democrats, Deputy Prime Minister David Whangapa, has been confirmed into the vacant leadership position.

"Whangapa is viewed as a charismatic and intelligent replacement, well able to reach out beyond the grassroots to the popular vote, including his Maori constituency. He needs to if the Social Democrats are to have any chance of recovering from their political decapitation at the hands of the unashamedly ambitious Green Future party leader Bella Simcox.

"Clearly the Social Democrats have been reeling from recent events including the media storm around the environmental problems in the Waikato. It is to Grafton's and the party's great credit that they are not in total disarray following recent events. Indications are that they have already been able to re-constitute themselves to demonstrate a fresh start, and must be viewed as bona fide contenders for the next election despite what the other parties may wish to think.

"However, the size of the challenge facing Whangapa is ably illustrated by our most recent opinion poll. The Social Democrats have slumped from fifty-four per cent of the vote following the last election to a miserly seventeen per cent today, badly burned as they have been by fallout from Waikatogate, as the environmental issue has come to be known. There is clearly a lack of confidence

in the party at present, but the change is viewed as positive as the party was most unlikely to have any chance in the upcoming election with Grafton still at the helm.

"What the poll also shows — and, it has to be said, this was taken before yesterday's leadership change — is that Grafton himself has fared rather better through the recent drama than the party, retaining twenty-seven per cent overall approval in the preferred PM stakes. This may be a sign of respect for the dignity and humility with which he conducted himself through what has clearly been a very difficult period, and his willingness to fall on his sword rather than disingenuously passing the buck as lesser mortals may well have chosen to do.

"A few moments ago Whangapa gave his first press conference as leader. He started with a flourish as you might imagine saying that yesterday was history and that today he wanted to make a fresh start — an obvious attempt to sideline Waikatogate. He continued by saying green issues were not the prerogative of minor parties and it was his pledge to bring them into the political mainstream. Whangapa acknowledges that the country's clean green image may have been tarnished by recent events, but is firmly of the view that New Zealand will require a concerted multi-party approach to rebranding itself if it is to get past the issues of the moment. He affirmed that the Social Democrats were more than willing to co-operate on ground-breaking new green politics where the value is clear.

"In contrast, Green Party leader Bella Simcox wasn't the least bit conciliatory at her most recent press conference, declaring that she saw no point in collaborating with the other parties for the sake of it. And why would she, you might ask, with approval ratings for the Green Future Party soaring to forty-seven per cent in today's poll with her personal rating as preferred PM ramping up to forty-one per cent — higher than it has ever been before. To her credit she has done a remarkable job of garnering popular support, especially around environmental matters.

"Under questioning, Simcox — political mud wrestler that she

is — made it clear that the Green Future Party would be the agenda-setters going forward, and that other parties would have no alternative but to fall in. She also continued to castigate and demonise the Grafton government, accusing them of shambolic mismanagement of not only the environment, but the nation at large.

"Simcox did not have it all her own way, though, coming in for some intense interrogation, possibly for the first time, with the press gallery asking for detail around her policies. Where's the meat? was the call. Simcox responded to the assembled reporters in true barnyard political fashion, retorting that she was not into old parties or policies; she was into something new. Little detail was forthcoming on what that something new might be.

"Lest there be any doubt, she reasserted that she would have nothing more to do with the losers of the Social Democratic Party. When pressed again on her specific position and policies on the broader issues of government, she was much less forthright. The consensus of the gallery was that she might not yet have a 'big idea' for the country, or, at least, an idea she is willing espouse at this stage.

"What did come through was that Simcox is most at home trading on the worst instincts of xenophobia and nationalism that the naked environmentalism of recent times seems to throw up. Clearly she would prefer to keep the spotlight firmly on this issue as we run into the election rather than expose herself by broadening the policy discussion.

"Certainly, environmentalism has been her 'cause célèbre', and given the rapid turn of events, one has to wonder how much thought she and her party has given to the fundamentals of running the country. Time will tell whether the environmental issue will be enough on its own to get her into power.

"For the record the One New Zealand Party is lumbering in third place with approval ratings of seven and ten per cent respectively.

"Overall and in perspective a useful first showing for

Whangapa, but nonetheless first blood in the campaign has clearly gone to Simcox who has all the running at present."

Sam listened with a growing sense of contempt for the Green Party leader, who was prepared to go to such lengths to get control of the country. He had been gored by her once, and it had left him totally convinced that she had to be stopped and that he wanted to be the one to do it.

He pulled into Wiremu's Raglan drive, where his mate's car was parked but his surfboard was not. Surf must be up, but he seriously doubted that he was up for a ride today. He limped stiffly from the car, deciding that a walk on the beach could be just what the doctor ordered instead.

CHAPTER 45

WITH A body built for *haute couture* and her intriguing accent, Shelley had all the prerequisites to hold the floor. Yet she knew immediately she entered the office of Biosecurity Operations boss Peter Smart that she'd be needing something extra today.

Plainly Chief Smart wasn't having the best of days. He sat fulminating at his desk, flinging monosyllabic orders to a bevy of scurrying sidekicks doing their best to please. Tension hung heavily in the air, and as Shelley greeted Smart his hollow eyes and tense mouth left her in little doubt that this was a man under pressure. Smart was a man who wanted no complications; searching desperately for answers, not questions.

"Hello, Ms Lai. We were hoping you'd be the bearer of good news today."

"Not exactly, sir, but all the same I would like to brief you on an important development!"

"Oh, really?" His tone was neutral. "First, please remind me — where is it exactly that you fit in?"

"I'm a research associate at ILAWR and 2iC on the monitoring programme that first picked up the contamination problem you're dealing with."

Smart frowned.

"From memory it's Sam Miro who's principal investigator on the programme, isn't it? So where's he today?"

"True. Sam is — was — PI. But there have been some changes that I'm not at liberty to discuss. He's been stood down."

"I see."

"The work must go on, though, and I have a new report

for you of the utmost importance. That's why I thought it best to bring it to you personally!"

"How so?"

"The report charts a further increase in contamination of the Mangawara Stream. If you would allow me to walk you through it, I think you'll agree the matter requires top priority."

Smart regarded her with a dismissive air. Frankly, he'd had about enough of it all and didn't want to know.

"OK, but let's cut back for a second. Who's running the show at the moment?"

"I am," responded Shelley, on the defensive. "Until we reorganise, you understand."

"And you do have a PhD, right?"

"No. Why do you ask?"

"Presumably the report contains new data. What confidence can we have in it?"

Shelley was immediately indignant.

"Chief Smart, the data has been generated using the same GLP systems we always use. It more than meets our quality standards."

"I hear you and I also need you to understand that this is my turf and I call the shots. We have multiple priorities and calls on our time and can't allow ourselves to be distracted by red herrings."

"Red herrings! Why do you say that?"

Shelley was boiling now, and wisely chose to stay silent. It was clear that the Chief of the Environmental Response Team, totally indifferent to her approach, was not even prepared to give her a hearing. Shelley stared at Smart, uncertain where to take the conversation. Finally he wrapped things up.

"Ms Lai, I want to thank you for bringing the report over. I can assure you we will take a look at it in the fullness of time."

"Chief Smart! That's exactly the point. We don't have time on this matter. I urge you to give this your utmost attention. The Mangawara Stream has the potential to poison Auckland's water supply."

Even as she spoke, she could tell she was wasting her time. He had moved on; might as well have been on a different planet.

The aides had seen it all before and swung instinctively into action, ushering her through the office door and out towards the car park. As she left, Smart called after her, "Have a nice day, Ms Lai."

She didn't bother to reply.

"I'll make sure he gets to it as soon as possible."

This from an embarrassed assistant as they parted at the main entrance.

Yeah, right.

Shelley was fuming as she walked on towards her Corolla. What hope was there with him in charge? The man was a total disaster. She would check in with Judge and Sam and let them know that they couldn't expect any help from him.

CHAPTER 46

KEN JUDGE had dedicated two days to compiling a full dossier of evidence against Simcox. As he neared completion, he knew this damning indictment of the Green Future party leader and her cronies was more than enough to bring them down. Contemplating the course of events laid out before him he felt an almost physical sense of revulsion for the woman who was prepared to go to such lengths in her unbridled quest for power. Simcox had shown herself prepared to compromise the future of the country for the top job. In his view this amounted to treason.

His summary had to hit the mark for best effect and the real question now was how to get through to Jeremy Grafton. He'd be fully occupied supporting David Whangapa with his election campaign. Judge reached for his phone.

"McWilliams here."

"Hi, Roger. It's Ken."

"Hey, buddy. How's retirement?"

"Huh. You keep saying that! What retirement, I find myself asking. I've never been busier."

"So what can I do for you, Ken?"

"I'm on to something big here and I need to talk to Jeremy Grafton. Do you have any influence at that level?"

"I still catch up with his Chief of Staff from time to time. Why do you need to talk to him?"

"It's to do with our friend Bella Simcox!"

"Why am I not surprised? You must have been joining some dots since we last talked. What have you got that warrants talking to Grafton?"

McWilliams was not so subtly plying his craft as a trader in innuendo.

"I'd prefer to say nothing, except that it's massive."

"Yeah, you said that. But Grafton is hard to get to at the moment. You'll have to give me something more than that."

"This is a highly sensitive matter, you understand!"

"Sure, but, Ken, you'll only get one shot at this so you can't go off half-cocked. The last thing we want is for them to tell us to take a hike."

Ken knew Roger was right, but he didn't want to give away more than he had to at the moment. "OK, OK. Tell him I can connect Simcox to the contamination in the Waikato."

"What! You sure?"

"Fuck, Roger, what do you think. Of course I am!"

"Ken, this is serious. I can't just go scaremongering, you know."

"For God's sake, Roger, don't you think I know that? Tell him that if we are to talk it has to be face to face and, here's the thing, it's important enough to make the critical difference in the election!"

"Now you're talking," said Roger, with renewed interest. "I'll get back to you soonest."

Ken hung up, satisfied he had done his best. Now he needed to update Sam, but as he reached for the phone, it rang again.

"Roger."

"That didn't take long!"

"The thorny issue of the election is occupying their minds to say the least. They know they're on the brink of a massive defeat and a second string party is about to take control. If that happens it'll be nigh on impossible for them to get back. These are desperate times indeed, so they're searching for answers if you know what I mean. If what you've got really is as important as you say, it might be exactly what they're looking for. McCarthy and Grafton are going to phone you in five if that's OK. Give him a thumbnail sketch and if you get past that they'll be wanting you to hop on a plane to Wellington. You can do that?"

"Sure!"

And with that Roger was gone.

Ken made himself a coffee and was taking his first sip when the phone rang again.

"Grafton here."

"Hello, sir. Ken Judge speaking."

"Hi, Ken. I recall we've met a few times though not recently. What are you up to?"

"I've been bundled disgracefully into early retirement, sir. It's a long story and part of what I want to talk to you about."

"OK, Ken, but I don't have much time, so please cut to the chase."

"Right. Sir, I came to you because this is bigger than Ben Hur and I don't know who else I can trust. The accusation I'm about to make is not made lightly and is completely evidence-based. We have a full dossier to back it up."

"Go on."

"Sir, the eco-calamity in the Waikato was no accident. It was a planned and co-ordinated act of deliberate environmental sabotage perpetrated by Bella Simcox."

Ken waited for the reply that was a long time coming as Grafton and McCarthy processed what he was saying.

"Sir," he added, "I have no political motivation in bringing you this information. In fact, I'm a paid-up member of another party. I bring it to you because in spite of everything you still represent the administration and something has to be done straight away. I am hopeful I can get traction with you as for a number of reasons I'm not sure where else to turn."

"Traction, traction. That's an understatement."

Grafton was still coming to terms with what he was hearing.

"How did you tumble on to this?"

"I mentor the young scientist who is principal investigator on the sentinel farm monitoring programme that picked up the contamination in the first place — one Sam Miro."

"Oh, yeah. The award winner. I've heard of him. So?"

"Sam was first alerted by the covert activities of a foreigner we now know comes from the Soviet Union. He discovered the man has a secret microbiological fermentation plant in the Waikato that's cooking up the bugs used to contaminate the farms. He caught him in the act on camera so we know it's deliberate and almost certainly premeditated. Eco-vandalism at a minimum, sir; or eco-terrorism, if you prefer."

"That's huge. But what's it got to do with Simcox?"

"Two things, sir. Firstly young Miro spotted Simcox and the foreigner — Caradijc — together in a news clip. That's what first alerted us to her dirty dealings. But the killer punch is this. Sam was at Caradijc's hideout gathering evidence the other evening when Simcox turned up. He got a snap of them together in the plant. Slam dunk."

No response from Grafton.

"It doesn't end there," Judge continued after a momentary pause. "A further strand in this relates to me and ILAWR. Caradijc was masquerading as an ILAWR employee to get into the farms we were monitoring. A few weeks ago I was forced into early retirement and as it turns out my replacement is another of Simcox's cronies — one Iris Dent — who is also in the photo I refer to. So getting rid of me was also part of the plan. And finally, as if that's not enough, the method of 'leaking' the report that caused the ruckus in the first place was straight from Dent to Simcox. What I'm saying to you, sir, is that Simcox has carried out a carefully planned and co-ordinated programme of deception and deliberate environmental contamination involving ILAWR aimed at bringing down your government. Successfully, too, wouldn't you say?"

There was another long pause, followed by a bout of swearing.

"That bloody loser," said Grafton. "I'm going to enjoy watching her squirm when she has to admit what she's done. This is exactly what we need. You can substantiate all of this?"

"Absolutely!"

"OK. Come down Friday and bring the full dossier. There'll be a ticket waiting for you at Hamilton Airport."

"Sir. One last thing. There has been an attempt on Miro's life and we don't know who we can trust. He's been badly beaten up and is now in hiding. Please hold this info close for now even within your office."

"Understood. One thing from us, too. We should make sure the accusation is heard in an impartial and independent manner. For that reason I'll book you in to see the Ombudsman first if that's OK. Leave it to me to organise."

"Yes, that's fine."

Without even a goodbye, the ex-PM was gone.

CHAPTER 47

DEEP DOWN, in spite of the friendly exterior, Roger McWilliams was as venal and exploitative as the next man. It was survival of the fittest in the jungle that was Wellington and he sniffed an opportunity in Judge's revelations. He needed a slice of the action. Knowledge is a tradable asset and he decided to make the most of the information from Judge. Not that many chances had come his way of late and Ken wasn't overly generous for the quality of service he'd been getting.

His phone was in overdrive as he threaded an upward path through the Green Future Party hierarchy to Bella Simcox. Using a mixture of persuasion, coercion and Wellington-speak he deftly navigated her legion of minions until finally he was put through to the woman herself.

"Simcox here. What can I do for you?"

"To be accurate, it's what I can do for you!"

McWilliams detected a momentary hesitation before Simcox replied.

"And what might that be?"

"Ms Simcox, you've been connected to Waikatogate. The evidence is not yet out there, but I know how and when that is to happen. There is an opportunity to shut down the revelations. Are you interested?"

This time the silence was prolonged.

"McWilliams, isn't it? I haven't a clue what you're talking about and if you think you can call me up and blackmail me with your insinuations you'd better think again."

"Oh, sorry, Ms Simcox. I must have got it wrong. In that case I beg your pardon; I won't bother you again. Goodbye."

"Wait." Another interminable silence and then she said,

"So what do you want from me?"

Bingo.

"Fifty grand in cash by lunch time tomorrow for the name of the contact. Can't have you rotting in jail now, can we?"

"OK, OK. Where to meet?"

"Pravda Cafe, 12.30pm. Oh, and make sure you come alone. You don't want the info to be inadvertently leaked. Do you?"

CHAPTER 48

Sᴀᴍ ᴘᴀʀᴋᴇᴅ at the Ocean Beach Surf Club and made his way awkwardly down the path, resolutely ignoring the nagging reminders of his recent beating. The sand wasn't much easier to traverse and as he pushed on through the dunes he began to wonder if walking on the beach was such a good idea.

Raglan had always been somewhere special for Sam. Therapeutic even. It was all about being there and as he reached firmer sand and the walking became easier the wild beauty of this sensational location began once again to weave its own particular brand of magic. With the breeze riffling playfully through his hair, the afternoon sun warm on his back and a frothy surf rinsing his toes, Sam found the stress and pain of the last few days starting to ease.

He surveyed the expanse of water and a distant line of board riders as he went, knowing Wiremu would be out there somewhere. Eventually he spotted a random surfer hook into a wave and recognised his mate's distinctive mop and characteristic style from afar as he worked the break. Sam strolled on more purposefully now; keen to catch up with his friend and confidant.

As he approached, Willie caught a big breaker, tracking expertly along the crest until eventually the wave spat him nonchalantly over the back. When he surfaced he kicked on for the shore and was rearranging himself at the water's edge when Sam stepped up.

"How are ya, Willie?"

Wiremu spun round, startled.

"Hey, boy! What you doing here? Work day, isn't it?" His eyes narrowed as he inspected Sam closely. "OMG. What happened to you? Is it sand in my eye or were you hit by a tsunami?"

Perhaps because Ocean Beach was a second home, or perhaps it was because he'd been too preoccupied to think things through, but it hadn't occurred to Sam that his bruised and swollen face would raise eyebrows here in surfer heaven. Wiremu noticed his recoil.

"Sorry, mate. Forgive me, but you must admit you've looked prettier. So what's happened — a bike prang?"

Sam put a hand on Willie's shoulder.

"Boy, have I got a story for you!"

"Let's head back home and you take me through it."

Back at Wiremu's place, Sam began to download the whole sorry tale of the last few weeks to his Raglan surfer and photojournalist buddy.

Sustained by takeaways and cold beer they talked long into the night. At first Willie was content to be there for his cobber, listening impartially. But as the twists and turns of the saga unfolded before him, the investigative psyche of the journalist began to kick in. He was beside himself with glee at what was being gifted here — the story of a lifetime and from such an unexpected source. A story that presented a major opportunity. A story that needed careful handling.

Finally he could contain himself no longer.

"You do know this is a blockbuster, don't you, Sam? You're telling me all this for a reason, right? Have you given any thought to how to handle the story and what you might want out of it?"

Sam stared at his feet as he reflected on what his friend had just said. Eventually he responded.

"Ah, you're hurting my head, Willie. All I wanted was someone to talk to. I haven't had a moment to myself since this fiasco began… Haven't given any thought to what might be in it for me."

"Now's the time to ask though, believe me."

"I hear you, but all in good time. You must know it's still breaking news and I need to see things through. There's much to be done before I can spare a thought for myself."

"Sure, but I can't help worrying. I can see how deep into this you are, but what you need to get your head around is this. What happens afterwards? Your world has already changed. When all this is over it might not be possible to slot back into the same old routine."

"I hear you… You may well be right, but give me a break, Willie. I need time, you understand. Who wouldn't if they'd been through what I've been through in the last few days? For a start, Simcox and her cronies almost succeeded in topping me, so I'd like to ensure they get what's coming to them."

He took a thoughtful swig of his Steinlager.

"Though as it happens nailing Simcox could be the easy part with my mate Ken Judge off to Wellington next Friday. The second thing is that I want the mess at the farms cleaned up and that'll be no mean feat either. The biggest challenge, though, is neither of these. It's something else again."

"Oh, what's that?"

"Beyond a shadow of a doubt it's the Mangawara that's the major. As I said, the bug in the stream has the potential to poison Auckland's water supply. Think about it. If that happens, no bull, it'll be like napalming the big little city. No one will be immune. We can reasonably expect that a great many Jaffas will get crook and there may even be fatalities. I'm not sensationalising, Willie. What's more, with me suspended, I'm told no one is taking the risk seriously. MPI Biosecurity don't want to know. This is my doomsday scenario, Mr Reporter. We're on the brink of a maelstrom and there's a sense of inevitability about it, like the crash of a runaway train. That's why the Mangawara needs my undivided attention."

With that revelation out there was a protracted silence that Willie eventually brought to a close. He cut back to what interested him most.

"Sam, I have a couple more questions. Have you considered the role of the media in this? You do know it has an important role to play in taking Simcox down, don't you? Sure, step one is getting the authorities on to her so that's all good, but then what? This thing won't be done and dusted until all the facts are out there and her public and supporters can make up their own minds. It'll take the court of public opinion to really nail her, especially as we're running into a general election."

He reached for the last slice of pizza.

"I guess what I'm saying is, you came to me, Sam, so I feel like I have a part to play in this now too. Please don't forget my day job. I'm with Newstand these days and that's a massive corporation — one of the top five media conglomerates on the planet; starting to challenge Murdoch. The point I'm making is that we have the clout to help."

Wiremu wiped his mouth and took a swig of his beer.

"Sam, if what you're saying stacks up then I want to see that scumbag Simcox consigned to the scrapheap as much as you, not the least of which is because she's stuffing up my country. In short, the story has got to get out there and soon. Newstand has serious reach to all the main players — TVNZ, *Auckland Tribune*, CNN, BBC, Internet; they're all linked. Plus we're also dabbling in the newer media — blogging, Twitter, etc. So what do you say, Sam? Give us a slice of this and we'll make it worth your while."

"I hear what you're saying. Don't want it getting out of hand, is all. How would you suggest we go about it?"

"It's understandable you need to be sure it's properly handled. You should give me the full report so I can have a story ready for when your mate goes to Wellington."

"Huh! Willie, I didn't come down in the last shower, you know. As soon as you take the story to your editors they'll want to go live with it."

"True, but there are methods of keeping a lid on things. For example, with something as big as this we can sign an agreement that embargoes the story until you give the word. And, as your friend, I'll tell you what the best form of insurance is. You can give me sufficient info to craft the story as breaking news, but hold back the critical bits — photos, for instance — until you press the go button. Then if somebody stuffs up further up the chain you can always go to the competition and that'd completely devalue our story."

"OK. Sounds fair enough. Now for me. You were asking what I might want out of this. I'm thinking the best thing would be to set up a charitable trust to fund environmental research."

"Cool idea, Sam, but don't go running ahead of yourself. How much do you think the story is worth?"

"Isn't that your department? You tell me."

"I'll have to take it back to the big chief, but I'm guessing fifty grand. That'd be about normal for a celebrity story."

"Come on, Willie! For that I might as well just put it out on the Internet!"

"No, no. Don't do that, bro! What sort of figure do you have in mind?"

"This isn't just another A-lister wedding, you know! This story is going to change our nation. To me it's worth at least twenty times that, plus a share of resales. Don't you reckon? As a suggestion, why don't you talk to your paymasters and let's see where we get to. Tell them I said the real driver for me is the high cost of doing research."

"You're a hard man, Sam. No wonder you won the big award the other night. Bella Simcox might think she walks on water, but she didn't bank on your voracity, did she?

"What do you think you'll do about the Mangawara-Auckland water issue?"

"I need to think that through. Not sure what's possible at the moment, but whatever the solution you can bet your bottom dollar there'll be real stretch in sorting this one out."

"You can't help yourself, can you, bro? Science is in your blood."

"Sure is! Anyway, thanks to you I'm beginning to get on top of this thing."

Of all the sounds in nature it was probably the symphony of the beach at night that Sam found most therapeutic. But at around two the beer spoke and he was forced up in search of the bathroom.

Back in bed he lay with hands behind head listening intently as the symphony played out before him. The rhythm of distant waves and the whistle of sea breeze in the trees, overlaid by an occasional lament from a possum and the jangle of wind chimes. A cacophony in C major.

Relaxing as it was to be serenaded, the matter of the Mangawara nagged at him. Despite confidence now that Simcox would be held to account, the massive risk that the Mangawara posed to public health was bothering him. What was obvious from Shelley's feedback was that the risk was not being taken seriously and for the problem to be averted it would take something special from him.

In the predawn he tossed the problem around. He could ignore it. After all, it was hardly his crisis to deal with now. But he knew that for him, turning his back was not an option. Next he speculated that Lady Luck would come to New Zealand's rescue; after all it is supposed to be God's own country. A favourable change in the weather would stop the bloom in its tracks. Yet he also knew this was not something that could be left to chance.

Finally he cut to the chase. Fortune favours the brave.

This was major and he could not stand idly by and allow the drama to play out unchecked. It was his duty to do something to sort it out.

Sam sighed. Easier said than done. He shifted restlessly between the sheets.

The only real question was what to do and how?

In his mind, Sam played out different scenarios.

He recalled a recent conversation with Max. The young PhD student had recounted his observations of a newly identified bifido bacterium which, at least in the lab, was lethal to the exact form of enterotoxigenic *E coli* 0157:H3 now proliferating in the Mangawara.

Maybe the new bug had the potential to clean up the Mangawara. Perhaps they should give it a test run and then release it.

Big problems require bold solutions and this answer was suitably big and bold — some might say audacious. But how, then, to produce Max's bug in amounts sufficient to make a difference?

What was required was access to a fermentation facility and no one was going to let him anywhere near one right now.

Where could he get fermentation done on that scale?

Where indeed?

And then it struck him — Caradijc.

Satisfied he was finally making progress, Sam turned over and got back to the serious business of sleep.

CHAPTER 49

Extortion was not Roger McWilliams' usual modus operandi and he was understandably nervous. But these were desperate times and he doubted now that Bella Simcox would be a long-term player on the Wellington scene. Better to cash in on this opportunity rather than invest for the future. He arrived at Pravda a little early and settled on a table up the steps that allowed an easy view of the entrance.

Sitting there alone his anxiety mounted as the allotted meeting time came and went and the only thing to turn up was his second long black. Finally at 12.50pm he was about to call it a day when a seriously large man in a dark suit and shades strolled purposefully into the café carrying a briefcase. He sat down heavily at the table.

"McWilliams?"

"Yes."

"Ms Simcox is unable to attend so she sent me instead."

"I will only talk to her."

The heavyset man regarded him distastefully.

"Don't be a tosser! If you think a woman of her standing is going to be seen doing a deal with the likes of you in public you're a bigger dreamer than we gave you credit for. Who else would be wanting to give you fifty K in a Wellington café? Mr McWilliams, I have the funds you requested in this case. All I require is the information you promised in exchange and we can go our separate ways."

He eased the briefcase over with his foot.

"Check out the contents, do the deal and I'll be off."

McWilliams reached down and opened the case to reveal wads of red one hundred dollar bills. He closed it with thinly disguised glee.

"I assume it's all there?"

"Don't be a wanker. Give me the information."

Avoiding his gaze, McWilliams addressed the wall in a hushed tone.

"The person you need to meet is one Ken Judge, ex-Director of ILAWR. He is coming into Wellington this Friday on the early flight from Hamilton."

With that the man-mountain stood up and strode from the café without another word. McWilliams sat there with the briefcase and thoughts of Judas; the new depths he had plumbed. Then he, too, stood, picked up the briefcase and left, intent on beating a hasty retreat from the scene of his betrayal.

He didn't get far.

Roger McWilliams never knew what hit him. He was half-way across the road when a dark Nissan Safari with solid bull bars lurched maniacally from an adjacent car park. The car charged into him, pounding him into the tarmac before careering on, its massive town and country tyres rising up and passing easily over the luckless victim. Flattened, his body gushed crimson blood from gaping wounds.

The monster SUV didn't hesitate for so much as a second, using the body for traction as it roared on towards the corner and down to Lambton Quay.

In slow motion bystanders reeled from the horror before them.

Further down the street a motorbike spurted into life and sped towards the road kill. A helmeted pillion passenger reached down and grabbed the briefcase from McWilliams' lifeless hand and then the bike too screamed off around the corner.

CHAPTER 50

UNUSUALLY THERE was an absence of wind and a fair ration of sunshine in Wellington as Ken disembarked the 8.30 flight. He walked confidently through the terminal past a myriad of suited business commuters and the odd gaggle of tourists. How could today not be good? He was armed with the decisive report and scheduled to meet all the right people to bring to conclusion the sordid events of the last few weeks.

He headed purposefully for the taxi ramp; down the stairs and out past the luggage carousel towards a bevy of corporate cab drivers displaying placards and calling out the names of their next booking. To his surprise he heard his own name and turned to see a rotund and uniformed chauffeur in shades displaying a placard.

"Dr Judge?"

"Yes."

"Please, sir, this way. We have a cab waiting."

Nice touch. Ken half-smiled as he followed the driver out to a late-model Commodore.

"Fine day."

"Yes, sir. Despite what they say, Wellington blows me away."

Ken settled into the back seat and soon they were heading out of the airport and down towards the main road roundabout. Behind him a large dark SUV slipped surreptitiously from an adjacent car park and fell into line, discreetly shadowing the taxi as it continued towards the city.

Ken allowed himself to relax, but was pulled back to reality as the cab, instead of turning left for the city, sped straight on through the roundabout continuing at pace towards Miramar and Shelly Bay. As they hurried past the *Tangaroa* he spoke up.

"Excuse me. This isn't the way to the Beehive. Where are we going?"

"No worries, sir. We have a surprise for you!"

"I see." Ken reached into a bag for his schedule. "I have the Ombudsman at ten fifteen and it's nine thirty now so please move it along."

He sat in silence, troubled by the change of plan, disregarding the scenery as the taxi motored on along the coast road towards Shelly Beach. Finally it pulled into a secluded lay-by containing nothing more than a council maintenance truck.

"What the hell?"

The Commodore crunched to a halt on the gravel as the SUV pulled in beside, its doors swinging open.

Alarm bells rang. This wasn't a good scene. Must have been abducted. He stared in mounting disbelief as his worst fears were confirmed. Leaping from the Nissan Safari and striding menacingly towards him was none other than a psychopathic Iris Dent and two minders.

The rear door of the Commodore was yanked open and Judge was dragged, half-standing, half-sliding, out of the vehicle, and thrown on his knees before Green Future party leader Bella Simcox's henchman.

He looked up to meet Dent's glare. Her look of serpentine disdain left him in no doubt that he was in clear and present danger. Judge was racked by an icy tremor of fear.

"You fucking idiot!" Hands on hips, she glowered over him. "Did you really think we could be stopped so easily? Let me tell you, the bullshit ends here."

Ken stared up at the overbearing figure silhouetted against the sun.

"Let's start from the beginning, Judge, I want you to tell me everything you know."

"Not a chance. I'm not intimidated by your theatrics."

"Theatrics, theatrics," she sneered. "Well, you should be!"

The cab driver stepped forward with Judge's briefcase. Dent snatched it from him and quickly located the report. She riffled through it and confirmed it contained much of what she was looking for. Turning back to Judge.

"That's a good start, but this is a hard copy. Where can I find the file?"

Ken remained resolutely silent.

"And yes. I've learned that runt Miro is still with us, too. I want to know where to find him as well."

"You can't be serious. What do you take me for?"

"A loser."

She laughed and signalled to one of the minders. Judge collapsed on to the gravel in agony as a baseball bat drilled into the small of his back. Before he could gather himself it crashed down again onto his kneecap then up into his crotch. Uncertain what to clutch first, he lay there gasping. Struggling to gather himself.

"This can be as easy or as hard as you like, Judge."

"Give it up, Dent," he managed. "You've no chance. If I was you I'd be out of here. You're fucked, so why don't you cut your losses and run like the coward you are?"

By way of answer, she grabbed the baseball bat from the bully beside her and swung it into his ribs.

Judge scrabbled in the shingle, desperate to retreat from the physical onslaught.

"OK," she said. "One last chance. Where can we find the computer files and where is Miro?"

On the edge of unconsciousness, Judge knew words were no longer of any use. Dent was well beyond reason and there would be no appeasing her. So slowly, deliberately, he gave her the finger instead.

Dent's nostrils flared and her mouth creased into a derisive sneer. Pregnant with malignant menace.

"If you won't tell us then you are of no consequence."

And with that she swung the bat viciously into his head with all the primal power of a major league baseball player. His face exploded, teeth ricocheting across the car park, blood spraying the horrified onlookers. His head rocked insanely back and he collapsed, twitching, onto the ground. Dark blood pooling beneath him.

"That's that."

Dent let the baseball bat fall from her hand as the three men numbly exchanged glances.

She took a moment coming to terms with her actions, considering her options.

"Search him for any other info. Also get someone round to his Hamilton home immediately. We want all computers, drives, hard copy records — anything that might incriminate us."

She surveyed the scene.

"Good of the sisters from the council to loan us a mulcher. Get it revved up and we'll get rid of him."

Though still reeling from Dent's unbridled violence, her sidekicks silently obeyed.

They dragged Judge's lifeless body over to the mulcher and fed him in head first. The machine roared as the characteristic green and pine of mulch turned blood-red as a human being was transformed into recyclable garden material before them, spraying out of the machine and into a half-full bin.

The macabre irony was not lost on Dent. With trademark indifference she asked, "What are you lot staring at? We're reducing his carbon footprint is all... How bad can that be?"

She turned away, reaching for her cellphone, then called back over her shoulder, "Put a few branches through as chasers to clean things up. No one will be any the wiser."

As her hired thugs watched the recycling with mounting revulsion, the mulcher protested, bogged down uncertainly and stuttered for seconds before, finally, stalling. The perpetrators of Ken's final solution exchanged uncertain glances before hesitantly returning their gaze to the machine.

"Fuck, it's only half done him," said the cab driver.

Judge's legs and feet still protruded from the jaws of the mulcher.

"It must've jammed on his coat or something."

Dent turned back, irritated by the delay and was shocked back to reality by the unimaginable horror of what she saw. In that instant the insanity of her actions caught up with her and she lost it too, dropping to her knees and shaking perversely.

"Fuck, oh fuck. Come away now. We're out of here."

She staggered to her feet and retreated.

"Hurry, hurry!"

Eventually, back in the car and driving off, she started to get it together enough to report in to Simcox.

"That's the second in two days, with McWilliams. I hope you cleaned up. We don't want any comebacks."

"No worries," Dent lied.

"And that's enough, do you hear? We don't want Wellington turning into a Wild West town, do we? You'd better keep a low profile for a few days. Here's an idea. Why don't you and the guys head up north and hook into that precocious little prick Miro. Finishing the job on him is another essential if we're to keep a lid on things. That raises another issue, too. We need to know what's going on in Wellington. Do we have a sister in the PM's office?"

"Yes. We have a sleeper there called Mariana Touala. Risky to activate her though; that's why we haven't done it so far."

"That may be so, and on the other hand if we'd done it earlier we'd have avoided the drama with McWilliams and Judge. Probably it's a good time to activate her so she can keep us up to speed on what Grafton's playing at."

"We might as well. The loser's only going to be in office for a few more weeks anyway so it's now or never."

"OK. Talk soon."

As she stared out of the window of her Beehive office, Simcox asked herself how it had all come to this. It shouldn't be so hard. She shouldn't have to push like this for the top job. After all, she deserved it. She had put in the hard yards and made such great personal sacrifices. The time was right for her now and yet the struggle went on. Why?

It could all have been so different. Long ago she had found true happiness as she cradled her baby boy, gazing entranced at his innocent face, the blond wisps of hair, and striking eyes. But they took him away. The one thing she loved. And she'd had no word. Ever. Where was he now? In his late twenties, he'd be building a career and breaking hearts for sure if he had his father's killer looks.

They had taken him away. They would pay for it. She told herself that over and over again.

At 11.30am with still no sign of Ken Judge, the Ombudsman phoned Jeremy Grafton.

"I'll get right back to you," said the ex-PM. He called for an assistant.

A few minutes later Grafton's secretary returned, disconsolate.

"He arrived in Wellington on time from Hamilton and in so far as anyone can tell, left the airport."

"He must have been intercepted." Grafton buried his head in his hands. "Get on to security right away."

He called the Ombudsman back.

"Something's happened all right and I'm thinking the worst. I seriously doubt we'll be meeting with Ken Judge today."

CHAPTER 51

SAM WOKE with a new sense of purpose and got straight on to the computer. Biosecurity had had long enough to action the clean-up of Mangawara, he figured, and as nothing seemed to be happening it was time to elevate the matter.

He recalled meeting the CEO of the company responsible for Auckland water at an environmental conference some time ago and after trawling through his contacts eventually located his details — nigel.waring@waterqual.co.nz. He pounded out an email.

'Hello, Nigel. You may recall we have met though not for some time. I am writing on a matter of the utmost seriousness from a water security perspective. Until recently I was Principal Investigator on a sentinel monitoring and research programme surveying the microbial ecology of a cluster of Waikato farms. To cut a long story short it was my work that surfaced the E coli and GE contamination of the farms that are at the centre of the current biosecurity alert.

There have been difficulties and I need to declare I am currently on suspension from ILAWR. That is not the reason I am writing though. The purpose of this email is to inform you of developments in the contamination problem that are without doubt of critical importance and yet to my knowledge are not being acted upon by Biosecurity New Zealand. Moreover I am contacting you because I recognise that these issues are of relevance to your organisation given it has responsibility for the integrity and safety of Auckland water.

In short, what my team discovered is that the dangerous enterotoxigenic E coli 0157 strain at the centre of the farm scare has now entered the Mangawara Stream and 'bloomed' to the point where levels of microbial contamination can only be described as exceptional as far down the stream as its junction with the Waikato River. Owing to the geographical proximity of the stream mouth to the Auckland water intake on the Waikato River I am sure the seriousness of this matter from a public health perspective will not be lost on you.

I am aware that the Biosecurity New Zealand Operations Chief Peter Smart was informed of the new developments via a hand-delivered report (attached) some days ago and yet we are not aware of any initiatives to contain the contamination or for that matter to inform you. It is for these reasons that I feel compelled to write this morning and to appeal to you for action.

In the short term until a clean-up operation can be implemented I think the only prudent course of action would be to shut down the water intake. Only through such a measure can you be confident that you have done all in your power to minimise the health risk to Aucklanders.

Yours sincerely,

Dr Sam Miro,

Environmental Research Scientist.'

Progress of a sort. Sam got himself another bowl of cereal and a second coffee. A few minutes later a scuffle of activity from outside announced Wiremu's return from running the dog.

"Hey, bro. Don't suppose I could borrow your car for a day or so? It's possible someone's on the lookout for mine."

"Sure. I won't be needing it. What've you got in mind?"

"This morning I contacted WaterQual and appealed to them to shut down the Auckland water intake. Dreams are cheap, though, I don't hold out much hope on that score. Nor do I have much confidence that the authorities will do anything useful on the Mangawara even if they do get their shit together and action a clean-up. I don't think they have the tools they need to make a difference anyway. It seems to me there's nothing else for it but to start my own contingency planning. So today I'll be kicking off the process. Should be back in time for dinner."

"That's just as well, because I've been meaning to tell you, you're cooking tonight."

"No worries!"

An hour or so later Sam pulled into the lay-by on the road outside Andrej Caradijc's hideout. He knew that if he was going to do anything useful about the Mangawara problem he would need to access some process scale fermentation facilities. Given his ILAWR suspension this was indeed a big ask. So here he was back on the scene of the recent drama, hoping to find Caradijc's plant abandoned but functional. A long shot but worth a try.

As he sat in the lay-by at the end of the drive he could tell immediately his best laid plans were in vain. Things were not at all as he expected — for his Eastern bloc adversary was still in residence. The ute, the dogs and the washing on the line; it was all a giveaway. Business as usual, so what's plan B?

Sam reflected on the situation and his last visit. Vaguely he recalled an argument between Simcox and Caradijc and concentrated on that. She had wanted him to pull the pin on the hideout and to get the hell out of New Zealand. And Caradijc became agitated and told her she was reneging on her deal to help with his immigration problem or whatever. As far as Sam could tell nothing had changed at the farm. It didn't stack up.

He was guessing that since the events of that evening, Caradijc would be well over Simcox and Dent. Surely he was feeling totally let down by them, Sam surmised — a bit isolated too. Clearly he's not taking instructions from them any more or he wouldn't be here. So it's all good. Not such a bad scene after all; in fact, it could be exactly what he needed.

He spent an age pumping himself up before deciding to take the bull by the horns. Whether he was stark raving mad or not he would never know, but in a moment of utter abandonment he started the car and drove boldly into Caradijc's hideout. He parked near the carport and stepped out to survey the scene.

"You! What d'ya want?"

Caradijc stood unsteadily on the back porch, looking even more dishevelled than usual. Two empty bottles of Smirnoff clinked down the steps in front of him.

"Yes, it's me."

Sam grimly surveyed the train wreck that used to be a bio-terrorist.

"I want to talk."

Caradijc gazed at him through cavernous eyes and week-old stubble. He squinted through an alcoholic haze into the morning sun.

"Did our friends do that to you?"

He pointed at Sam's technicolour face.

"Yeah, a long story. They dealt to me real well, but I'll get over it! You don't look so flash yourself, you know! Putin you're not!"

Sam could tell he had struck a chord with Caradijc, who chuckled at this minor joke. Then he gave up the struggle to stay upright and collapsed onto the step before erupting into a wail, half-laugh, half-cry, as the tensions of the last few days washed out.

"Yes, it's the vodka," he slurred, "but let me tell you, I look a lot better than the comrades I've lost along the way. Sverdlovsk claimed them, you know… Thought I was building something special here; a better life. Now I've lost that too… I'm not like you. I don't have a career; not going anywhere. "

Sam listened patiently, understanding more of Caradijc's paralytic ramblings than the Russian probably realised. Strangely, in spite of everything, he had no antipathy towards his former adversary, possibly because of respect for their common area of science.

"I've been impressed by your work, Miro, but what brings you back here? What could you possibly want from me?"

"Plenty," said Sam firmly. "I've got unfinished business."

"Good, good. I'm looking for a job." He waved a third bottle of Smirnoff. "Tell me about it."

"Not until you're sober."

Sam could tell Caradijc was a mess, pale and cold. Barely coherent. He brushed through him into the kitchen, rummaging in cupboards and fridge for coffee and food. When Caradijc joined him he pushed a mug of black coffee across the table and stuffed a sandwich into his hand; deftly removing the bottle as he did so and slipping it out of sight.

Then he settled down to wait.

He glanced at his watch. Ken must be finished with his first meeting by now. He reached for his mobile to check in, but Ken's number cut straight to voice mail. That's good. He must be still going. He left Caradijc brooding over his food and drink and went out to satisfy himself the fermenters were still intact. When he returned his newfound friend was sleeping it off, head on his arms, snoring heavily.

He backed into the next room and tried Ken again. Still no response. There must be better ways to spend the afternoon. He dialled again and got Shelley.

"Hey, gal, how's it going?"

"Oh, Sam, I was hoping you'd call!"

"Want to meet for a coffee?"

"That'd be great!"

"Right. Hamilton East in an hour!"

With that he left a note for Caradijc telling him he'd be back the next day. Then he drove on out of there, confident now that fortune does indeed favour the brave.

CHAPTER 52

NIGEL WARING was a man under pressure. The spring had been unusually dry leaving the West Auckland reservoirs low and WaterQual Auckland heavily dependent on the newly commissioned Waikato supply line. The last thing he needed was a question about water quality. Now, staring out at him from his computer, was an email from someone he hardly knew about something he didn't want to know.

What's more it contained accusations about his mates at Biosecurity New Zealand that, if true, would be hard to sweep under the carpet. Grief that he didn't need right now. What he did know was that he could be dealing with an overall shortfall in supply if he was to shut down the Waikato source. And that wouldn't do. He decided to give Peter Smart a bell and waited impatiently to be put through.

"Hi, Nigel. How're you bearing up?

"Could be better. I hate surprises, so help me out here. What's this about the Mangawara being contaminated?"

"What d'ya mean? Who told you that?"

"I have a report in front of me that was apparently handed to you a week ago. Why didn't you give me a heads up on it?"

"Oh, that. No worries, it's of no consequence. The work was done by an unsupervised technician working in a programme without a leader because he was kicked out of ILAWR on a disciplinary matter. It has no credibility at all. Sending the report to you is just sour grapes!"

"Still. Not sure I can take the risk as the buck stops with me on safety. If the report is correct I'd have to shut down the Waikato intake and buggered if I want to do that. Unless I must. I've just got it up to speed and the West Auckland reservoirs are a real problem this year. Shutting it down would risk disrupting supply and cost me my bonus. What do you reckon we should do then?"

"Trust me on this, Nigel. My reading is that the report wouldn't make good toilet paper. Here's a thought. How about pooling resources and doing some more monitoring?"

"Done! Send me a contact and I'll get my deputy on to it."

"Let's talk again in a week if the testing turns anything up."

"Righto! See ya."

Satisfied, Nigel Waring returned to the business of the morning.

CHAPTER 53

WHEN SAM arrived Shelley was waiting. She threw her arms around him, and, when they kissed, her lips parted beneath his. Tongues briefly met. The message was clear. So much had happened, pent-up emotions were making their presence felt. The kiss was so sweet, he took another. Shelley responded eagerly, pressing herself against him. When they finally parted they were flushed with stirring emotions.

Sam cupped her face between his hands. A hint of jasmine and green tea playing across his nostrils.

"Sometime soon we will have to talk this thing through. We need to be sure it's right."

"True," Shelley agreed. "But it feels oh so good right now."

The urgency of the moment passed and she took a good look at him; recoiling in shock at the state of his battered face.

"Wow! Did they do that to you? Oh, my lord, I'll kill them, I swear!"

"It's coming right," Sam shrugged. He was touched. It seemed a long time since a woman had shown any concern for him. "I have to say I've had enough of the attention it attracts though. Anyway, you'd better look out. Soon I'll be back up to speed and then there'll be no stopping me."

"Can't wait." Shelley arched her eyebrows suggestively.

"In the meantime, will you settle for coffee and cake while I check in with Ken? And can you get it, please?"

He handed her a twenty and then found a quiet corner in the café to dial his mentor; again without success. Why didn't Ken answer? He must know we'd be hanging out for an update. Moodily, he found an empty table and sat down. Soon Shelley returned to take his mind off things with a substantial helping of carrot cake and two spoons.

"So how is Ken?"

"Busy, it seems. He went to Wellington today to talk to Grafton and the Ombudsman. I'm desperate to know how it's going, but he hasn't called in yet."

"Me, too. I need some closure here. I'm still being pressurised, you know. Comrade Dent called again yesterday and tried to bully me into telling her where you are. I reminded her you'd been suspended so I didn't have a clue. I guess she believed me because she left it at that. Trying me on the off chance, I suppose. She sounded distracted. I wonder what's going on."

"As you can see, they had a good go at topping me and by now they must know they failed. So I've been keeping a low profile. With Ken in Wellington we should be getting closer to a result."

"Hope so!"

"None of that is why I called you, though."

"I know. You're thinking about a week at a tropical resort and wanted to invite me along." She squeezed his arm and giggled. "So sweet of you, Sam."

"Tempting. Very tempting indeed. Unfortunately, a holiday might have to wait. We've still work to do. I'm fretting about the Mangawara and have decided that to get it sorted we'll have to do something fairly dramatic ourselves."

"Given everything that's going on, what can we possibly do that'll make a difference?"

"What do you mean — everything!"

"Face it, Sam. It's not as if you can just pop into the lab and take over."

"True, but necessity is the mother of invention. I think I've found a way and need your help."

"OK, but you're losing me."

"A couple of things have happened that could mean we may now be in a position to do something useful. The first — I'm not sure if you're aware, but Max has discovered a new bacterium that is lethal to this form of *E coli*. While it still needs validation he has done enough on a laboratory scale to suggest it has real potential for bioremediation. The best thing we could do," Sam continued, with a glint in his eye, "is field trial the bug, and this might be a never-to-be-repeated opportunity to do just that!"

"Now that is exciting. How do you think it works?"

"Good question. We're far from certain, but it's definitely not competitive overgrowth. It seems much more specific than that. Could be a secreted toxin or similar and if so it has enormous potential for application…"

"Mmm, I see. That is cool. Problem is that at best Max will have minuscule quantities of the isolates frozen down and I'm guessing truckloads will be required to make any difference." She raised her eyebrows. "So, Sam, don't we come back to the same thing? You'll need to ferment the strain up at scale to get sufficient to be of any use and we don't have access to facilities."

"Didn't, but I do now, I reckon. That's the second thing I wanted to talk to you about. You'll recall that I followed the bloke who was causing the contamination in the first place and found his hideout…"

"Go on, tell me," Shelley broke in. "His fermentation plant is free to a good home."

"Close, Shelley, very close. And it gets better. The chap is still around, too and we've done the bonding thing. Turns out he has all the required experience. In fact, he built the plant. Ten to one I'll be able to get him to grow up Max's isolate for us."

"Sorry, sorry. You're losing me again. Why would he?"

"Yeah, confusing I know. You see, nothing is what it

seems. Caradijc — that's his name — is a recent import from Russia, brought over on false pretences by Dent's friend to cook up this little scam. But he has immigration problems and she's left him in the lurch. They had a serious falling out and there's no love lost between them now, if there ever was. The poor chap is seriously disaffected so I've befriended him. So I've not only found the fermentation plant we need but also the best qualified person to run it."

"You're too much! That is a coup. Realistically it'd take us weeks to optimise a fermentation process at that scale, but he's probably got all the know-how required at his fingertips."

Shelley leaned back and thought it through. Slowly she nodded. Sam leaned forward on his elbows, hands clasped, and went on.

"Hey, but here's the thing. What I need you to do is get samples of Max's isolates for me so I can get them over to our new friend to do some work on. Better we don't involve Max; I'm reluctant to pull in any more people than we need to. It wouldn't be fair on them."

"True." She reached across and put a hand on his. "Plus it's bringing us closer together. You know I'd do anything for you, so no worries."

He smiled at her holding her hand and then, lost in each other's company, they moved on to more personal matters.

Eventually Sam glanced at his watch.

"Hey! Shelley, you know I could stay forever, but there're other things I need to be doing. I have to go. Can you text me when you get the samples? I'll collect them and whizz them out to our man."

"Sure. Realistically we're looking at tomorrow morning now."

"That's fine! Oh, and thanks, Shelley." He folded her hands in his and brought them up to his lips. "You make it all worthwhile!"

"Take care of yourself, Sam Miro. You don't half push the boundaries, you know. I do worry. Oh, and don't forget to let me know how Ken is getting on."

"Understood."

And with that he was off.

CHAPTER 54

HE NEVER had a clue what he was going to cook until he stepped into the supermarket. It all depended on what was on offer; matching a wish list with the pragmatic realities of cost and availability. The rump steak and spinach were good today and the curry spices easy to find. So tonight it would be a saag, he decided, and soon he was back on the road to Raglan.

As he drove Sam's mind wandered, but by the time he reached the divide Ken was foremost in his thoughts. Where is the bugger? He must know I'm hanging out for news and it's already past five. The least he could do is give me a heads up. Sam pulled over while he still had reception hoping upon hope for a message. There was none. Next he hit the recall button, nervously stretching as he did so. Again to no avail. That Ken is beginning to be a worry, Sam told himself as he cautiously pulled back out onto the road and on towards the beach.

As he pulled into Wiremu's drive a murmur of conversation spoke of company on the deck.

"Hi, you." He carried the groceries passed them into the house. "There can't be many better spots to chill out than under a Raglan sunset."

"Hey, Sam. Come and say hello. This is my colleague Sally Lock from Newstand — the media company I work for."

"Hi, Sally. How's it going?"

"Great. Wiremu's been filling me in on you and your recent dramas. Sounds like quite a saga."

"You bet! You couldn't make this stuff up, could you? To me it proves once and for all that fact is stranger than fiction."

"That's prophetic, Sam. It'll make a headline."

"Yeah, I suppose so. Anyway, you guys carry on and I'll get some dinner going."

"Sounds like a plan, Sam. Oh, and there's a cold beer in the fridge for you!"

"Thanks."

As he sautéed onions and spices Sam could hear them talking things through out on the deck. From the discussion, it was evident that Lock was excited by the revelations and her questioning was insightful; aimed at teasing out the angles for future stories. There were the scientific and technical aspects; a political intrigue; the environmental perspectives and interpersonal activity. It was all there and all good, with Lock more enthralled by the moment as the tale unravelled against a crimson sunset.

Soon enough he had coated the meat and left the curry bubbling enticingly on the hob so he could join them outside.

"Sally tells me she's taken up the matter with the top dogs at Newstand and they've expressed interest."

"That's good. What'd they say about my proposal for a research trust?"

"As always, Sam, the devil is in the detail. To be fair they haven't seen anything yet so they can't be sure what they're dealing with."

"OK, understood." Sam pondered what he could do to progress things. "I've found a copy of a confidentiality agreement on my memory stick. Let me edit it up and we can sign off on it. Then providing we can get to the point of agreement with your bosses I'll print off a copy of the key report for you to take with you."

"That should do the trick!"

A few minutes later with the CDA signed Sam had a hard copy of the report in front of Sally. She was quiet as she skimmed the document, and when she looked up it was with a glint in her eye.

"This is everything you said it was, Sam," she said, "and more."

Then turning to Wiremu, she added, "Put me somewhere so I can talk this through with the chief!"

"Sure."

He high-fived her, and then showed Sally to his office at the rear of the house. When he returned Sam was in the kitchen putting the finishing touches to the curry.

"She'll have them hot to trot."

"If you say so, Willie, but then I don't know them like you."

"Time will tell."

"True. Anyway, dinner's nearly ready. Give her a few more minutes and then I'll serve."

When ten minutes had passed with still no sign of Sally they knocked on the door and pushed it open."

"Oh, hi, Sam. I was about to come and get you. Let me put you on speaker and introduce the chief operating officer at Newstand."

"Sam, nice to meet you. My name's Vernon Chan."

"Hello, Vernon."

"I hear you've been holding back the forces of evil virtually single-handed and are about to blow the lid on this elaborate hoax. All credit to you for getting the exposé this far."

"Thanks for that. And yes, that's about the size of it. To me this is all or nothing. It really is about the future of the nation."

"Sam, I'll be perfectly frank with you. I want to thank you for allowing us to consider the story, but even though we're the biggest daily in the country we can't stretch to anything like the million or so you're asking for."

"That's too bad. You see, I've been thinking too and where I've got to is that I couldn't even begin a research programme for a million anyway. So it seems we're miles apart and heading in the wrong direction. Let's forget the whole thing. That way we can get on with our dinner!"

There was spluttering down the line at the hardball tactic followed by a moment's silence as Chan considered.

"Let me tell you what the problem is here, Sam. Looking at the story critically it's almost a bit passé, if you know what I mean? When it's released you'll be legend for a day and then confined to history like everyone else."

"I'm surprised to hear you say that, sir, given its gravity. Maybe you don't get it. This is about the future of our country and what could be more important than that?"

"That's all true, Sam, and you've done well, but from a media perspective it's not breaking news, but mission accomplished. You see, when it comes right down to it, we're investigative journalists. So what would really sell this to my Board is something to show that the newspaper is more actively involved."

Sam considered the feedback.

"And if I gave you that, what'd it be worth?"

"How long is a piece of string? Sky's the limit, to be honest, but only if the story is a blockbuster."

"Mr Chan, I have other things I need to focus on, so here's the piece. Last chance. You'll know from the report that we have concerns about the safety of Auckland water. That concern has risen to status critical. We've been totally unable to get any traction on this from the authorities and so we're going to have to deal with the problem ourselves."

Sam paused while he considered his next move.

"What's more Simcox's Eastern bloc chap has come over to our side and is going to help me ferment up a newly discovered bug — the only thing I know of that has any chance of treating the contamination. Sir, this isn't history; it's cutting edge science being rolled out before you as we speak and I can offer you an exclusive as the story unravels. Wiremu and his cameras could be following us around. All it will take is for us to do the deal. So to recap: what you will get is the report plus an exclusive on this new angle as it plays out in real time. Seems like a scoop and a half to me; anything but *fait accompli*."

"You don't hang about, do you? I have to admit that does sound more like it!"

"Great. So let's cut to the chase or our dinner will be ruined."

"OK. Put it on the table, Sam. What are you looking for?"

"I'll try to make it palatable. I want you to establish an independent trust fund and it'll take five million to do it. The trust will be governed by a board and its purpose will be to sustainably finance an environmental research programme. You can be board chair to oversee your investment and I'll be chief scientific officer. The objective would be to fund research off the interest in perpetuity so that technically the principal would remain your asset. It would be like any other investment so that should keep your shareholders happy."

Silence at the other end. Sam ploughed on.

"We could call it the Newstand Environmental Research Fund — NERF — or similar if that would help. That way you'll get the PR upside from the investment as well. How's that then, Mr Chan? Sounds like a win-win to me and what could be better than that?"

Sally and Wiremu exchanged admiring glances, impressed with his vision and clarity of purpose, not to mention his negotiation skills.

The reply came back after only a brief delay.

"Done! Subject to Board approval, of course. My God, you've got some balls, Sam Miro. You're quite the salesman, aren't you? This'd better work out or it'll be more than my life's worth."

"No worries and thanks for the compliment, sir. Let's exchange an email agreement and then we can leave it to

Sally and Wiremu to get the paperwork lined up. Now can I get back to my curry?"

Vernon Chan chuckled. "You bet! Sam, we'll be in touch."

Sam left them to deal with the detail and exited fast. In the hall, he excitedly punched the air with his fist.

"Primo!" he bellowed. Now, with any luck, he'd be able to focus on cleaning up the mess at the Mangawara. And then getting his life back in order.

He picked up his phone to call Ken with the good news. Once again it cut straight to voice mail. What's up with that man? Sam wondered. Where is he when he's needed the most?

CHAPTER 55

HE WAS up and out of there at the crack of dawn, knowing Wiremu was cool with him borrowing his car. He figured that if he got a rustle on he would be able to swing by Ken's for an update on Wellington and still be at Ruakura by the time Shelley surfaced.

When he got to Ken's house he was surprised to find his mate's car was not in the drive, nor did he answer Sam's knocking. With a growing sense of trepidation Sam continued on to his next meeting, now deeply concerned. He and Ken were in this alone and there were so very few people out there he could turn to.

When he was close he called Shelley.

"Morning, Sam." That songbird voice could lighten the darkest of thoughts. "I have the samples. Told Max I needed them for the genomics, so he was cool. Tell you what. Why don't I meet you in Hamilton East about nine? You can collect them there. It's busy during the rush hour so nobody'll even notice."

"Great idea. I'll be there."

He hesitated. Was now the right time?

"Oh, and by the way, Shelley, I need to talk to you about something else as well. See you soon."

A couple of minutes before nine Sam spotted Shelley's ageing Corolla outside the shops and managed to park behind. He slid in next to her and gave her a thoughtful hug. Hesitantly, he continued where they'd left off.

"Shelley. What I want to say is — well, it's personal. OK?"

She perked up immediately. "What's up, doc?"

"I think you can guess I have really strong feelings for you. And I wanted to know..."

"...if I feel it too?" Her smile was wistful and disarming. "Oh, Sam, you must know I'm crazy for you."

She bent forward for a kiss. He complied and then moved gently away.

"Please wait, Shelley. You see there's something I need to say... Something I need to come clean about... Recently there's been someone else. Don't know where it's going, to be honest, but it's complicated. Also she's tied up in the current drama. I do want us to go to the next level, but please understand I have to work this thing through first."

Shelley looked at him quizzically, trying to make light of something she didn't want to hear.

"Don't tell me — it's Iris Dent, isn't it?"

"Huh! You're joking." Sam sighed with relief. "You're making me out to be an even bigger dork than I am already. No. Her name's Georgie. She's the daughter of the farm manager at the Mangawara Trust Farm."

"Ah! So that's the lucky girl."

He held her hand. "Shelley, to be honest, I could never see it working out with her anyway; it just happened. A moment's madness. I've been feeling guilty because Georgie was helping out on this too and got a bad dose of *E coli* poisoning for her trouble. Maybe you saw it on TV? She's the girl who's been dangerously ill in hospital."

"Oh. That's totally rotten. And you feel you have to stand by her?"

That's about right. For now anyway. I just need some space, is all. Anyway, thanks for listening. I'm glad I told you. It's quite a load off."

She cuddled up to him, subdued, but leaving him in no doubt how she really felt.

Soon he had to be going. As he drove away, he snatched a glance over his shoulder. Despite the brave face he could tell Shelley was upset. Seemingly her world had been turned upside down again.

Twenty minutes later, armed with the outline of a plan and what he believed would be the biological antidote of choice for the toxic 'bloom', Sam was back on the road to Caradijc's.

CHAPTER 56

IN WELLINGTON ex-PM Jeremy Grafton was up early and heading for his office. When he got there Chief of Staff Richie McCarthy was already waiting.

"Hi, Jeremy. I've had Don Ridgway from the Security Intelligence Bureau on the Judge case since yesterday. Apparently they were going all night. They're conferencing in shortly. Care to join us?"

"Yeah. This thing is killing me. I saw Judge as our great white hope!"

Shortly afterwards the phone rang.

"Morning, Mr McCarthy, sir. Mariana Touala here. I have Don Ridgway from the SIB on the line. Shall I put him through?"

"Yes, please, Mariana. Hi, Don. I'm sitting here with Jeremy. What've you got for us?"

"Morning. Quite a bit, sir. Richie, I'm emailing you a link so you can check out some images.

"We can now confirm Judge did arrive on schedule at the airport. But look at this; he was intercepted by a corporate cab driver and left with him. Have you opened the link yet? See the top two images. That's definitely Judge, here with the driver and, there, getting into his cab. The driver is a person of interest to us, a bit of a sleaze, confirming Dent and Simcox have friends in low places. We got the vehicle rego and, unsurprisingly, it doesn't check out. Definitely not a bona fide cab. So I think your worst fears are confirmed, sir. Ken Judge is not a no-show. He's been abducted and could be anywhere by now."

"Fuck!" Grafton was rarely exasperated enough to swear. "Where on earth is this thing headed?"

"Where indeed? And there's more," continued Ridgway. "If you'll allow me, sir. Watch this clip. The security camera footage shows the cab heading out of the airport and down towards the city turn-off. Now look what happens at the roundabout. The cab doesn't turn for the city; it continues on towards Miramar. That will help us no end in narrowing the search. Oh, and another thing. Notice the SUV pulling out behind the taxi. It sticks to the cab like glue and tracks it on through the roundabout and out towards Miramar."

He allowed them some time to examine the clip before continuing.

"Needless to say that vehicle didn't check out either, but a screen on it did throw up something of real interest. I don't know if you're aware of it, but there was a hit and run in central Wellington yesterday. The footage confirms that it's the same SUV at the centre of that enquiry, too."

"Really? Who was hit?"

"A policy adviser cum political consultant called Roger McWilliams. Heard of him?"

McCarthy and Grafton exchanged a swift glance.

"Yes. It was McWilliams who put us on to Judge."

"Really! Sadly, he won't be giving you any other leads as this is now a murder enquiry. I had figured there might be a connection. Oh, and one more thing. The CTV coverage in the central city is getting better all the time and we've got coverage of the hit and run. You won't want to see that, but you might be interested in what happened before. That's the last clip. What you see is McWilliams going into a café followed a while later by a dark-suited heavy carrying a briefcase. Now I ask you, where've you seen him before?"

"That's the airport cab driver."

Grafton confirmed it without a moment's hesitation.

"Then what we've got here is a conspiracy pure and simple — unbelievable as it might sound. Everything Judge was about to tell us would've checked out, I'm sure. Don, you have to find those lowlifes before this gets any further out of hand."

"Please, let me finish, sir. Notice that the guy went into the café with a briefcase yet it was McWilliams who carried it out. That suggests something changed hands in there, possibly cash, so the whole thing gets murkier by the minute. Sir, I have no clue to what it is between you and Judge but it appears to have a high price on it. McWilliams was taken out because of what he knew. What's more I doubt you'll be seeing Judge again, either. You'll need to find another way to access whatever it was you were expecting to learn from him."

"Agreed. We'll be on to that. In the meantime, please give your full attention to finding those men. Don, I know you want more from me but, believe me, I would give you more if I could and in due course I will. For the moment all I can say is this now represents the highest level of threat to national security!"

"OK. But, sir, please be reminded we're not just offering a detective service here. What we're about is counter-terrorism in the national interest. It seems to me we have a lot to talk about, don't we?"

"Don, I agree. But one thing at a time, eh?"

CHAPTER 57

THESE DAYS Nigel Waring was kicking back a little. No more early starts for him. He'd had enough of corporate life in his previous roles and the move to WaterQual was a lifestyle choice. These days he preferred a slow start. Juice and granola followed by Pilates. Then the papers and a latte at his local café while he waited for the traffic to clear. It made perfect sense at his stage of life — and after all, he deserved it.

What he disliked most was nasty little surprises to disturb the ordered flow of life. And this morning when he got to the editorial section in the Auckland paper a particularly nasty surprise awaited him. The subject was progress on the Waikatogate biosecurity scare and its implications for Auckland. Why can't the press stay out of matters they have no understanding of when experts are employed to act in the public interest? They should just butt out and leave us to do our jobs…

He read on. The article was measured, containing no accusations or revelations; nothing but quality commentary. What it did do was raise awareness and seek reassurance that the best interests of Aucklanders in this crisis were being properly managed from a health and safety perspective.

The bastards! Trying to brew a storm in a teacup or test public opinion on the topic. And it's just possible they know more than they're letting on, thought Waring. Maybe it was time to press on with the water quality testing.

By the time he arrived at his office this particular morning Nigel Waring had put together something of an agenda.

"Get me Dan at the Manukau plant," he barked at his PA in lieu of his customary 'Good morning'.

"Right away, sir."

A few minutes later the PA reappeared in his office door, her expression pained.

"He's called in sick, sir."

"Oh, so what's his second in command's name again? I know — Michelle Bain. Get her for me instead."

"Naturally I tried that, sir, but guess what? She's off crook, too."

"Don't give me that. Get me the pump room engineer then. What's his name again?"

"Give me a moment, sir."

The PA struggled to remember who it was, too. She checked and rang and a few minutes later returned to Waring's office, increasingly frustrated.

"It's Peter Brown, sir, and you'll never guess. He called in with a bug as well."

"For Christ's sake. Who's running the show then?"

"Of course it's mostly controlled remotely from here, sir, and there's usually four or five people out there. Obviously not today. The only one on site is Farouk Shafei, the Iranian engineering student."

"You're joking! Why wasn't I told of this? You mean Auckland's entire water supply is in the hands of a temporary import from behind the Axis of Evil? What hope have we got? Anyway, get him on the blower right away."

"I'm putting him through."

"Hello, sir," came the tentative greeting from the speaker phone.

"Shafei, isn't it? Where is everyone?"

"Seems they're all unwell, sir. It's only me here today."

"Only indeed. You're not wrong there. Stay close to Frank Sutter — do you know him? He's the Regional Distribution Manager based here. He'll tell you if anything needs to be done."

"I will, sir. I know it's not so funny now, but we were

joking about this, sir. They were changing one of the main inlet valves from the Waikato feed yesterday. Would only let me watch. It stuck open for a minute or so and they got drenched. Like children around a New York fire hydrant in summer. I said they'd better watch out or they'd catch their death and it seems I wasn't wrong, sir."

"Hm. Get them to call me first thing tomorrow when they get back in, Shafei. I have an urgent job."

Bugger! There goes the water testing for another day. Waring returned to his office and called for his coffee.

CHAPTER 58

WIREMU ENJOYED a lie-in, too, but he heard Sam leave and the dog was hanging out for a run. When burying his head under the pillow would work no longer he eased into his boardies and trainers and headed out for his morning jog. The route was usually the same. Down through the dunes, onto the beach and along the foreshore finally looping back up to the road and home past the dairy for milk and bread.

A proper dog's life, and Wiremu's constant companion was in canine heaven plundering whatever the tide had thrown up the night before. The trip took the best part of an hour and by the time Wiremu ran back down the drive he was desperate for a shower and breakfast.

He knew today was going to be different when he almost ran into a dark SUV as he turned back into his drive. His concern was reinforced when he stepped back on to the deck to be met by two burly strangers in dark suits and shades.

"Hi. Great day for it," he offered with mock good cheer. "Bit hot for those jackets though, isn't it? How about a cuppa to wet your whistles?"

Inwardly, he was uneasy. He could sense an attitude with this pair. Decaff might be best.

"Wicked morning for a run. What can I do for you anyway?"

"What you can do is tell us where Sam Miro is."

Ah! The worst was confirmed.

As the first man got to his feet Wiremu couldn't help but notice he was built like a brick outhouse and was more than a little threatening. He braced himself for trouble. The dog also sensed a problem and hackles rose signalling its displeasure. The door was ajar; they'd obviously had a look around already. Thank God Sam was gone.

"Sam Miro? Never heard of him."

"Tell that mongrel to shut the fuck up. And when you've done that you might consider why Miro's car is parked in your drive if you've never heard of him."

Good point. Good point indeed.

"Over here, boy." While he fondled the dog's velvety ears he thought hard.

"Oh, that. You're not from around here, are you? This is Raglan by the Sea. Things are different here. Do you know I haven't got a clue whose car it is. It was left here by a bloke a couple of weeks back when he came to do some surfing. I wasn't around. Who knows? Maybe he'll come back and collect it one day. That's how things are around here, you know."

"Don't fuck with me, boy!"

The intimidating reply was reinforced by the ominous tapping of a baseball bat on the deck.

"That's all I know. I can tell you've had a look around. You'll know then that — what's his name? — isn't here, so you might as well be on your way."

"Could be, but I tell you what — if I find out you've been hiding him, I'll be back and, believe me, I'll cut off your balls and feed them to the dog. Are you hearing me?"

"Sure am."

"Write it down somewhere so you don't forget."

And with that Dent's henchmen were on their way.

Wiremu reached for his cellphone and thumbed in a text.

'Don't come back here. Had a visit from some unpleasant lowlifes — Simcox's goons? They'll be watching 4 sure. Keep me posted on where U R. Best. W.'

CHAPTER 59

THIS TIME when Sam arrived at Caradijc's his newfound friend wasn't completely wasted. There was a new light in his eyes that suggested he might be open for business.

"How are you?"

Sam was relieved that Caradijc hadn't done a bunk in the meantime.

"That food was you, wasn't it? It worked wonders."

"Hit the spot, eh? Thought it might. I brought some more and a few beers to keep us going. No vodka, you understand. I'm kind of hoping we could kick a few ideas round and that maybe I could enlist your help on a project."

"Why not? Got nothing more pressing. But why me?"

"Ha! Why you? Now there's a question. Put it this way. If I want my lawns cut or my house painted I can pick up the phone. On the other hand, if I need a truckload of a particular bug cultured up there aren't so many people I can turn to. That's why. Anyway, let's start at the beginning. I don't know that much about you, Andrej. Can see you're not your average Kiwi though, so how about filling me in on some of the gaps?"

"Sure. But why now, after everything? I still don't get it."

"It's a long story. Let's just say I've got my problems too."

"Never would have guessed."

"We'll get to that later, but let's start with you, Andrej. It must have been one hell of a journey from cold war Russia to twenty-first century New Zealand. It'd be great to understand your background a little better."

"OK. You know I'm into microbiology don't you? Well I did some of my best work at a place called Sverdlovsk. Heard of it?"

"Rings a bell. Can't say I know much about it though."

"Doesn't matter. It was a centre for the practical application of microbiology, but old technology, if you know what I mean. Pre-genomics. What we did was bacterial culture on an industrial scale. Hard to explain why. That's why I think it'd be easier to start with you. Let's park me for a moment. What's your specialist interest then?"

Sam regarded Caradijc, surmising he was still not relaxed enough to totally open up.

"OK, if it'll help. The thing that lights my fire is understanding how bacterial species interact and change under different environmental conditions. To me it's just so amazing. If we cut back to classical micro for a moment the central assumption was that a bug was a bug. They didn't change; it was like they were set in concrete. The belief was that the only constraint to separating and identifying individual bacteria in all their diversity was ever more discriminating culture techniques. Ultimately, or so the dogma went, if the techniques were good enough you'd be able to isolate all the species in the microbial world and perhaps even individual strains. How wrong was that assumption? You'd know most of this anyway, but let me explain."

"Yes." Caradijc's interest was growing. "Go on."

"To me the single biggest development of the last few years has been the emergence of the concept of the microbiome. This has resulted from the newer techniques of genomics where we haven't been analysing the DNA from individual species one at a time, but from the whole microbial community in a sample all at the same time. It's so much less laborious and avoids the need for much of the culturing used previously."

He checked that Caradijc was still listening.

"Then what we do is use sophisticated association software to unravel the myriad of info that results and identify the individual species in a sample. We're calling this eco-genomics and the main families of bugs in a community we designate as ecotypes. Some of them map back to the classical bug types. But many don't, you understand."

Sam was on a roll. He could have been back in his university classroom or guest lecturing.

"Here's the thing. The key scientific advance of the last few years has been the realisation that bacterial species are far from static. On the contrary, the new genomics has shown that in microbial ecosystems the bacteria mutate and exchange DNA at a phenomenal rate — like species are going out of fashion. They are so dynamic and promiscuous. It turns out that the sharing of DNA is one of the key ways bugs evolve. It's not only individual genes being exchanged either, but whole chunks of DNA such as the ribosomal RNAs."

Sam was positively bouncing with enthusiasm as he knew Caradijc was hanging on his every word.

"Man, it's like a biological arms race. New species arise all the time spreading like wildfire through the prevailing environment. Their 'fit' is tested, 'trade-offs' challenged; if they pass then they flourish and if not they're gone in the blink of an eyelid. Here today; gone tomorrow!"

Silently the Russian opened up two beers, pushing one towards Sam.

Sam took time out to refresh the inner man before continuing.

"A major for us has been realising the fluidity of DNA exchange. Indeed, it's causing us to question the whole notion of the individuality of species. If you were to do a stocktake of bugs in a community at any one point in time what you would see is a range of distinct species. Try doing the same thing again a while later, especially if their environment has changed some in the meantime, and the profile of bugs will be quite different. Man, it's like evolution on caffeine."

"Sounds more like revolution to me," said Caradijc. "I had no idea. What do you think the key drivers are?"

"I guess classical Darwinism applies to some extent — survival of the fittest and all that — with individual species looking for selective advantage. Anything that gives them a leg up and helps them get their portfolio of genes into the next generation has got to be good. What we have noticed is that if the micro-environment is stable then the rate of change is relatively low. Introduce a perturbation to the system — say stronger UV light or a new antibiotic — then it's like you've started a tsunami. The rate of DNA exchange and natural selection ramp up massively, species come and go; the abundance of individual species changes and eventually the whole system moves to a new ecological equilibrium state."

Caradijc began to set out the food that Sam had brought to the table, and gestured for him to sit down and join him. The two scientists talked on into the afternoon reviewing the concepts and debating the implications of microbial genomics. A bond was growing between them. Finally, Sam stood up and stretched. His throat was dry from talking.

"Will you excuse me a minute? I have to ring a friend."

Still no Ken. Something bad must have happened. What was he going to do about that? He noticed the text from Wiremu and immediately replied.

'Think I've found a farm stay for a couple of days. S'

He turned back to Caradijc. "Another beer?"

"Why not?"

They returned to the kitchen table with their drinks and Sam handed the baton back to Caradijc.

"What about you, Andrej? What's your main interest?"

"I was more at the application end of microbiology, Sam. Biological remediation, in fact."

"OK. Biological control. That's of interest, too. Of what?"

"Oh, all sorts of things. Let's just say pests."

"And your specialty?"

"Process scale culture systems. In my time at Sverdlovsk we developed the only truly industrial scale microbial production systems the world has ever known. To give an example, in our peak year of seventy-nine we produced something like one thousand tonnes of highly active dried bacteria."

"My God. You have to be joking. What on earth for?"

"For application in WMDs, of course. Biological weapons, comrade. I thought you realised... But in the end, what for? is indeed the question. It was like a sick joke. Granted it was a different era, but how could our masters have seriously believed that producing enough weapons-grade anthrax to extinguish all humanity was a means of protecting us — a biological deterrent? I do not know. And how could we have been so stupid as to believe them?"

"And I thought the Soviet biological weapons programme was all just a rumour!"

"No, Sam, it was all too real. But all we succeeded in doing was losing many excellent young people along the way. So many died on the programme, Sam, especially in seventy-seven. We had a serious leak then, the biological equivalent of Chernobyl. If the wind had been blowing the other way the whole city would have gone. Instead it was 'only' the PhD quarters that caught the anthrax cloud. One hundred and twenty of my colleagues were infected. We lost them all, Sam, one by one. Some days I'm accepting of it. On others the dark clouds of guilt wash over me and I struggle. Why was I exempt? Let me tell you: because I was on duty. Now I'm the only survivor, and I wish I wasn't. It would have been so much easier if I'd perished with them."

CHAPTER 60

DESPITE HER best efforts Jacquie Schofield was struggling to find quality time with her children these days. As she pulled into the parking area at Shelly Bay, she was hoping that with the spring evenings drawing out things might be about to improve. For the children a run on the beach, a climb on the rocks and, if weather permitted, a splash in the waves was what it was all about.

As the Legacy crunched to a halt on the gravel the kids were already unbuckling their seat belts, keen to get out and get on with it. Little Johnny was clutching his football and as soon as he was out of the car sank the boot in to it sending an expert grubber scudding across the lay-by towards a parked council truck.

"Watch what you're doing with that," his mum shouted, doing her best to unbuckle the baby and keep up with Johnny. "We don't want the ball getting out on the road, do we?"

Instead the ball skittered into the truck, slewing sideways and under the trailer, chased briskly by the young All Black wannabe. Johnny was shimmying back out when his mother and two sisters finally caught up.

"What've you done to yourself?"

Kim pointed to a not insignificant smear of blood down his front.

"Nothing!"

"Cripes, Johnny, we can't take you anywhere, can we? We haven't been here a minute yet!"

On a closer inspection Johnny was equally shocked and proceeded to scan knees and elbows for any evidence of gash, slice or graze before declaring himself fine to continue.

Kim piped up again.

"Is that your phone ringing, Mum?"

"No. It's in the car."

"Mum, what's the pong around here?"

"No idea! Yes, it does reek a bit, doesn't it?"

Finding the source of the ringing inevitably became the next challenge with the kids looping around the truck trying to zero in on the ringtone before settling on the trailer-mounted mulching machine for closer inspection. Johnny started to climb up onto the back, but was headed off by his mother.

"Come on, Johnny. You know better than that. You shouldn't be climbing up there."

As she yanked him down from the back of the trailer they both spotted the source of the ringing. Protruding from the jaws of the machine was the lower half of a body. It took a moment to register what they'd clapped eyes on.

Jacquie's mind was in denial.

"It's nothing, it's nothing."

She dragged him away, doing her best to dismiss the oddity as a weird prank. But a swarm of disturbed flies and the unmistakable colours and smell of death all led her inexorably to a different conclusion. Repugnant as it might seem they were staring at a body — half a body — stuck in the mulching machine with a ringing phone still tucked in its pocket. Johnny suddenly threw up, and together the family turned and bolted for the car.

In the relative safety of the Legacy, Kim began to sob noisily.

"Mum, what was that? Should you call the police?"

Her mother's response was terse.

"What do you think I'm doing?"

CHAPTER 61

SAM WAS silent. He had nothing to offer as counsel or consolation to Caradijc, who had experienced such institutionalised horror. Equally clearly, he realised that, like the village elder from some lost jungle tribe, there was so much more to be learned from this man than met the eye.

"Another beer?" he asked. "Andrej, how'd you meet Bella Simcox?"

"I think it was a couple of years ago when she was on a fact-finding mission to the Ukraine; interested in bioremediation, as I recall. We were introduced by someone from the Ministry. We stayed in touch and eventually she offered me a consultancy with her Green Future Party here in New Zealand. Full of false promise, she was. Do this, do that and I'll take care of everything so you can bring the family out and make a go of it here in New Zealand."

"What'd she want you to do though?"

"At first she didn't seem to know. But over time, working with her motley crew of party associates and some women's club or other, she began to harden plans for a grand design to destabilise the government. It was all, how do you say it, hush-hush. Cloak and dagger stuff; reminded me of the old days back home. I could tell the key players were from different government departments, don't have names but know I would recognise them if I saw them again. You will have met one of them for sure — that woman Dent. She was here the night you visited. They call her the enforcer."

"Yes, I know Iris Dent. No favourite of mine, I can assure you!"

"You astonish me. I'm sure there's a heart of gold in there somewhere!"

"Yeah, right."

"Planting her in ILAWR was part of it, but you've probably figured that out already, as was getting your research programme funded."

"That was the unkindest cut of all for me. Really pisses me off, because it means I've been a pawn in their game all along too. Makes a farce of my career in research, doesn't it?"

"You'll be looking forward to taking Simcox and Dent down then. Getting them what they deserve!"

"You aren't wrong there. And with any luck nailing them is already well in hand."

"Who knows what this will mean for me now? I'm beyond caring. Relieved that it's all over."

"Good man. Let's cross that bridge when we come to it. I'll do what I can, though right now that doesn't mean much. As things stand, we could all be part of the fallout."

Sam handed over the last beer and smiled at his new research partner.

He went on, "What I'm still trying to understand is what Simcox wanted you to achieve. That is; what your brief was. I'll come to why I need to know in a moment, but it would help to understand."

"They had a good grasp of what you were measuring in your research. What they wanted me to do was make sure you got some positive results in your assays; a few hits that she could trumpet in Parliament."

"OK, I get that. But why 0157?"

"All sorts of things were possible, and at the end of the day what I wanted to do was make sure you got some positive results, but not by using anything too dangerous!"

"0157 is bad enough."

"I didn't want anyone to get hurt, Sam, but the contamination had to make a strong enough statement for Simcox to be happy. On the positive side, it's not contagious in any real sense and the farms are miles from anywhere. So I thought it would be OK. And I don't know whether you noticed, but I included a generous helping of antibiotic to keep things under control."

"I did note that and, as it happens that's exactly why we still have work to do. Because it's not under control. In fact, exactly the reverse. What you don't know is that the *E coli* has bloomed down through the local streams and into the Waikato. It's a major, believe me."

Andrej sank his head in his hands as he took in this new revelation and its implications.

"How do you know that?"

"If we can get onto your computer I can show you some data. Briefly, we have the genetic signature of your strain so we can identify it wherever it is. And what we've found is that levels don't decrease downstream from the farm as you might expect. What they do is increase — not just incrementally either, but massively, right down through the catchment to where the local stream runs into the Waikato."

"Who'd have predicted that? Any ideas how it could have happened?"

"That's the big question, isn't it? Your strain has obviously found conditions to its liking. This is a complex system and who could have second-guessed nature's influence on the introduced species? Clearly it's down to some kind of gene environment interaction, but why conditions are so favourable to your bug I don't know."

Caradijc was deep in gloom as he listened.

"What we've learned is that the introduced *E coli* mutated and picked up some extra genes by horizontal transfer making it even more toxic and better-placed to dominate in its new microbial community. Certainly there's been much chopping and changing going on in your strain at the DNA level. I can think of a couple of possible reasons."

Sam was nervously flexing his hands as he spoke.

"We've noticed it's picked up some new antibiotic resistance genes. Probably by including the antibiotic you've applied a selective pressure that it's been able to respond to; perhaps at the expense of other bugs. Another reason may be copper. The local farmers apply it liberally as an 'organic spray' and it's building up in the soil and waterways. What we've noticed is that copper is a growth stimulant for your strain and inhibitory to many of the other bugs in the area. Again, a selective advantage for your bug."

Caradijc suddenly got to his feet and commenced pacing up and down the narrow kitchen. He was obviously thinking hard. Sam went on with his exposition.

"The X factor for me could be the special environment of the Waikato wetlands. We're only just beginning to understand what goes on in there but, believe me, it's special. Mystical even, and from time to time it creates a perfect storm of conditions to support the growth of some species to a tipping point where they get completely out of control. We see this periodically with the algal blooms and now we've got a bacterial 'bloom'. Kind of novel, I know; it'll make a great publication. One thing's for sure, for whatever reason, conditions in the wetlands are perfect for your strain and levels have exploded. My friend, we're facing a smoking gun; or better still — a runaway water tanker headed for Auckland."

Andrej sat back down, his face expressing mixed emotions of guilt and scientific curiosity. Sam was content to be silent, knowing they were drawing close to the point of his visit. After a time Caradijc spoke.

"What I don't get is — what it is about Auckland. Can you run that by me again?"

"OK. The Mangawara Farm drains out through the streams and wetlands into the Waikato River. As it happens the intake for Auckland's domestic water supply is just downstream from there. We've done some modelling and predict that with bacterial loadings of this level even given dilution in the Waikato and the water treatment plant there is still likely to be sufficient 0157 to cause health problems in Auckland."

Sam noticed Caradijc wilt as the revelation of what he had done hit him with the force of a southerly chill. His grand experiment could turn into a final solution for Auckland. Sam continued as if to dispel any residual doubt.

"It's been a dry winter, you know. The reservoirs in West Auckland are extremely low, which leaves the city particularly dependent on the Waikato source."

Again Sam waited, hoping Caradijc would take the necessary step into the next stage. Eventually it came.

"Question is, Sam, what can we do about it?"

Ah! He was on to it.

"Exactly, Andrej, exactly…! I have some ideas. I can show you some recent data we've put together on one of our bifidobacteria strains and then we can talk about how we might use it."

"Go for it, Sam. If there's anything I can do..."

And Caradijc listened in awe as Sam walked him systematically through the highly novel findings that Max had made on the bifidobacteria. He recognised immediately that Sam was right — the newly discovered species had amazing potential for bioremediation and was probably their best bet for cleaning up the rampant *E coli* in the Mangawara.

He was thinking hard, and eventually responded.

"I'd need to do some tests though. Your bug is an effective inhibitor in the Petri dish, but we can't be sure how it will work in the swamp."

"True. Only I'm not sure we can afford to wait."

"Understood. I'll do some simulations to predict the amount of your material we would need to have any effect.

The *E coli* has one hell of a head start. I will base the modelling on a range of projections of bifidobacteria survival and see what comes out. And in the meantime I'll start to ferment up some of your new antidote for testing purposes."

"Now you're talking!"

Though he forced himself to sound enthusiastic, inwardly Sam had real concerns. The last thing they could afford was delay and, quite likely, the bifido bug was the only thing separating Auckland from Armageddon.

"Andrej, it's now or never. We have to knock this bugger off as soon as we can. That's our calling."

He waited to let the gravity of the situation sink in and then Sam turned back to more practical matters.

"What's your best bet of how long it will take to ferment up sufficient material to treat the river, Andrej?"

"That is difficult to assess. Assuming your bug grows well, possibly three days to its first field test. It is difficult to know how many releases we'll need to complete the job."

"OK. I've got some material here for you to work with."

"That is good. Let's start growing it up and tomorrow I'll begin testing it against my strain. Can you get me a sample of Mangawara water? It'll have the mutated form in it and I need to evaluate how it has changed."

"Done! Oh, and tomorrow, Andrej, I'd better push off and take care of some other things. Can we catch up again later in the week?"

"I will attempt to fit you into my busy schedule." Andrej winked. "I have so much else to do."

Sam's hunch about Caradijc's usefulness had paid off. The Russian scientist had turned out to be a good ally and working partner. He knew exactly what had to be done and was working all hours to prepare the new treatment for trial release; doing his level best to make amends for past indiscretions as he went.

We've all got areas of vulnerability, Sam reflected, as he lay in bed with the first rays of a dawn sun streaming in through a tear in the curtains. And so it is with Andrej; dreams of a new life in New Zealand now seemingly dashed. Sam made a private vow to pull out all the stops to help him when this thing was over. He knew the knives would be out for Caradijc.

Time to get up and moving. Sam couldn't risk Simcox's thugs catching up with him again. With the continuing uncertainty about Ken's whereabouts and a growing fear for his safety, Sam was beginning to think he could be the only person left in a position to expose Simcox's deadly scam. He'd need to fire off a few emails and then it might be a good idea to find somewhere new to lie low for a day or two. Perhaps he could give Georgie a ring and head back to ground zero. After all, the farm would be the last place anyone would think to look for him. He really had to talk to Georgie anyway.

Best, too, if he tried to contact Grafton. For all he knew Ken never even made it to Wellington so it might be the smart thing to do.

He heard Caradijc rattling cups and plates in the kitchen so he showered quickly before heading down to check on progress.

"Morning."

"Morning, Sam. Coffee? Your bugs are growing nicely, so today I'll run some tests and start ramping up the fermentation. Do you want to help?"

"Believe me, there's nothing I'd like better, but there are a stack of other things I need to attend to. Do you mind if I leave you to it for a day or so? I will aim to be back tomorrow evening to help you with a first release the day after. How does that sound?"

"As good as it gets."

Caradijc buttered the toast, understanding Sam's

priorities but, nevertheless, a touch disappointed that he would have to wait to share the marvels of his mock-up lab with his new-found companion.

"Andrej, before I go, can I get onto your computer? I need to keep things moving."

"Why not? Now, come eat."

They ate breakfast without conversation, brains in overdrive. So much depended on the success of the next few days.

Finally, Sam cracked the silence.

"Man, I feel so alone in all this, you know. We're entering the endgame and, Andrej, I wanted to say — I couldn't do it without you. Thanks, mate."

"Sam, for me it's the opposite. I have someone I can talk to for the first time in ages. I used to do only what I was told. Now is my time to be bold; to step up and put a few things right. So thanks for giving me a second chance."

He came round to where Sam stood and lifted him up in a bear hug.

"Spasibo za to, moy drug."

"Hey, put me down."

Chuckling, Andrej complied and stepped back. Sam held out his hand.

"That's how we do it here."

The two men shook hands, grinning.

"Now, back to business. We're both clear on what has to be done, aren't we, Andrej? Auckland's staring down the barrel and without us it'll be in big trouble. The odds are totally stacked against us but we'll just have to deal with it." Sam punched Andrej lightly on the shoulder. "It's the Battle of Britain and St Petersburg all over again."

"And not a Spitfire in sight," Andrej replied, entering into the spirit of things. "Our secret weapon is the humble Petri dish." Sober again, he added, "My friend, let's not get too ahead of ourselves. We don't even know yet that the bioremediation will work in the field."

"Yes, and at least Londoners knew what they were up against. At present Auckland is caught like a possum in the glare and the city doesn't have a clue what's coming. I've rung the alarm bell, but no one is listening. That's my first priority this morning. I plan to put that right as soon as I'm online. No more stuffing around. This time I'm going to the top."

"Better get on with it then," said Caradijc, pointing to his computer. "I'll be out in the barn."

'From: Sam Miro PhD
To: Medical Officer of Health — Auckland
Subject: Auckland Water: major public health risk

Dear Sir/Madam,
I refer to my email (below) to Nigel Waring; Head, WaterQual — Auckland. I have evidence of a potentially catastrophic failure of Auckland water security related to contamination by a new and dangerous form of enterotoxigenic E coli 0157:H7. This clear and present threat to public health was first communicated to the Biosecurity NZ Operations Chief with responsibility for the Waikatogate biosecurity breach — Peter Smart — some ten days ago and to Nigel Waring five days ago.

It is a source of major concern to me that I see no evidence that the risk is being taken seriously and so it is for this reason that I feel compelled to write to you today. I have no clue as to why they have not acted on the information I have provided. I have no doubt that the gravity of the situation will not be lost on you and that you will pursue the matter without delay.

Yours sincerely,
Sam Miro,
Environmental Research Scientist.'

Sam then pasted in the relevant email and clicked on Send.

One down and one to go. He went into newzealand.govt.
nz and got the ex-Prime Minister's email address.

'From: Sam Miro PhD
To: Right Honourable Jeremy Grafton
Subject: Urgent — Various

Dear Sir,

*We haven't met but I am aware that my colleague Ken Judge
has recently been in touch regarding the background to the
Waikatogate biosecurity event. I also know that Dr Judge
travelled to Wellington to brief you more fully but it is a matter
of great concern to me that I haven't heard from him since. I can't
be certain that he even made it to the meeting with you.*

*I believe Ken has already given you an outline of the
circumstances behind the biosecurity breach and so I expect you
will be as anxious as me to get to the bottom of this matter.*

*Given the above I seek an opportunity to meet with you
directly at your convenience so as to provide you with whatever
information you may require to pursue the matter.*

*Additionally, sir, I need to advise you that there is a second
and related issue before us of potentially even greater concern
than the Waikato event itself. That is — the public health
implications of the Waikato event for Aucklanders. Needless to
say I would also appreciate being allowed to brief you on this. In
short, there is now a very real risk of Auckland water becoming
contaminated with a dangerous new form of the bacterium
E coli as the contamination spreads.*

*Sir, to put it bluntly if this is allowed to happen it will cause
nothing short of a public health catastrophe.*

*Together with my colleagues I have been trying to raise the
alarm on the spread of contamination with Biosecurity and
Auckland Water for some days now. To no avail: my concerns
have seemingly fallen on deaf ears. Consequently I am now of the
opinion that the only way left to avert this disaster is by the direct
intervention of your office and so I seek your help on this.*

Please feel free to contact me at your earliest convenience. I can be reached at this email or directly via my mobile — 021 995 389.

Sincerely,
Dr Sam Miro,
Environmental Research Scientist'

CHAPTER 62

Mariana Touala, Second Assistant to Richie McCarthy, Chief of Staff in the Office of the ex-Prime Minister, was vetting unsolicited emails to Jeremy Grafton. As she panned through the inbox she spotted a message from a Sam Miro. This was the man Iris Dent had instructed her to be on the lookout for. Touala spent barely a moment examining her conscience before she printed a copy for Dent then hit Delete, unceremoniously consigning the email to oblivion.

A few minutes later she was acting out her usual role, and answering the first phone call of the day.

"Don Ridgway, Security Intelligence Board. Can I speak to Richie, please?"

"One minute, sir, I'll put you through."

"Good morning. Richie McCarthy here."

"Richie. I have news. We've found Judge. Thought you'd want to know straightaway."

"Great. Go on."

"No, it's not great. Not great at all actually. He's been topped. They found him — to be accurate, half of him — stuck in a mulching machine near Shelly Bay. Can't tell whether he was fed in dead or alive. Identified him from the cellphone stuck in his pocket."

"What!" Richie gagged, his bacon butty and morning latte threatening to rebound. "Gross, Don. It seems Simcox and Dent will stop at nothing. Anyway thanks for letting me know. I'll update Jeremy and get back to you."

Eavesdropping from the front office Mariana Touala decided Dent would appreciate a heads up on this development, too. She thumbed off a text and remained on alert.

Richie went straight in to report the news to Jeremy Grafton. Touala heard the raised voices and a stream of expletives from the ex-PM. This was serious stuff. Quickly she scuttled back to her desk as the door opened and McCarthy took his leave.

"Get straight back to Don," Grafton roared after him. "Judge's offsider Sam Miro must be out there somewhere. Tell Ridgway to find him, like yesterday." And in mounting frustration he added, "Before they do! We need to get to Miro immediately or we're lost. Nothing else matters, Richie, so go for it!"

"I'll give it my utmost, sir."

Sitting at her desk Mariana tried hard to stay calm. She was soon reassured by a text from Dent.

'U did well, sister. Meet U at Starbucks on The Terrace 10.30 to discuss.'

CHAPTER 63

WITH HIS coffee mug refilled Sam reached for his mobile. Time to book his accommodation down on the farm.

'Hi G. How's things? Can I swing by to catch up? S'

Half a minute later he got her response.

'Hi U. Y not? Yes, drop over. Gr8 2 C U. G'

As he slid the phone back into his pocket Sam wondered how he'd find her and what to tell her about Shelley. PC to discuss developments; but how would she react? Only half an hour later he was pulling into the drive overlooking the Mangawara Farm and about to find out.

The moment the door opened and she threw herself against him, he knew this wouldn't be easy. He held her for a few seconds and brushed her cheek with his lips before easing gently away.

"Georgie. You look great. Back to your best after all the drama. Tell me — how are you?"

"Tell you?" She nudged against him again. "Hell, Sam, I want to show you how I am."

Her arms wound round his neck and she kissed him full on the mouth.

The last thing he needed, yet as her warm body pushed into his space he felt his resolve evaporating. Man, he was so pathetic.

"Georgie," he began. "We mustn't... We need to talk..."

Before he could add another word she had wrapped him in a passionate embrace, French kissing him deeply while allowing her hands to reacquaint themselves with his body. When she found what she wanted, she purred with pleasure, leading him by the hand to the front room couch. There she began to tug at his clothes before falling back and pulling him down onto her. All resolve now gone he slid unthinking into the moist inner warmth of her body.

If anything it was better this time; recent fantasies playing out into reality with an intensity that he had barely imagined possible. Her skin was satin beneath his fingers as she bucked and moaned on top of him. He was tireless, and triumphant when she came; sliding her off the couch and on to the rug. But she wanted to do it all again. Harder and faster this time until they collapsed panting, flushed and glistening, sighing deeply with satisfaction.

Sam took a moment, gazing down at her splendid form framed by the bright afternoon window sun. And in that instant the only person he could see was Shelley; now always on his mind.

And the guilt returned. What have I done, what have I done? He was nauseous with the realisation of his betrayal.

"That was crazy mad," said Georgie, giggling. Oblivious to his deepest thoughts. "Well, what's the verdict, Sam? How was I?"

"One hundred and ten percent. Over the lurgy, I should say. There'll be no stopping you now!"

Gently he slid her down beside him and reached for his T-shirt.

"Georgie, I do really want to talk to you. It should have been first," he said, pulling it over his head. "But you took care of that."

With his underpants back on, he stood up, stretching, and stepped into his jeans. Through the window the farm spread out before him; a cluster of MPI Biosecurity staff going busily about their business. He slipped his feet into his sneakers.

"Georgie, how has it been for you, truly?"

"In a word — horrible!" She got up, he trying to avoid her insolent beauty. "Dad has taken it oh so badly. He's bitter about everything — especially the stranger. Been nudging the single malt along, too, if you know what I mean. I'm worried about him."

"You're right to worry. And, I'm sorry, I've got more bad news to share. The first is that the *E coli* bug has bloomed into the Mangawara, so it's spreading. And that's a major."

"Oh, God. What will it mean? More people at risk?"

"You've got it. And, Georgie, the contamination is spilling into the Waikato so it could get into the Auckland water supply."

She stared at him, open-mouthed.

"What is ILAWR doing about this?"

"Ah! That brings me to the second thing I was going to tell you. There have been big problems at work — a lot of people in denial and worse. The upshot is, I've been suspended."

"So we can take that flyaway holiday now?"

"Chance would be a fine thing. Problem is, I can't get anyone to take the Mangawara problem seriously, so I'm trying to fix it myself."

Sam hesitated. This was where it got tricky.

"Georgie, I couldn't do that alone, so I've teamed up with a partner."

He stopped. Georgie raised an enquiring eyebrow.

"I need to tell you who the partner is — the man you call the stranger. His name is Andrej Caradijc and we're now working on fixing the contamination together."

As she listened Georgie stiffened, paling in anger and disbelief. Sam could tell immediately he'd overstepped the mark. Her pained expression left no doubt how she felt about the revelations. Momentarily the colour rushed back into her face, and she bristled with anger.

"You bastard."

"Georgie, I know what you're thinking but, please, listen."

Too late. The damage was done and as he reached out for her, Georgie totally lost it.

"Surely you can't be serious. That bastard destroyed our farm, not to mention Dad and also had a good go at me! And now you're in cahoots with him. I can't believe I'm hearing this. Why him, Sam, of all people? Go on, tell me. Next you'll be saying it was all a terrible mistake and he's not such a bad bloke after all."

Sam tried to reason with her. "Calm down, Georgie. Let me explain."

"No. I don't want you to. I can't handle this right now. I just want you to go. Fuck off out of here and don't come back."

She was beside herself, and who could blame her for that. She'd been through so much, and he should have realised he was expecting too much to ask for her understanding.

"OK, Georgie, OK. I can see you need your space. Later, please take a moment to think what this is really about. It's bigger than any of us. It's about saving Auckland no less and I need Caradijc for that. I'm so sorry I've hurt you, Georgie, and you're right. I should go."

He didn't dare attempt a kiss or a hug. He left Georgie sobbing on the couch, closed the door behind him and drove away.

For Georgie it was all too much. She'd found someone she believed in and now she'd been let down. The room darkened as she lay sobbing on the couch, stirring only after closing time when her father finally stumbled back to the farmhouse.

"Hey!" She wiped away the tears on her sleeve. "Guess what, Dad? Sam dropped in today. I couldn't believe it. Thought I understood him but obviously not. He spilled the beans that he's now teamed up with the man who ruined our farm. Dad, I feel so used and let down!"

Phil stared at her, incredulous, unsteady, wavering, the flush of however many shots washing out of him.

As the sense of what she had said sank in, he spoke with deliberation.

"I'll kill the pricks, I tell you… I'll kill them both."

Then he turned and staggered to his bedroom. He lay there staring into the darkness all night.

CHAPTER 64

SAM DIDN'T know what to do. He should probably check into a motel and chill out. A good night's sleep wouldn't do him any harm. This decision made, he parked under a full moon at the Mangawara, and stepped out to survey the effervescent shimmer of the water. Who could imagine the morbid danger that lurked beneath the surface of this peaceful stream?

He stared down for what seemed an age, playing out likely scenarios for the next few days until he was jolted back to reality by the shrill notes of his mobile.

"Hello."

"Is that Sam Miro?"

"Yes, who's this?"

"Richie McCarthy. I'm Chief of Staff in Jeremy Grafton's Office."

"Oh, hi, I was hoping you'd call. I guess you want to talk about my email."

"Which email?"

"Er, the one I sent to Grafton this morning."

"That's strange. I haven't seen it. What address did it go to?"

"Cor, I dunno." Under stress, Sam often became sarcastic. "How many does an ex-PM have?"

"It's odd that no one ran it by me, but these are strange times as I think you know."

"Agreed."

"I suggest you resend it to outreach@securityintelligencebranch.govt.nz. It's completely secure; give you my word."

"Should be able to do that from my phone. Anyway,

let's cut to the chase. Time is running out. I need to talk to Grafton on a matter of the utmost urgency; a matter of national security."

"You mean Waikatogate?"

"Look — Richie, is it? — please listen to me. Waikatogate is history. That ain't the half of it any more. People stand to die here, big time. I need to talk to Grafton urgently. Do you hear me?"

"Loud and clear!" McCarthy was well on the back foot now. "But forgive me, Sam. As we don't appear to have received your email we haven't got the background."

"Richie, am I missing something here? You rang me. What'd you ring for if it wasn't about the email?"

"Sam, let's cut back. Forget the email for a moment. Grafton needs to talk to you urgently, too."

"There's a thing. Can I ask why?"

"It's about the biosecurity matter, but I'm afraid I have some bad news for you first. Do you know a Ken Judge?"

"Yes. He's a close friend of mine, and my mentor."

"Regrettably something bad has happened to him."

Sam's stomach churned and he tensed. He had suspected Ken had gone belly up and now his worst nightmare was about to be confirmed.

"Tell me what happened."

"I'm sorry. Ken Judge was found dead today."

Sam stared sightlessly at the glowing orb of the moon, angry and frustrated. Finally he cleared his throat, and said, "It wasn't an accident, was it?"

"No. There are suspicious circumstances!"

"Suspicious, my arse. Could you give me some time here?"

He stood in the moonlight, shoulders heaving, struggling for control and thinking hard.

Finally he resumed his conversation with McCarthy.

"Richie, no disrespect, but I don't know you from Adam.

I need to do a run-through here — check your ID and that. I tell you what. Get Grafton to leave a message on my voice mail. I'll recognise him. When I have that I'll resend the email I'm referring to and also the report Ken was going to present to him in Wellington yesterday. Then you'll know where I'm coming from on this and we can try talking sense in the morning."

"Sam, Sam!" The response was rapid-fire. "That's a good plan, but, please, be careful. You'll be toast, too, if they track you down."

"Yeah, I know," Sam retorted. "I've already had a taste of their hospitality. Not much chance of them finding me though. I hardly know where I am myself."

CHAPTER 65

THE BROODING shadow of a late spring storm amply reflected the collective mood in Grafton's Beehive office. The ex-PM had put in a call to David Whangapa to update him on developments and the outlook was grim.

"Whangapa wants me to stay on this and he'll continue with the electioneering," Grafton reported to Richie McCarthy and Security Chief Don Ridgway. "Good call I say. I want first dibs at stringing Simcox up."

The three of them were working through the night studying Sam Miro's reports and emails. As the storm's intensity grew so too did the groans of utter disbelief as the trio delved deeper into the documents. Finally, Grafton could stand it no longer and launched into an explosive tirade.

"That egregious, hypocritical bitch. How could she? You couldn't make this up, could you? And here was I thinking the Greens were custodians of the environment, but no. That sick fuck Simcox has been doing her level best to torpedo it, clean green image and all. What is it with her? I swear she must be on something."

"Enough of the histrionics, Jeremy," counselled McCarthy. "Don't want you popping a rivet, do we?"

"What she's done is so utterly incomprehensible. I'm going to make sure she gets everything that's coming to her plus some, I swear. And enjoy every last minute of it, too."

"Who can blame you for that?"

The trio settled down to reflect on the information laid out before them. Calmer now, Grafton continued.

"There can be no doubt that Miro and Judge have built a compelling case. Their truth is much stronger than her lies and has to be pursued. We have everything we need. It's a question of how best to use it."

"Yeah. That Sam Miro's an absolute bloody rock star, isn't he? He's been picking away at this in virtual isolation. Nobody's taken him seriously yet he hasn't walked away. He's stuck to his guns, doing his level best to blow the whistle on the whole affair. I can see where he's coming from. No wonder he's suspicious of everyone. We have to get to him before that psychopath Simcox does and roll out whatever protection and support he needs. Without him we'd be totally down the gurgler by now."

"And may be still if we don't play this right," offered Ridgway. "The next few days will be critical."

"That's true," said McCarthy. "We're not out of the woods yet. And keen as I am to nail Simcox she has to be only our second priority now. The first is to sort out Auckland's water. We have no option but to close down the Waikato feed immediately or risk a real disaster. A pandemic or whatever you like to call it. Could require some water rationing, but hey! The health of Aucklanders has to be the priority. What's the name of the Medical Officer of Health up there again — Claire Steiner, isn't it? Get her on the line. And also that tosser from WaterQual — Nigel Waring."

"Will do. Mind you, it's two thirty in the morning. Should we wait?"

"No. This situation is critical."

"OK, OK. I'm on to it."

"I tell you what; that Peter Smart from MPI is another one whose head is going to roll over this. He won't come out of this smelling of roses. So up himself; took no notice of Miro and team. On a power trip, I bet. He's been doing his own thing regardless." He snorted. "Fiddling while Rome burns!"

After a time Don Ridgway came back into the room.

"Got them on the line so if you're ready I'll conference them in."

"Go for it."

Grafton began.

"Sorry to call you at such short notice, but we have a crisis on our hands."

"It must be serious if it couldn't wait until morning."

Waring obviously didn't care to be disturbed at such an early hour. Claire Steiner hastily intervened.

"How can we be of assistance, sir?"

"Here's the thing," said Grafton. "I have email correspondence and reports in front of me from a certain Dr Sam Miro who is the scientist who first picked up on the biosecurity issue in the Waikato. He's indicating the *E coli* contamination has spread and could pose a risk to the Auckland water supply. Mr Waring, what are you doing about it?"

"Oh, Miro! Is that all?" Waring scoffed. "Nothing but hot air, sir. Miro trying to stir up a storm because he's aggrieved, is all. You know he's on suspension? Pissed his boss off at ILAWR. My take on this is that he's another disaffected prima donna wanting to get back at his superiors. Typical cathartic behaviour."

Grafton drew a deep breath. "You quite finished, Mr Waring?"

"Er, yes."

"If I can stop you there. With all due respect you know diddly-squat. If I'd wanted your opinion on Dr Miro I would have asked for it. But that's not what I'm asking. What I would like to know is what you are doing about the possibility that Auckland water is contaminated."

The silence indicated that Waring had finally got the message.

"Er, sir, we're planning a major response here. I've only just learned of the threat myself."

"Oh, really? That's interesting as the email in front of me indicates you were informed seven days ago and Peter Smart from MPI Biosecurity five days before that."

"Er, yes — it took him some time to contact me, and...'

"Cut the crap, Mr Waring. I can tell you categorically that it is seven days since Dr Miro contacted you directly with the information. My question is simple enough. What have you been doing about it since then? Have you been in touch with Dr Steiner?"

"Sir, if I might add something here?" Steiner interposed tentatively. "Myself, I only became aware of this potential threat yesterday, again via an email from Dr Miro."

"Yes, I see that, Dr Steiner. So my question is to Mr Waring and I repeat — what have you and your WaterQual team been doing for the last week? Enlighten us, if you please."

Waring remained silent, wisely or not. McCarthy could tell Grafton was struggling to keep hold of his temper. Too late.

"Nothing to say? Then let me give you my take on this. Your answer has to be sod all, doesn't it, Mr Waring? Face it. If Dr Steiner as Medical Officer of Health hasn't heard from you, then presumably none of the relevant risk management protocols have yet been actioned. Have they?"

"Mr Grafton, sir, I agreed to a monitoring programme with Smart a few days ago, but he hasn't got back to me yet, and now I have staff off sick at the Manukau Reticulation Plant."

"Enough. Your response is a total sham, isn't it? For all you know their absence could be related to this matter. Now, can you assure us of the safety of water from the Waikato feed? Yes or no?"

Another long silence until Waring finally muttered, "No."

"Thank you, Mr Waring." Grafton cut the beleaguered water chief short. "I'll expect your resignation on my desk in the morning."

Waring's jaw dropped, but he had the sense to say nothing.

"Dr Steiner, under the Public Health Act I am declaring this a Public Health Emergency and placing you in charge of the response. Effective immediately. Under the provisions of the Act you will be aware that the powers I am vesting in you give you full authority over all relevant jurisdictions including government, local body, army and public and private organisations that might be required for your response. Go for it, Dr Steiner. All I ask is that you work directly with Richie McCarthy here in implementing whatever measures you deem necessary to manage the event. Godspeed and I hope we're not too late. We will do whatever is necessary to support you and manage any collateral damage. You have our full confidence."

"Thank you, sir. I have only one question for the moment and then I'll get on to it. Mr Waring, please provide me with the name and contact details of your second in command at WaterQual."

"I'll email them to you immediately. Oh, and Mr Grafton, sir..."

"Mr Waring, I have nothing further to say to you. Good night."

The conference call was over.

CHAPTER 66

NOT EXACTLY the Hilton and certainly not as good as being in your own bed, but the bench front seat of Wiremu's ageing Falcon was the business in the circumstances, assisting Sam to a better than average night's sleep.

The morning sun began to defeat the Mangawara mist and peek over the car's windscreen. Sam did his level best to sneak a few more minutes but the early light conspired against him. Turning his back, he settled back and was soon drifting again when his phone rang.

"Hello," he barked.

"Sam Miro?"

"Yes."

"Jeremy Grafton calling."

"Prime Minister — sorry, ex-PM... Heck, sir, what do I call you?"

"Jeremy will be fine in the circumstances."

"Thank you, sir. I've been waiting for your call."

"Pleased to make your acquaintance at last, Sam. I've heard a lot about you, young man. First things first. I'm so sorry about Ken. I know you were close."

"Yes. We really connected. And when this sorry affair began he was one of the few people I could turn to."

"I can see that. It must have been hard for you. Ken is going to be a huge loss. We'll have to think of an appropriate way to honour him. Sam, overnight we've been reading your emails and reports. New Zealand owes you a huge debt of gratitude."

"Thank you, sir. I've got to say I've been through a bit lately. Seen better times, you know."

"Me, too, as you can imagine. And it's all down to the same thing, if you get my drift."

"Yes, sir. I think we have a common objective here. I'm happy to help you in any way I can, sir."

"Brilliant. The first thing is we can't risk losing you. I want to bring you in."

"That'd be great, but not immediately, sir. I need to sort out the Mangawara first. If you read my emails you'll know Auckland water has to be the priority."

"Which reminds me, I need to update you, Sam. We acted on the Auckland thing overnight — declared a public health emergency and shut down the Waikato feed."

"Great. That's the kind of decisive action required. The next step has to be remediating the river. We can't wait or the new strain may become endemic."

"What have you got in mind?"

"I need to brief you, sir, but the upshot is we have other research going on that's resulted in us finding a natural bio-control agent for the toxic strain. It's got real promise, sir, and I propose to use it to treat the bloom."

"That sounds amazing, Sam, but realistically it's a mile from the lab bench to the field, isn't it? I'm guessing it'll take years to bring it to the point where it'll be useful."

"Not really, sir. Desperate times demand affirmative action. We've done enough background work to establish proof of concept and ensure it's safe. The problem is we'll be needing serious quantities of the bio-control agent so I've had to figure how to grow it up at scale. Took me some time to work that out though having been sidelined by ILAWR. But I'm on to it now."

"There's no stopping you, is there, young man?"

"Doing the best I can, sir."

"So much we need to work through. If you can't come to us, we'll have to come to you. Where can we find you, Sam?"

"How's this for an idea, sir? Tomorrow we're going for broke; releasing the first batch of the new bug into the

Mangawara. I know it's an imposition, sir, but I don't suppose you'd like to come up and see for yourself?"

"Classic. The appliance of science, eh? I'd like that, Sam. I need to see the problem first hand anyway, so it would be great to look over your shoulder. Where will we find you?"

"Do you know where the Mangawara is?"

"Vaguely."

"North of Hamilton at Taupiri. Turn onto Orini Road from Gordonton Road just before it runs into State Highway One. Continue alongside the wetlands for three or four kilometres and you'll see an old cottage down to the left on the river terrace. We'll be out in front of it during the afternoon. If we need to talk we should be able to use the cottage."

"Great. It'll be good to find out what you're up to. Till tomorrow then."

Mariana Touala had got exactly what she wanted and quietly replaced her extension phone in the reception area of the Grafton's Beehive suite. No one had noticed her listening in and she couldn't wait to update Dent.

In the Falcon Sam made another call. He and Wiremu needed to get the show on the road. Time to get some cameras set up to record the proceedings tomorrow.

CHAPTER 67

THE DAWN was far less impressive in Auckland than Mangawara, though no less an invitation to activity. The city woke and stirred.

Sione, like most of his neighbours in Manukau, was doing his best to break the cycle of dependency and build a better life for his family. Sometimes, though, while out with the road gang in his hi-vis vest, freezing his duff off one minute, burnt to a crisp the next, he struggled to remember the point of it all for five hundred dollars a week.

Still, he was doing all right, it was better than the dole and the islands; on a good week he had a few bucks left over to send to his mum and for a few cold beers with his mates. One of life's little pleasures that made it all seem worthwhile.

So it was after work on Thursday that a bunch of the lads piled into Sione's beat-up old Bluebird and headed for the RSA.

He'd had a few; couldn't remember how many and no dinner either when he got home; nothing but a couple of glasses of tap water. And now here it was Friday morning and he needed to get a move on or he'd miss the gang's pick-up at 6.30am.

Nothing seemed to work. Truth was, Sione felt like crap. He wasn't usually this bad; surely it couldn't be bottle flu? He'd only had a couple...

And then it came upon him like a tidal wave, a sudden overwhelming rush; an urgent need to throw up and let go at the other end.

Not good. Not good at all.

Afterwards he sat limply on the edge of the loo, drained

of all colour. His stomach churned like a concrete mixer. Finally, when there was nothing left to come out, he hauled himself over to the basin, splashing water on his face, and cupping it fresh from the tap to rinse out his mouth. Oh, that was so good. He must have drunk a gallon. Then he half-crawled, half-swaggered back to bed, resigned now to the reality of no work today. Better knock off the booze. That was his last conscious thought before he passed out.

Sione wasn't the only one off colour in Auckland's south-west. Jaffas all over rose as usual and headed for the kitchen and bathroom; to the taps as usual. Some were OK, others not the best, depending on how much water they'd been exposed to in the last few hours.

Still others felt totally gutted retreating to bed or the comfort of a nearby couch; to the shower even in a vain attempt to freshen up — totally unaware of the threat that lurked within. Then came the shock of no more water from their taps.

CHAPTER 68

With mixed emotions and a touch of trepidation Shelley Lai picked up the phone to call Georgie Towhai.

Shelley had had more than her fair share of false hopes and disappointments. Overall, she did her best to stay positive and not let the bad luck get to her. Perhaps it was true; you make your own luck as you go along. Yet you can only play with the hand you're dealt and Shelley did seem to have had some dud cards in her time.

On the other hand, Sam was definitely an ace. They went well together, with good chemistry and shared interests. And Shelley wasn't about to stand idly by and let her one big chance of a better future slip through her fingers. She had to do something.

"Georgie here."

"It's Shelley Lai from ILAWR. How's the convalescence going?"

"Do I know you?"

"No, but I do know what you've been going through, so I thought I'd ring and see how things are."

"What could you possibly know?"

"You're right, probably not the half of it, but listen, Georgie, I can understand you're carrying some stuff right now. I wanted you to know you're not the only one who's been hurt by recent events. That's why I thought I'd call — to say you're not alone; to try to show a little solidarity and support."

"Oh, yeah? So who else has been hurt?"

"For a start, Sam Miro."

"Sam Miro! You cannot be serious. How could I have been so stupid as to help him? I'm still peeing blood four weeks on, my dad's turned into a psychopath and the farm is shut down for I don't know how long — all because of Miro. And you want me to cut him some slack. And now it turns out the selfish bugger is in tight with the guy who contaminated the farm in the first place. Talk about being gutted. I've been totally betrayed."

"What? Oh, no, no, Georgie. It's not like that. Sam's only working with that guy now because he's got no alternative. The Mangawara clean-up has to be the priority. The two of them are working down there on it twenty-four seven."

Georgie listened then responded, enunciating each word clearly and with finality.

"Get this straight. Sam Miro doesn't exist for me any more. If I never see him again it'll be too soon. You can tell him that from me!"

And as if to emphasise her position she slammed the phone down. Hard.

Shelley hung up even more ambivalent. Certainly she'd got the assurance she wanted and, what's more, she hadn't had to work for it. Georgie was finished with Sam. Good result, yet she was troubled by Georgie's hurt and anger.

Back on the farm, Georgie marched into the kitchen where she found her father staring aimlessly out the window; the cup of coffee on the table cold and untouched.

"You want Sam Miro and the other guy? You'll find them down at the Mangawara."

CHAPTER 69

An hour after talking to Grafton Sam pulled into the now familiar drive of Caradijc's south Waikato hideout.

Andrej had more than fulfilled his expectations. After Sam had left, he'd launched into fermenting up and testing the new strain. He'd worked almost nonstop for the last forty-eight hours. Two tanks of the antidote sat on the back of the ute as mute witnesses to his progress.

"Andrej! Man, you've really been going for it."

"You are not wrong there. I have done a fair amount of testing, too, and I would say this new bug fits the bill. Besides high potency it has good specificity and I believe it is robust enough to stand a range of wetland conditions!"

"All systems go for a trial release then. That's a relief having talked it up around the traps."

Praise from the old master was praise indeed and the two men worked on amicably together until evening. They talked as only friends and colleagues can, finally crashing near midnight. They slept secure in the certain knowledge that tomorrow would be a watershed moment for them and for New Zealand.

Next morning up early and in buoyant mood they drove out to the Mangawara, windows down and music blaring.

"You couldn't have chosen a better day to save the country, Sam."

"Yeah, there'll be no stopping us now. That's good stuff in the tanks and all I want to do now is deal to the Mangawara."

"I also. I owe the country this."

As the ute lumbered down through a wetland paddock to the stream both men completely failed to notice they had company. Tucked behind some shrubs on the far side of the paddock was another vehicle whose occupant tracked them suspiciously through binoculars.

Andrej parked beside the stream.

"What's the plan of attack, Sam?"

"No point dumping our entire stock into the river on spec, is there? I suggest we release one tankload at the top of a natural run and let it drain through. We can collect samples over a reach during the day and then do bug counts to gauge its effect tonight. Sort of a time course. What do you think?"

Andrej nodded.

"A good scheme. The key will be to get evidence that the treatment works. Armed with bug counts we may be able to extrapolate to required doses and develop a plan of attack for the entire area. Did you notice that helicopter on the way here? Aerial top dressing could be the answer. With a helicopter and a truckload of the bug we would be able to treat the entire wetlands down to the mouth of the river in just a few days. That would be something, indeed."

"Andrej, that's one cool idea for scale-up."

"Not totally original, Sam. We were planning helicopters over London and Paris for the anthrax, you know. Project Yellow Rain."

"You're joking. There must've been some pretty sick people running your outfit."

"That is correct." Andrej spoke gravely. He had been part of that sickness and now he wanted to make amends. He sighed. "So let's get on with the trial release, Sam. See if I can't do some good for a change."

They returned to the ute to unload the first tank.

They were getting down to their work when out from behind the parked vehicle stepped a threatening figure.

"You don't give up, do you?"

Gaunt and dishevelled, Phil Towhai glowered out at them through the sights of a shotgun.

"Phil. What are you doing, man?"

"Putting some things right I should have done ages ago."

He was standing so close Sam could smell the whisky on his breath. He poked the gun menacingly in Sam's face.

"OK, mate, but put the gun down and let's talk about it. This isn't what you think."

"I've got nothing to say to you, Miro. It's too late for that. I'm not your fucking mate, either. Never was, never will be. All I know about you fuckers is you've ruined my farm and nearly finished off my daughter. Now's the time for payback."

Sam was taking it in. This was definitely for real. Phil was shaking with rage; about to lose it completely.

"You don't think I can do it, do you? Blow your fucking brains out. Believe me, I can. I don't care about anything any more."

"I do believe you, Phil, but what exactly would that achieve? And what about Georgie? Let's talk about what we're doing here and then you'll understand."

"Nah. No point, I tell ya. And don't you dare talk about Georgie. You're not worthy. The only thing I want to know is why you fellas chose us. We don't deserve it, been through enough..."

He brushed a free hand across his face, while his other finger wavered close, very close to the trigger.

While Sam was considering what could be done to calm Phil, Andrej was surveying other options. He'd been in enough tight spots to recognise what was playing out here. No point trying to reason with a man beside himself with anger and loaded with booze. They'd be lucky to get out of this alive. Talking would only delay the inevitable.

Sam was speaking again to Towhai, his words soothing and slow. As he did so Andrej edged slowly over to the ute and came up with a length of pipe. He didn't delay. Leaping forward he delivered a king hit to the side of the angry farmer's head.

But Towhai had seen enough pub brawls to know what was coming. As soon as he sensed movement he spun towards Andrej and squeezed off both barrels just as the pipe ploughed into his head.

The shots clapped out across the river flats sending a dozen pukeko into a panicked tailspin. Andrej heard none of it. The blast ripped through his face and folded him back against the deck of the ute before he collapsed forward on the rebound. He was dead before he hit the ground, convulsing grotesquely as his lifeblood spilled out.

One barrel had been enough. The other careered into the tank releasing a torrent of fermentation product down over Andrej, across the stretch of land to the bank and out into the stream.

Phil Towhai never knew what hit him either. He recoiled from the blow, head arching back and eyes rolling in. The gun fell from his hand and he rolled lifeless into the water drifting face-down out into the flow.

Silence and numbing mind-echoes only.

Sam sank down on his haunches, head buried deep in his hands. Macabre images played over and over in his mind, and when he drew out a handkerchief and wiped Andrej's blood and brains from his face he vomited deep and hard from the pit of his stomach.

Oh, God. What had he done here? He reeled from the sudden horror of it all.

Up on the road in the camper van he used on assignment, Wiremu had recorded the carnage on film. He peered intently out from behind his movie camera to check if Sam was OK.

What the fuck had happened? That wasn't in the script. Should he intervene?

Sam had been adamant that getting the news footage was to be a covert operation; that Wiremu should not show himself under any circumstances. Yet his impulse was now to run down and help his mate.

To his relief as the dust settled and the panicked squawks of the birds subsided, he could see that Sam at least was still alive. To Wiremu that was enough and he decided to sit tight.

Sam couldn't tell how long he remained slumped against the ute, cold with shock and grief. One man had become his friend; the other was Georgie's father. And now they were both dead. Oh God, how to deal with it all?

How could it have gone so badly wrong? This was supposed to be a day of triumph, when together he and Andrej achieved reparation and regained reputation. That was the theory, anyway, before Phil Towhai had intervened, blasting away sanity and sense.

He was consumed with remorse, unable to process accurately what had just happened and who exactly was to blame. His mind pressed replay as he ran through the sequence of events again and again. How could it have been different? When did he miss the moment for change? He rocked in despair, gasping for breath, half-choked with unshed tears.

Slowly and inevitably he started to come around. Drawn back to reality by the compelling matter of the stream. Peering out through clouded eyes he gazed out at a scene that was surreal beyond his wildest expectations. He got slowly to his feet like a man well past his best and staggered over to the water.

By now the *E coli* had transformed the Mangawara with a bank-to-bank overlay of phosphorescent biomass.

If not for the lethal threat the bloom posed, the gently flowing tapestry of olive-green could easily have been mistaken for a thing of beauty. Through the morning light the surface film glimmered and gleamed like some high street Christmas light show in soft focus, a kaleidoscope of fluorescent colour.

And then he noticed it. The surface film immediately before him was disturbed, displaying a marked ripple effect where the spilled contents of the tank met the bloom. Something extraordinary was happening at the interface; a rare interaction.

If he could have been miniaturised, he would have been able to witness it at first hand. But for now he could only surmise. To his trained eye the surface effect was evidence of a distinct reaction between the bioremediation agent and the toxic *E coli* — an assumption made stronger by a change in colour and a build-up of soapy scum at the point of contact — the characteristic flotsam and jetsam of dead coagulated bacteria.

My God. He turned instinctively to share the moment with Andrej — then nearly threw up again at the sight of his friend; the half face that remained distorted in a weird approving grin. The Russian scientist had paid one hell of a price for his involvement, both criminal and compensatory.

But the treatment of the wetlands was definitely working.

"We've done it, you bastard, we've done it. Max's bug is coming up trumps against the contamination."

If only Andrej were able to stand beside him and share his triumph. But Andrej Caradijc was gone. The man was never going home.

CHAPTER 70

IN MUCH of South Auckland there was doom and gloom.

"They say it's something in the water."

The man who spoke was jostling for position in a supermarket queue.

"Got to pick up some bottled water for the wife. She's about due and beside herself with worry about this lurgy, whatever it is. What it might do to her and the baby."

"You think you've got problems. My old man's got the rust and I can't so much as give him a drink."

"Give it up," someone called dismissively from further back. "Everyone's got a story."

Impatience was mounting and the crowd was restless.

No one had time to respond. The relative order at the supermarket entrance was dispersed by the roar of a truck in the car park. The ramshackle vehicle screeched to a halt and swung round to reverse hard into the store front window. Glass exploded into shards and trolleys were flung in all directions as it powered purposely through.

Once inside, its doors flew open and a gang of hooded youths burst forth. Like locusts descending on a wheat field they stripped the supermarket shelves of bottled water and anything else they could grab as they went.

Struck first by frustration, the resentment of the shoppers changed rapidly to overwhelming rage. The priority of their queue had been violated and, determined to get a share of the spoils, they charged after the looters or stood helplessly by, waiting for someone, anyone to restore order.

The security cameras dispassionately recorded the decline of social order as good people turned bad and mob rule took a hold; mirroring, if they did but know it, similar scenes of panic and lawlessness all over South Auckland.

And all for a few bottles of water.

There was also despair and chaos at the nearby medical centre.

"This is hopeless."

The receptionist had long since given up on attempts to clean the floor.

"Maybe we should get the numbering system up and running. It's getting out of hand."

"Go for it, Sue, but best we start triaging them too." Charge Nurse Megan Andrews motioned towards the patients sprawled on crowded chairs and benches. "Some look so much worse than others."

To Sue they were all goners, crowding the corridor by the toilet, impatiently banging on the door, or puking into plant pots. She snapped on a pair of latex gloves and donned a face mask. Megan did the same. It did little to protect them from the stench.

"I phoned Pakuranga," Megan said quietly. "It's the same for them, so no help there."

Sue groaned.

"What the hell's going on, Megan? And here was I hoping for a quiet day. I've got to pick up the kids at five."

"Ssh."

Megan turned up the volume to listen to breaking news on the waiting room TV.

"Auckland woke this morning to a contagion of water-borne poisoning. The severity and extent of the emergency is still emerging but what we know is this. Overnight it was reported that reticulated water in South Auckland had become contaminated with a dangerous bacterium.

"The reason for the contamination is not yet clear, but owing to the obvious health concern, emergency services responded by

cutting water supply to all areas from the Bombays to Waitemata Harbour. The scale of the emergency is massive affecting not less than two and a half million people. The contaminated water is known to cause severe reactions, especially skin irritation and gastro-intestinal, with the threat of serious, ongoing side effects and long-term consequences. Our information is that the region's health clinics and hospitals are struggling to cope.

"The Prime Minister has declared the situation a civil emergency and support services and supplies are being rushed in from other centres. In a further update we can also report that there has been panic buying of essentials including water from retail outlets and this is leading to widespread civil unrest. The police have been mobilised in force.

"Finally we can confirm that the motorways are jammed with a series of accidents further exacerbating the congestion.

"We cross live now to Dr Claire Steiner, Auckland Medical Officer of Health, who is co-ordinating the response to this emergency. Dr Steiner, could you outline what measures you are taking?"

"Thank you for the summation. I can also add that, sadly, there have now been a number of fatalities so the severity of the problem should not be underestimated. The key issue on everyone's mind must be — what can I do to protect myself and my family? The first and most important thing is to avoid all further contact with tap water. The mains supply has been cut, but there is still the possibility of exposure from any water remaining in taps. This should be avoided at all costs. We are not sure if boiling will suffice to make the water safe because of the possibility of toxins.

"Access to safe fresh water is a given in society so we fully appreciate this measure will cause hardship and distress. In response we have organised the distribution of fresh water through tankers and my personal commitment is to locate these at over forty strategic points in the community by dusk as an interim measure. Their exact placement will be widely advertised.

"We now have as a priority the main task of isolating the source of the contamination, restoring supply from safe and *secure sources and purging the network to prime outlets with the fresh supply. Realistically this process will take four to five days so I must ask the public for their patience and support.*

"The second dimension to the response is to ensure that there is sufficient medical capacity available to treat anyone displaying symptoms of poisoning. Owing to the scale of the event we have taken the decision to set up field hospitals and we are deploying the army to assist in this process. We anticipate no fewer than twenty of these and hope to have at least some of them in operation later today. Again locations will be notified. We are not yet clear on how many people have suffered health effects, but initial projections are that this will be high with symptoms ranging from minor to severe.

"On the positive side and to help with your understanding — E coli *infection has relatively low person-to-person infectivity compared with, say, influenza. As indicated problems occur following exposure to the contaminated water, for example drinking it or using it for washing. For this reason our main directive is not isolation from others, but strict avoidance of exposure to contaminated sources.*

"Finally we will be giving you frequent updates and I expect to be able to report further progress later in the day."

"Thank you, Dr Steiner. Can you give us an update on the cause of the contamination?"

"I regret I am unable to comment on that. Queries of this nature should be addressed directly to central government. My role is to implement the response."

Standing at the A & E reception desk, Sue turned to Megan, wide-eyed.

"My God, this is for real. People are dying. Where's it going to end? That's what I want to know. Mass graves in the Domain?"

"Oh, come on now, Sue. Don't go all dark on me. We've got work to do here."

CHAPTER 71

For Sam at the Mangawara the adrenaline was kicking in. He had never been this close before to mortality. Stoically he forced himself to stand by the husk that was Andrej Caradijc. He could almost feel the cold breath of death. He sank to the ground, shuddering and sick to the heart.

Nothing brought the reality of his situation home to him more than what had happened here. How much of this was down to his own inattention or to the reaction of others? Perhaps Dent was right; staying one step ahead was too hard and he should have walked away. Instead he was locked into this thing more than ever now and in emotional freefall; blindsided by the trail of destruction behind him: Ken Judge, Andrej Caradijc and Phil Towhai. Was he now exposing Georgie and Shelley to further pain?

His logical brain told him that he had to go on. He had to bring this thing to an end.

He returned to the stream and there he sat, white and motionless, rocking gently forward and back for comfort. He wanted only safety and his old life back. Some time alone with Shelley.

Eventually he was pulled back to reality by the sound of approaching voices.

"Hello, anyone there?"

Ex-PM Jeremy Grafton emerged before him, with a retinue of security men. They grouped around him, silent and enquiring.

"Mother of God," said Grafton. "What happened here?"

Sam tried hard to respond, to put Grafton in the picture. His mouth opened but nothing came out. Dispirited he returned to his view of the stream and the scanty satisfaction of his own gentle rocking.

The security men had now been struck by the cold realisation that this was a crime scene, sending them into a frenzy of activity, Glocks at the ready, to secure the site. Soon they regrouped around Grafton, on full alert.

"One confirmed fatality, sir, and we have a weapon for fingerprinting."

"Yes, yes. Find something to cover that body with, will you? Miro's a mess. In deep shock and I need to talk to him. I'll take him up to the crib and clean him up some. See if I can't get a cup of tea or something into him. Might be able to get some sense out of him then. In the meantime, do what you must to sort this out. OK?"

"Yes, sir."

"Best I send someone up to the bach with you to check it for threats, sir. Sean, you go."

"OK, but we'll be right. Whoever did this will be long gone. You let me focus on this young man."

He hoisted Sam to his feet and shepherded him up towards shelter.

Still on duty, up on the road cloistered in his camper van, Wiremu captured events as they unfolded. Wicked footage! He filmed the ex-PM assisting Sam slowly up the path to the river cottage. What a statement it made about who needed whom the most in this fiasco. Why else would Grafton be here?

As the two men approached the door to the crib he hurriedly shuffled from one stack of recording equipment to another in the back of his van. Go on, go on! Wiremu crossed his fingers. Sit on the porch to have your yarn; picture and sound quality will be much better there. Damn it, no! They headed right on in. It was so dark inside he'd be struggling to get a decent take from the remotes.

A loud crack from his speakers.

What the hell was that?

Sound works OK. Wiremu fiddled with the remote tuning of the cameras to improve the picture to match. In that instant the image recording kicked in with perfect timing for him to catch the uniformed form of Grafton's security guard crumple lifeless to the ground.

Then a woman spoke.

"Welcome, gentlemen. Pleased to catch up at last."

Wiremu quickly recognised that the derisory tone belonged to none other than the Associate Minister of Research, Science and Technology.

Bella Simcox.

He froze.

How in God's name did she get into the cottage? He recalled the distant thump-thump of a helicopter while he'd been filming Sam down by the river. That must be it. Oh, God. What next?

With his adversary before him Sam's brain stuttered back into life. There must have been a leak in Grafton's office for them to find him and Grafton so readily. Simcox's face was set in that trademark smirk. The men behind her stood at ease, grimly impassive. If we'd guessed she might be here we'd have taken a different tack. Too late now; and what did it matter? She had to catch up with us sometime.

Trouble is, they were caught in a trap.

He had hoped that when he and Simcox met it would be on his terms. Obviously that was not to be; it was here and now in this place, still reeling from the horror of Caradijc's death and Phil Towhai's too. The only bonus was that coming face to face with the instigator of all that had gone before had jolted him out of his stupor and was galvanising him back into action.

To hell with the consequences. If I'm going down, I'll go down fighting and do my level best to take them with me. Sam drew in a long slow breath while he considered his options, steeling himself for whatever fate would throw at him next.

Jeremy Grafton was also struggling to come to terms with this new predicament. He stared at the dead security guard and faced the fact he could be next. Why else would Simcox and her hired thugs be here? He was transfixed by the trickle of blood that had issued from the neat hole in Sean's forehead. The man had been with him for years.

Without knowing he was going to do it until it was done, Grafton lunged at Simcox, his thumbs grasping for her throat. Before he could reach her he was felled by the might of a baseball bat wielded by serious muscle.

Cowering from the threat of further blows, he could not restrain himself from expressing his utter loathing of this despicable woman.

"You utter self-righteous bitch! You bloody traitor."

She laughed derisively.

"You do know you'll never have any democratic legitimacy, don't you? A two-bit environmental terrorist is how you'll be remembered. A purveyor of hypocritical verbiage. The public will desert you in droves when they know the truth."

"But they won't know. Without you how do you think they will ever find out?"

From the door, Iris Dent clapped loudly.

"Oh, here's the other bitch," said Grafton. "No, that's too polite. We've seen what you did to Judge. You're nothing but an emotional retard. I'd string you up myself if I could."

Sam bent down to Grafton, intent on calming him. He needed time to think. To stay cool and work out what to do.

And then he remembered the cameras.

Simcox could hardly contain her glee at bringing her political opponent literally to his knees.

And Dent was openly admiring of her attitude, and

contemptuous of Grafton and Miro. They had the two men exactly where they wanted them.

Sam had feared that he, too, would lose control when he met up with either of them. He had so much anger stored up inside about Ken's death, so unnecessary; about the damage they'd done to the environment, to which, as an environmental microbiologist, he had dedicated his life. About what they had done to Shelley.

About it all.

He had vowed he would take them down by whatever means at his disposal; to hell with the consequences.

Instead, at this moment, he was imbued with a strange calm. He wanted to play on even if Dent and Simcox thought it was game over.

He turned to Simcox.

"How do you seriously expect to get away with this? Do you truly believe that scam is good enough to pull the wool over everyone's eyes?"

Dent answered on Simcox's behalf, her stance menacing and aggressive.

"Of course we'll get away with it. Nobody else knows anything and you're going to tell me the whereabouts of your report material. Who has it and where the electronic copies are."

"You must be joking. It's already out there."

Sam was bluffing. He knew full well it hadn't gone far.

"Oh, no, it's not. We stopped Judge in his tracks. So I repeat. Where are the files — hard and soft copies?"

Sam allowed himself to show some uncertainty, as if this was an earth-shattering revelation, totally undermining their position. Glancing down at Grafton he continued.

"Sorry, sir, seems we have no alternative. Might as well give up; tell them everything and save ourselves. That's all we can do now."

"Good." Dent smiled at this apparent capitulation.

"You're learning."

Casually Sam brought a finger across his lips, his eyes fixed on Grafton, willing him to bite his tongue.

Dent couldn't resist crowing.

"That's the boy. You know when you're beaten, don't you? No point wallowing in self-regret. You must have known you never stood a chance."

Sam ignored her and faced Simcox.

"One thing I don't understand is how someone like you, truly a Green, could hatch such a plot?"

"Green!" Simcox flicked a dismissive wrist. "To hell with the environment, it's already a disaster zone, you must know that. So we sprinkled some damaging stuff around a few farms. How bad can that be really — given the benefits?"

"What benefits? You're undermining everything New Zealand stands for." Grafton was fuming again now. "The last thing this country needs is a challenge to its clean green image and you as its tinpot dictator."

"Listen, you miserable toerag. The country was going nowhere under your vacillations. You've been an ineffectual blip on the political landscape and that's how you'll be remembered. No statue of you outside the Beehive. At least I'll make a difference."

"Is that what this is all about — recognition? You'll probably get nothing but a cartoon in the *Dominion* when the story breaks."

"That's enough from you." She signalled to one of the heavies, who took up a threatening stance beside the ex-PM. "Where's the report, Miro? We want all copies."

"You might as well take them for all the good they'll do you." Sam reached inside his shirt and pulled the memory stick from around his neck. "It's probably all over the Internet by now anyway."

"No way! Our IT people blocked all your accounts."

But Dent's nervous glance at Simcox betrayed self-doubt.

"Indeed?" taunted Sam. "As if that's the only means of making it public."

"No way!" shouted Dent. She reinforced her argument by ramming her baseball bat into Sam's groin.

He grimaced and recoiled, unable to refrain from clutching his balls. It was a fine line he was walking for the sake of a confession on camera.

"Simcox, we know you don't give a damn about the environment, but your constituents do. Don't you understand that Auckland's water supply is dangerously contaminated because of your actions? The city is under threat of poison even as we speak."

"Don't you dare try to pin that on me. A little collateral damage was inevitable. Who gives a proverbial about a few Jaffas anyway? They're all so up themselves."

"It'll be more than a few and even one is too many."

"Whatever. Now, let's get back to business."

Wiremu was beside himself as he received sound and action loud and clear, live streaming the theatrics back to the station. Sam was baiting them perfectly. This is our big break.

He recorded Dent returning from the front veranda and as he did so he dialled 111. The situation was clearly too dangerous to be allowed to continue.

"Come on, Bella, we need to get out of here. We're not going to get anything else of value out of them." She snapped at the hired thugs. "Finish them off. And make it look like a murder-suicide. Hurry! Grafton's security guards are coming."

Sam steeled himself for the worst. He outfaced Simcox defiantly, preparing a last ditch attempt to subvert Dent's resolve.

He went for the jugular.

"Come clean, why don't you? Confess. The only future you have in Wellington is in front of a jury. A confession might secure a little compassion."

"Wait," Simcox instructed the heavies, who had levelled their pistols. "Are you completely out of your mind, Miro, or what? You've no chips left to play yet still you prattle on. You keep on rolling out the bullshit."

As her goons stepped closer Sam pointed to the camera in the nearest corner.

"Take a dekko up there, Simcox." He pointed again and again. "And there and there. Cameras. This room is bugged. Everything is being filmed and streamed live as breaking news. Tomorrow you'll be a YouTube sensation going viral. So go on, finish us off, and you'll get a Grammy along with your life sentence."

The two women exchanged nervous glances.

"Pathetic," declared Dent. "You expect us to believe that?"

"See for yourself. The transmission van is up on the road. Face it, Simcox, it's over!"

Dent was ashen and shaking at Sam's revelation.

"Bella, what do you reckon?"

Simcox slumped heavily onto the couch, staring at Miro in disbelief. She had totally underestimated him. Had they really been taped? Why else would a backwater bach have cameras in it? She'd be crucified. There'd be no explaining this to the public. She was exposed, wide open to scrutiny. A tide of crippling self-doubt washed over her; but as yet no contrition. Only rage at being outfoxed.

Her gaze drifted to Sam, eyes vacant now. How could this boy — no more than an Ivy League preppie — have taken her down like this? She regarded him enquiringly for perhaps the first time, taking in the shock of blond hair and the fresh-faced complexion that not even river mud or blood splatters could mar. She was transfixed by the gaze of those most distinctive of eyes. One green, one brown. How unusual was that? Her mind drifted back to a maternity ward in smalltown New Zealand some twenty-seven years before and the memory of the man who had fathered her child.

"Tell me, Sam," she asked, as if elsewhere, "how old are you and are you adopted?"

"What? What's that got to do with anything?"

She snatched a gun from a nearby minder. "Tell me or I'll end it right now."

He shrugged. Resigned. One more invasion of his privacy, but hey! What did it matter.

"Yes, I'm adopted and I'm twenty-seven years old."

Sam thought she was in shock and taking refuge in irrelevancies. He watched transfixed as she bent double, gagging in self-pity as the revelation of what he had said crashed down on her like a tidal wave.

Grafton dared to sit up and stare at Sam, both men trying to make sense of this bizarre twist.

She was back in a South Auckland tenement. Fifteen going on twenty-five; a joint in one hand and a can of bourbon and Coke in the other. Hair mussed and T-shirt torn from the scrap outside. And now much worse, she was alone with the Killer Beez leader. The spoils of war.

She could tell he was on a mission. He wanted it all and wanted it now. She also knew she needed to play the game here, be staunch and take it like a trooper or else risk being done over too. Next he was easing her back towards a grimy mattress. Stained fingers unbuttoning tight denim shorts. She so wanted to be back home now. Anywhere would be better than this.

What else could she do but take it? He was all-powerful around here. Not to be messed with. So she shut down, let him force his way in and pump away like a wild man. Soon his back arched as, eyes wide open, he came deep inside her. Her face was buried in the mattress to hide the sobs and when eventually she turned he was passive, gazing down at her with something like affection.

Like he had done a good thing here.

That's when she noticed that in spite of all the anger and aggro he had the most beautiful eyes. One green, one brown: how unusual was that? Smiling down at her like beacons.

And then he was gone and she left too, never to set eyes on him again.

Make-up wrecked and face smeared, Simcox lifted her head and spoke to Dent.

"He's right, you know. What have we done…? It's all been for nothing. The whole world will be down on us. What could be worse?"

She staggered to her feet.

"Come on, all of you. We're out of here. Leave them, just leave them."

As she went by she paused just long enough to squeeze Sam's arm and to mutter in hushed tones, "You… you remind me of someone I once knew."

Then she ran for the back door, the bushes and the helicopter waiting in the paddock beyond.

Dent, open-mouthed, stared after her. The minders had already gone. She swung round to Sam and Grafton, fists clenched, eyes wild; wanting to hurt them and badly. After a tense second she turned and raced after Simcox.

Sam helped the ex-PM to his feet, and they staggered to the door as both women scrambled into their helicopter and headed for the clouds. He exhaled slow and deep, a sigh of utter relief.

Grafton was shaking his fist at the fast-disappearing machine.

"Go on, bugger off," he yelled. "You talk about me. Well, let me tell you, Simcox. You're history — a failure of epic proportions. And get this: you can run, but you cannot hide."

CHAPTER 72

SAM AND Jeremy Grafton gazed at each other in abject disbelief. Pale now and shivering they struggled to come to terms with cheating death. They sat side by side on the battered couch vacated so hurriedly by Simcox and took time to pull themselves together.

"Sam." Grafton began the conversation. "Call me slow, but what was all that about? Cameras, bugs, adoption... What's going on here?"

Sam could only shake his head. He didn't know where to begin.

Before he could string a few words together in answer Grafton's security men burst through the door.

"Fuck! What happened here? Who got Sean?"

"Bella Simcox's cronies." Grafton snapped to, resuming the mantle of leadership. "Secure the site. We'll give a statement to the police later. C'mon, Sam, we're out of here. Need to get to Wellington, like yesterday. Got to rein in Simcox and her gaggle of gays, get you what you need to sort out the Mangawara, etc. And turn those polls around."

Before long they were in the ministerial limo speeding for the airport.

Grafton didn't let up for a minute. He was a man revived, spiritually and mentally. He had literally got his life back. Sam acknowledged ruefully he was still waiting for his. The instructions were nonstop.

"Get me the acting PM. We need an immediate Cabinet briefing, got to let them know what's been going on. Now connect me to Don Ridgway. He'll have to lock down the Beehive. What next? Oh, yes. Claire Steiner — can you get her? We could use an update on the state of play in

Auckland. Get the media team on the line, too. A press conference is essential the moment we land at Wellington."

Sam rested quietly, ignoring Grafton's feverish activity, contemplating his own reflection in the window as the countryside sped by. He was haunted by questions. What had he done to deserve this? And what was it with Simcox? Most importantly, what was all this leading to?

Eventually, exhausted, he gave up, falling into a deep and dreamless sleep. The next thing he remembered was climbing groggily up the steps of the Wellington 737 at Hamilton Airport. While it was sitting on the tarmac he checked his cellphone.

There was a new text from Shelley.

'Tell me you're OK. Beside myself with worry. S. xx.'

He texted back.

'Thanx. Safe & well now but scary as. Want to talk 2 U badly.'

'Yes. Yes. Me 2.'

'U know it's over with G?'

'Guessed.'

'You're the one that's always on my mind. Want to be with U if you'll have me.'

'Oh yes. U must know I'm crazy for you. You're the one for me. I know we can make us work. Love. S.'

'Love you too! S'

CHAPTER 73

CHIEF OF Security Don Ridgway was waiting for them as the official limousine pulled up at the Beehive.

"Simcox and Dent are here. I didn't expect that. They've barricaded themselves into her suite. I've had the negotiators up to try to flush them out, but not a hope. What do you reckon we should do?"

"Let me at them."

Grafton barnstormed past the body scanners and headed for the lifts.

"Sir, sir, take it easy. They could be armed."

Ridgway set off behind him, but Grafton wasn't having a bar of it as he hit the button for the seventh floor. He was followed by Sam, now totally bemused, and a phalanx of minders shoving in before the lift doors closed.

Grafton was on a mission, hell-bent, charging out of the lift and through the foyer past a ruby-red circular couch to the door of Simcox's suite. He yanked at the door handle, nearly pulling it off its hinges before he realised the door was locked.

He pounded on the door.

"Give it up, Simcox. It's over. Come on out and face the music."

Nothing.

"You've nowhere to run, nowhere to hide! Can't stay in there forever either. So, come on, open up."

By then Sam and the others were milling around expectantly. Surely common sense would prevail now that the sisters of sin had had time to reflect.

Grafton turned to Don Ridgway.

"Give them five minutes, then you'd better go in."

He returned to the siege of Simcox.

"One thing I can promise you, Bella, is a fair trial. So don't make things harder than they need be."

He stepped back, taken aback as she answered at last.

"I won't be going on trial. No charges to answer. It's all a mistake."

"Yeah, right," Sam snorted. He couldn't help himself. "She losing it, I reckon. Why am I not surprised?"

"I can explain everything," Simcox continued. "Leave me alone for now. I promise I'll go quietly then. I don't want to cause any more grief."

Grafton's disbelief now matched Sam's.

"She's lost her marbles if she thinks she can talk her way out of this. Don, go ahead. Pull everyone back, get a jamb spreader and break down the door. Go in and get her. I'm tired of her theatrics."

Soon enough it was done and the Armed Offenders Squad rushed in, guns levelled, followed closely by Jeremy Grafton and Ridgway.

The office was empty.

The two women, forlorn, were standing beyond the railings on the balcony — hanging on for dear life.

"Come on in, Simcox," shouted Ridgway. He reached out to grab her. "There's nothing to be gained by this."

"Don't!" she warned. "You hear me? Or we'll jump!"

Iris Dent nodded pathetically.

"So sorry, darling. I did the best I could. This is the right thing. Now we can be together forever."

"No, no," Sam pleaded. "Don't do it." Even as he spoke he wondered why he was bothering. "It's not worth any more deaths."

Simcox turned her head to stare at her son.

"You don't know anything about me. If you did you would understand; you would have worked with me instead of against. This is all down to you and yet you're coming out the winner, at my expense. Oh, Sam. Why couldn't you have turned and walked away?"

"What can I say? That's not me at all, not what I was brought up to be."

She stared at him, expressionless.

"I don't get you, Simcox. What you did is beyond reason. What you did to my friends, to the country... Ah! I'm done. You deserve everything you've got coming!"

He turned and walked away.

Simcox spoke to Dent.

"Time to go, sister. No mercy here. On the count of three."

Dent nodded, resigned now to her fate.

"See you on the other side, Iris. One ... two... three... Go!"

A solitary figure arched out into the breeze, seemingly hanging there for a second before plummeting earthwards, arms and legs spread wide, mouth open in an unheard scream. A moment later she careered into the conical building, battering and dashing her way down the side before ricocheting off and cartwheeling unceremoniously into the pavement.

The assembled crowd stood dumbstruck by the abject horror of Dent's demise.

At her nod, Ridgway leaned over and pulled Simcox up.

"Thank you..." She nodded graciously and smoothed herself down. She sat down and said confidentially to Grafton, "It was all down to her, you know. I was a victim. Tried to stop her, but I just couldn't."

Grafton was awestruck by her gall.

"You never fail to astound me. You'd even betray the memory of your best friend to save yourself. Face it, Simcox; it's all turned to custard. Your precious reputation is in tatters. Your public will repudiate you. You're alone in this now. Stand up and face the music."

Then he turned and walked away.

"Come on, Sam, we're out of here. We've got to save the Mangawara and Auckland."

Simcox called after them, softly but pointedly. "All I really wanted was to be with my baby boy."

CHAPTER 74

AT FIRST glance it was a fine day for a funeral, but as Sam stepped out he noted the grey clouds gathering on the horizon portending moody and changeable Waikato weather for the send-offs he had now to attend.

First it was Andrej Caradijc. A private affair — as lonely as the man — organised by Sam ahead of the return of his remains to the Ukraine. There was no one else so once the handful of mourners had gathered Sam said a few words. He talked of a laconic chap who had learned to keep his own counsel by necessity; of a colleague with considerable technical ability and resourcefulness who had learned to make do.

He also spoke to his background; how he was a vestige of a bygone Soviet era and had a deep commitment to his family. Finally Sam made it clear that Andrej's only real mistake was to place his trust in someone offering a better life in New Zealand.

Next it was Phil Towhai's tangi at Mangawara under a threatening sky. This one was seriously sad. Hundreds of mourners behind dark sunglasses doing their best to remain staunch in the face of obvious despair. Daughter Georgie was desolate. Raked by intermittent wailing and sobbing, visibly swaying when not supported by an unknown older woman with blonde hair.

The speeches were clipped, angry even and spoke of a man of great personal strength who had striven to deliver a better life for his people in spite of deep personal hardship. A man with much to offer who had been taken too soon.

Sam watched through misting eyes from the periphery. Wanting so much to offer some little comfort to Georgie;

knowing full well he would only make matters worse. Much as he would have liked to be, he was not part of this. He could sense the closing of ranks by the iwi and respected that. Yet looking on as Georgie struggled to come to terms with her loss he felt a great remorse. He knew he could have done better.

And then the rains came.

In parallel, on a cold and blustery day in Wellington, separate services were being held for Iris Dent and Roger McWilliams. The news reports had not been kind to Iris. The funeral was most notable for the no shows. No Bella Simcox, no one from Gravitas and no representation from the party.

Only a few diehards who simply didn't get it. The speeches were curt, economical with the truth and no one shed a tear. On the coffin was a single handwritten note.

'Ms Simcox regrets she is unavoidably detained and unable to attend today.'

Roger McWilliams' wake was a family affair. Incredibly sad; his wife and daughters still coming to terms with the notion that he was caught up in the Waikatogate affair. That his moral compass had been called into question. Why? they asked. He was a good Christian man. Surely there was no need.

The sun was out for Ken and his funeral was different, for it was not about commiseration or a departure. This was about celebrating Ken's life and the eulogies reflected that.

As Sam said, Ken stood for something. He had made a difference. He had built ILAWR on the back of a deep understanding of science and politics and of people. Most of all he had succeeded because he had learned how to herd seagulls. Barely a tear was shed instead replaced by mirth and humour and recollections of what a privilege it had been to work with the man.

Jeremy Grafton also spoke. He talked of Ken's greatness as an unsung leader of men. Of how he had created a national icon in ILAWR the success of which could be measured by the innovative, freethinking researchers it produced. Ken's legacy was young scientists like Sam Miro with the leadership qualities to take up the challenge and ultimately find sustainable solutions to the environmental challenges New Zealand faces. This was an outstanding achievement.

And there were drinks, of course, but Sam had to leave. He had another appointment. Though he looked for all the world as if he belonged on the studio couch inside he wasn't so relaxed as he waited to be interviewed for current affairs TV. If this is what it meant to be a celebrity, it wasn't for him.

"This evening I would like to introduce Dr Sam Miro. For those of you who don't know we Aucklanders owe Dr Miro a debt of gratitude. He is the scientist who not only identified the environmental contamination that led to the recent poisoning of Auckland's water supply; he also actioned the clean-up. Thanks for coming in, Sam. From the reports of recent events you come over as an ordinary young man doing extraordinary things. We're wondering what makes you tick."

"Oh, thanks. Er, hello... Well I'll tell you one thing — beautiful days like today make me proud to live in New Zealand."

"Go on."

"Seriously, what drives me is a belief in the fundamental importance of the environment to the health and well-being of New Zealanders — and the need to protect this. It is just so vulnerable. Wouldn't it be great if, at the very least, we could leave New Zealand as we found it for future generations? Or just maybe in even better condition... That's what motivates me and I'd like to help with this by giving Kiwis the tools they need to make a better future possible."

"Great vision, but hey! That's a bit modest, isn't it?"

"When it comes down to it I was part of a team able to act quickly to avert an even greater disaster. Who wouldn't have done the same? Some of those team members aren't with us any more either so, with your permission, I'd like to take a moment to remember them and thank them from the bottom of my heart. Together a few of us recognised early on how serious the situation was and were able to do something about it."

"How did you do that?"

"As part of my research programme we were monitoring certain farms and identified changes in bug profiles that suggested something was awry. Fortunately related research meant we also had a way to rapidly intervene to start a clean-up."

"And thank goodness for that," continued the interviewer. "Your initiative prevented what was a dark day for Auckland becoming an even greater catastrophe, so we owe you — and your team — for that...

"Also we can't help wondering how this whole affair has affected you..."

"OK, I'll come to that. But first I want to make a plug for the science system in this country. Perish the thought, but some people have been known to suggest that our research isn't relevant to the real world we live in. I would like to point to this as an example of something that is working."

"You ask how I've been affected by recent events. One thing I can say is I gained enormous real world experience from the events. I've spent my whole life training as a scientist and wasn't sure I was equipped for the events that transpired. So that's a positive. I have learned so much — about myself and how to cope with adversity."

"So what did you personally take from this unfortunate episode?"

"There are a few things, and the most important relates to the role of science in modern society. You'll be aware that it doesn't sit well with everyone. There is the suggestion that humankind's technological 'progress' is actually to blame for many of the problems we face today. For example, global warming."

Sam turned to face the cameras squarely.

"I put it to you that notion is ill-informed and the current example is illustrative. True, it began with a misuse of science and technology, but that problem was down to political corruption. Let's be absolutely clear; science was not the problem. Science was the solution. Our current research not only identified the problem, but also a means of fixing it. To me that's the point: when science and technology are used appropriately they are of inestimable value to society."

He smiled at the interviewer knowing he had scored.

"I see. And what does the future hold for you, Sam?"

"I think the example I've given signals an important need — better engagement of researchers and scientists with the community. That's one thing I hope to do some more of. And to stay close to my own research, of course. More than ever I believe in what it can contribute to make a big difference for New Zealand. I want to set up my own research institute to speed up the rate of progress."

"Good for you, Sam. Tell me though; after all that's gone on do you still think New Zealand can claim to be clean and green?"

"That's a good question. To be honest, probably not. Perhaps some rebranding is in order, don't you think? It's all relative, though, and we do have certain advantages over other countries. For example, we're still young as a nation and, it's indisputable that we're first to see the light of day. Nobody can take that away from us. So maybe we should morph 'clean and green' into 'first to green' or similar... Why bother? I hear you say. To me it speaks to the heart of what New Zealand is meant to be — a leader in the green revolution."

He smiled again at the interviewer, knowing he had carried the day.

Watching at home, Shelley and Hua clapped exuberantly.

"Thank you, Sam Miro. It sounds as if you are offering an entirely new vision for the country. And it should be enough to keep you going for some time, too."

The interviewer stood up and gestured for him to come and stand beside her. He turned as instructed to face camera 4.

"Ladies and gentlemen, I give you Dr Sam Miro."

ABOUT THE AUTHOR

Dr Steve Hodgkinson

Steve's day job is as a biomedical scientist researching biopharmaceutical and nutritional approaches for optimising health. His main focus is in translating academic science into products and services that are useful and make a difference. He is also interested in finding new and exciting ways to communicate the complex role science plays in modern society. Although Steve has over 180 science publications, *Unearthed* is his first work of fiction. He is married with two adult daughters. On his days off he likes to get out on his sports motorcycle and enjoys a beer with his friends.